# THROWBACK

EDWARD J. MCFADDEN III

SEVERED PRESS
HOBART TASMANIA

# THROWBACK



*WWW.SEVEREDPRESS.COM*



*ISBN: 978-1-925840-35-3*

# 1

Humanity held its breath.

NASA Commander Jonah "Hawk" Hawkins floated before a monitor in Destiny lab aboard the International Space Station, his stomach crawling up his throat. The display showed the approaching space cloud, nothing more than a thin gray-white haze drifting across the black star-filled horizon like smoke. The big heads said the cloud was the size of fifty Jupiters, and the outer edge of the cosmic fart would blow past Earth at 190,000 MPH.

"T-Minus three minutes and counting. All systems are go," said Flight Engineer Svetlana Savitska. The cosmonaut's voice was rock solid as she stabbed her control panel with one hand while grasping a handhold with the other, a ponytail of blonde hair floating behind her. From Hawk's perspective she was upside-down, monitoring the equipment on the ceiling. All of Destiny's bulkheads had a function in the near-weightless environment.

Hawk said, "Max, any new data?"

"Nothing," the German ESA physicist said. The crew communicated via wireless headsets, and they all wore jumpsuits with various patches on their breasts and shoulders.

"Our probes? The sensor array? We're still getting nothing at all?"

"Static and random noise. No new predictions as to composition. Speed and density confirmed, again," Max said.

Hawk said nothing. Probes had been sent into the cloud as it moved through the solar system, and a minefield of sensors had been deployed, but they'd yielded no significant data or clues as to what effect the cloud's passage might have.

Earth was a blue arc at the bottom of the screen, and Hawk's chest ached as he watched the space fog advance on his home. He'd gladly given up chunks of his life to live in a soup can, and he'd never admit it to anyone, but Hawk missed his old ball of dirt.

Sea breezes and rain. Wind tearing at his face. Cold chilling his toes. Well, the station did provide that pleasure.

"Two minutes thirty seconds and counting," Svet said.

French Mission Specialist Michel Fulcello floated into the lab and took up position at his work station. "Everything's secure, sir," he said. Michel was the first French astronaut to serve on the ISS.

Hawk nodded. He didn't expect any turbulence, but he had Michel check the station anyway, making sure nothing was floating around and that all nonessential equipment was powered down and secured. It gave him something to do. Hawk had noticed early signs of space dementia in Michel; depression, lethargy, expressing feelings of isolation and loss of family and he needed to snap out of it.

"Mission control at Houston, do you copy?" Hawk said.

"Mission control here." Hawk could picture his old friend and rival Theo Rantic sitting in his command chair, staring obsessively at his status display.

"Nothing to report, control," Hawk said.

"Same here. We're on a party line, so speak now or forever hold thy peace."

Hawk didn't know how many governments were listening in. In addition to NASA, Roscosmos, JAXA, ESA, the CSA, many other agencies monitored their communications, as well as universities and private citizens and businesses. They were the only humans in space, outside the protective shell of Earth's atmosphere, and that made them prime observers, which made them news. Hawk and his crew were on point, the enemy a cosmic mystery.

Svet said, "Sir?"

Hawk nodded. Svet and Hawk had been together on the station for eleven months, and they'd reached marriage level on the mind reading scale.

"Roscomos, this is Flight Engineer Svetlana Savitska, do you copy?"

"We copy, Svet," a male Russian voice said.

Svet rocked back, her motion smooth due to lack of stress. Hawk knew the voice; it was Svet's husband, Vladimir. "T-Minus two minutes and counting and nothing new to report here," she said.

The U.S. and the Soviets had been partners on the station through thick and thin, good times and bad, and there'd been times the diplomats attributed the survival of the free world to the series of connected metal cans powered by solar energy and manned by an international team of space hounds who spent months drinking recycled water, breathing manufactured air, and tolerating each other's failing mental states and increasing body odors. All in the name of science, progress, international relations, and nationalistic ego.

"Roscomos wishes you luck," Vladimir said, the comm crackling under his deep accent.

"You as well. ISS out," Svet said. She pushed away from the bulkhead. Hawk had never seen the woman upset, but in these final moments before the cloud's arrival, one couldn't help but imagine the worst.

The space cloud continued to fill Hawk's screen, and a dread crept over him that turned his stomach to ice. Doomsayers, religious zealots, profiteers and politicians had put forth many end-of-the-world scenarios that filled the endless hours of TV talk shows and gave new meaning to the word paranoia.

But just because you're paranoid doesn't mean they're not out to get you.

Nothing like the cloud had ever happened in recorded history, and to Hawk, the unknown it presented was exhilarating and scary. Some preached the anomaly was Earth's salvation, and it would renew a failing world by boosting Earth's oxygen content, or adding elements to the atmosphere that could strengthen it against harmful radiation and cosmic rays. Some said God sent the cloud to destroy the world in the end times. All of this meant nothing to Hawk. He believed the anomaly's passage would be akin to Y2K. Years of buildup and expense, and one train broke down in Europe. Some argued that was because of preventative measures, but Hawk believed the entire thing to be an overreaction, like the cloud.

"Ninety seconds," Svet said.

Static burst through the comm. "ISS, this is Roscomos, are you seeing increased radiation levels on your long-range spectrometer?"

Hawk spun and looked at Michel, who pushed off and glided to another monitoring station, where he cued up a data set and asked the onboard computer to graph it. The low electric hum of the station and the occasional snap of static filled the silence as Michel studied his monitor and fingered his headset. "I'm not sure. The sensors are reading something, but whatever it is isn't matching with the identification software," Michel said.

"An unknown element?" Hawk said.

"Most likely a combination of many, otherwise I'd see a clear pattern in the numbers. In this case the sensors are detecting so many unknowns they're all falling below the materiality threshold."

"No density changes?"

Michel pushed to another bulkhead before saying, "No."

"T-Minus one minute," Svet said.

"All stations are go, and all recorders are green," said Max.

Hawk grabbed a handhold with both hands as if bracing for an impact. Sweat inched off his neck, yet he was cold. As his monitor filled with the gray-white fog of the cloud, his confidence fled. He didn't like the feeling.

Hawk had always wanted to be an action star, growing up watching *Rambo*, *Predator*, and *Platoon*, and playing war with the most elaborate collection of plastic guns and knives any kid would've envied. He also loved the sea, and those two things drove him to the Navy, where he'd become a pilot and then a SEAL. He'd given most of his life to the service, and it had given him adventures few had experienced.

But the cost had been great. Floating in the ISS, everyone he loved and cared about on Earth, doubt gnawed at him, as it always did. A worm burrowing through his flesh and soul, always asking if he was being selfish, or if his sacrifice had been worth it, giving up the time with his family? He barely knew his two children, and Andrea stayed with him because they loved each other, and she'd known what she was getting into. They'd had their first date, and Hawk had been deployed the next day and they didn't see each other or speak for a year before he'd shown up unannounced when he'd gotten leave.

"Prepare for passage in 10, 9, 8..." said the voice of mission control.

Hawk resolved in that moment that this would be it. He was only forty-seven, he wasn't dead. He still had time. He could turn everything around. What would he do? What could he do? Desk job? Pilot? Would he be happy? Would his family even want him around if he wasn't?

"...7, 6..."

It all came down to what was important. He'd wanted to go to the stars, and he'd done it, multiple times. He couldn't let the fear of the unknown imprison him. His mind spun, and he almost laughed. He floated two hundred and fifty miles above the Earth with nothing but a thin layer of metal between himself and the chilling vacuum of space, and he worried about the unknown. Hawk decided this would be his last mission, and he'd announce it live after the cloud passed. A little surprise to Andrea. He was coming home, for good.

"...4, 3, 2—"

A sharp burst of static tore through Hawk's headset. "Mcfly, turn down the amp," he said. Svet and Michel chuckled, but Max ignored him. The Russian and Frenchman had seen more American movies than he had. The only American entertainment Max knew was *Friends* and *Star Trek*.

The screens showing the external cameras were obscured in gray. Miniscule lights twinkled like rainbow colored stars in the cloud, and they reminded Hawk of how sun rays caught dirt and sand particles as they floated in clear water. There was no sound, no vibration, and the spacefarers looked to each other, as if to say, "Anything?"

The ache started in the tips of Hawk's toes and fingers, a dull throbbing that grew to a stabbing pain that spread up his arms and down his legs. Hawk's station mates felt it too, because Max rubbed his feet and Michel jerked and shook like his limbs had fallen asleep. Svet's hands were clamped to her head.

Hawk once had a minor case of the bends, and that pain was nothing compared to the agony that pushed into every corner of his body. He squeaked, and Max yelled as he spun across the lab and slammed into a rack of equipment.

Svet grabbed handholds, head down, but didn't make a sound.

Like a receding flood the pain eased, but lingered in the extremities where it began. Hawk was winded, and he pulled for air, his chest heaving.

Svet grabbed an oxygen mask and tossed it in Michel's direction, then slipped one over her face. Svet's instrument panel flashed red with warning lights. The station's power went out and Destiny lab fell into darkness.

Hawk took shallow breaths, conserving the oxygen in his body, preserving the air still available in the compartment. He'd never felt more alone, closer to death, as he floated in the blackness.

*Snap*. The control panel came on, then the lighting.

Svet's head glided up, and she went back to her station. "The system appears to be rebooting. We should be up and running in ninety seconds," she said.

Hawk waited as the blank monitor laughed at him. He had to see what was happening. He tapped his headset and said, "Let me know when the system comes up."

"Aye," Svet said.

Hawk pulled himself along the bulkhead out of Destiny lab, flying like Superman into Unity node one.

"Hawk, you copy?" Max said.

"Go ahead."

"The chronometer is…"

"What?"

"Malfunctioning," the German said.

Hawk made a right into Tranquility node three, twisted around, and braced himself against the bulkhead.

"All Earth-side communications are dead, and I'm getting no signal from any of the comm satellites," Svet said.

Hawk floated down into the cupola, a seven-window observatory that resembled the turret on the Millennium Falcon. When Hawk looked down at Earth his mouth fell open a crack, then he said, "I might know why that is."

The planet below was nothing but blue ocean from horizon to horizon, no land masses visible.

There had been a moment in Hawk's first flight test as a cadet when he believed he'd lost control of his plane. A panic filled him that was so all encompassing he froze, unable to react. Sometimes Hawk believed the paralysis had saved his life, stopped him from making some knee-jerk reaction that would have made things worse, but that wasn't how he felt now.

There were no brown mountain peaks on Earth's surface, no massive swathes of green life or tan deserts. No continental shapes outlined the globe, and the streams of white clouds covered only water. His house had been on one of those continents. Everything and everyone he loved.

All of it was gone.

# 2

Hawk found Michel's corpse floating in Columbus lab, tongue hanging out, eyes cloudy pools. There was no blood, no note. Hawk blamed himself for leaving the man alone. He'd seen the signs of space dementia, and he should have sat with him, never left him alone, but Hawk was lost in his own grief and couldn't remember what he'd done for the last half-hour.

None of the astronauts spoke of it, but each space hound had a way out, a last resort death pill for when no other option was available. The French poison of choice was a cocktail of cyanide and cloglestrial, a new acid that destroyed living tissue and replicated. Hawk had considered taking his pill, but he was just too scared, his grief and worry for his family consuming him, the shock of their situation still too new. That same shock that had pushed Michel over the edge made him focus.

The spacefarers sealed Michel's body in an airlock, out of sight. Hawk said a short prayer and looked at each of his shipmates and saw fear and doubt. What had kept them from taking their pills?

The station passed the terminator into night, and the outlines of several large landmasses bunched together stood out in the blackness below. It was as if Earth had been tipped over and all the continents ran to one side. At the sight of land, Hawk breathed a sigh of relief, but his thunderous nerves returned as the reality of the situation broke through his cocoon of denial.

Hawk tried to push Michel from his mind and went about his business in stunned shock as the International Space Station moved through space at 17,000 MPH, with the Earth, or what had once been the Earth, slipping by below. The stars looked the same, but the station's instrumentation was showing something different. According to the onboard computer the star map had changed, and the chronometer showed numbers that were so far off the chart Hawk assumed it was broken. No satellites responded to their pings, and there'd been no signs of life.

Daylight revealed the problem in full color. Swathes of green, brown, and white filled the surface of the planet, but the land masses were bunched together and didn't look much like Earth.

"Looks like a broken Pangaea," Max said. "Or something like it." When Max wasn't flying around in space, or pressing the limits of the known universe at the large Hadron Collider at CERN, he was a professor at Oxford, and his areas of expertise extended well beyond physics.

"When everything on Earth was together? That was long time ago, nyet?" Svet said.

"Very long."

"You think the planet below is Earth? How could it be? You're saying we traveled back in time?" Hawk said.

"I'm saying the landmasses below resemble what scientists think Pangaea looked like fifty million years ago as it broke apart into the continents we know now. We *were* orbiting Earth, and the current configuration of land masses is somewhat recognizable. What are you suggesting? The station was transported to another point in the galaxy and placed in orbit around a different planet that just happens to resemble Earth of the past?" Max said.

"Govnó," Svet spat. "Délo drjan'." Svet lapsed into Russian when she got excited.

"Shit is right. And "things don't look good" is an understatement," Max said.

"Is there another option?" Hawk was pleading, because he couldn't get his noddle wrapped around the other possibilities.

Svet and Max said nothing.

The earthlings sat bunched together in the cupola, watching the oncoming twilight zone cut across the horizon like a dark blade. Svet pressed her face against the thick glass, and Max rubbed something from his eye. Wherever or whenever they were, what wasn't in dispute was they were alone. Michel's suicide had driven home they only had each other, and it might be that way for a long time. Hawk smiled ruefully. Might be that way forever, and that burned his chest as he thought of his family. Were they OK? What had happened to the Earth he'd known?

The space station crossed the terminator and the planet surface went dark save for moon glow, a giant erupting volcano, and…

something else. Hawk leaned forward, his heart pounding. Toward the center of the largest land mass, a bright multi-colored light blinked in a rhythmic pattern.

"You see that?" he said.

"Da." Svet pulled back from the glass, her hair floating around her head like Medusa's snakes.

"What could it be?" Hawk said.

"My first thought is it looks like a beacon," Max said.

"Me also. I thought of Morse code," Hawk said.

"This changes things. Someone—"

"Or something," Hawk interrupted. "Humans aren't due to hang around these parts for millions of years if we have our location and time period right."

"It got here somehow. It's not a natural formation, and that's the only clue we have. Whether the planet below is Earth or not doesn't matter," Max said.

Svet said, "How you know the light isn't natural?"

Max said nothing, but looked to Hawk.

"We don't, but we only have so much food, so staying up here isn't possible long term. Why wait? If we make it to the surface it would be nice to have some food to get started," Hawk said.

"What if it is trap?" Svet said.

"Set by who?"

"Or just some cosmic rock?" Max said.

"Or we can't breathe air?" Svet said.

"Possible, but unless one of you can see something I can't, we have but one option. We need to put on our spacesuits, abandon the station, and go planet side."

Hawk let that idea sit out there like a fart in church. Both Svet and Max were military trained space veterans, and giving up just wasn't in their DNA, so the debate didn't last long. After they rested they'd begin preparations to abandon the space station, the place they'd called home for almost a year. Using the Soyuz capsule docked at the station as a lifeboat, the two astronauts and one cosmonaut would fall to an Earth they no longer recognized as their home, leaving the remains of their friend behind in his orbiting grave.

As Svet pointed out, they weren't certain what the air composition was on the planet's surface, and thankfully the space station was equipped with spacesuits that had been designed for the Mars mission and were much more advanced than the Extravehicular Mobility Unit (EMU) spacefarers had used for many years. The new suits were much lighter, had a sleeker life support backpack, and could provide air into perpetuity via advanced oxygen scrubbers. Everything was powered by a new top-secret high-tech battery locked into the life support backpack so it couldn't be examined.

As he waited, Hawk felt the stars looking at him like millions of dead eyes. He peered down through the thick glass and saw the giant volcano spewing orange lava. About fifty clicks to the east the light beacon sparkled like a diamond.

Hawk would figure out what it was, or die in the attempt. He had nothing left to lose.

"Brace for impact!" Hawk said.

Their morning had started with an early scare when the electronic docking claw wouldn't work. After two hours of rerouting systems they finally managed to free themselves and begin their voyage. They had breathed pure oxygen while Svet played with the landing claw, so Hawk had ordered them to put on their spacesuit helmets and life-support backpacks as a precaution.

Hawk's fear that the landing parachutes that would allow the capsule to soft land had been damaged, or were covered in ice, proved unwarranted. When they had opened, and he felt the pull of tension on his harness, Hawk forgot, for a couple of minutes, what might await them upon landing.

All space station modules had been closed off, and all systems turned over to the computer, so Michel's tomb could theoretically remain in orbit for years due to the large solar arrays that captured the sun's energy above the horizon. With the station modules sealed from one another, it could sustain damage in one part but still not be destroyed.

Hawk shifted in his harness. His spacesuit was uncomfortable and he hated wearing it, but the precaution was worth the inconvenience. The capsule shook and vibrated until it thumped upon impact with the Earth. For an instant, the ship teetered and Hawk thought the capsule was going to tip over. After a few tense seconds the ship settled itself, but on a fifteen-degree incline. They had landed on something.

The capsule rocked like it was hit with a battering ram. The space ship fell on its side leaving Max and Svet looking down at Hawk as they hung in their seat harnesses. "What the hell..." said Max. The interior of their vessel echoed as something pounded on the hull. Hawk strained to see through the tiny porthole in the hatch, but saw only blue sky and white clouds.

An eye filled the porthole, and Hawk yelled. A red pupil rolled against a black cornea and settled on him, then narrowed. The capsule shook, and the eye splattered against the window, pieces of red skin and black eyeball sticking to the glass. They were jerked in their harnesses as the ship was lifted from the ground, and then they were free falling. Hawk and Max realized what was happening before Svet and they held tight to their restraints.

The capsule landed on its side and Svet shrieked when metal crunched. Silence fell, and they waited for several long minutes, expecting at any moment to be tossed like a pebble. Red light from the warning klaxon spilled across the cabin, painting everything in a ghostly red glow.

The capsule vibrated and the sound of thunder echoed through the cabin and Hawk jumped. The sound was unmistakable. A huge beast had just cried out in anger or pain or fear. Blood and blue sky filled the porthole, but it darkened as it fell into shadow. Another roar, and this time it was much closer. Hawk held his breath. Svet had her eyes squeezed closed and Max looked like he was praying, though Hawk knew the scientist wasn't religious.

The vibration eased, the thunder faded. The red alarm klaxon and rays of sunlight sent daggers through the capsule. Several minutes passed. Hawk said, "Check yourself out before you climb out of your harness. Make sure all the seals on your suits are tip-top." He snapped free of his harness.

Static filled Hawk's headset, then "Yup," from Max, and "10-4," from Svet. Hawk pulled a key from the pocket of his spacesuit using a short tether, and unlocked the storage container bolted under his seat. Within were two Ash 12 machine guns and an MP-446C Viking handgun, a spare magazine, related holster and shoulder straps, ammunition, a knife, and a bottle of Russian vodka. Hawk smiled at the thought of the anonymous soldier at Roscosmos that had put the vodka in their last shipment of food and supplies.

The guns had been a different matter. Firearms in space were frowned upon and the International Space Station didn't stock weapons. Svet had found the machine guns and pistol hidden in her personal locker with a note from her husband. The cloud had everyone on edge, and Vladimir wanted her to have protection because he couldn't be there. Svet informed Hawk as soon as she'd found the guns, and they'd told Max and Michel.

Hawk strapped on a leg holster he'd modified to fit over his spacesuit and slipped the loaded Viking into its cradle. Then he slammed a magazine containing lightweight supersonic bullets with aluminum cores into one of the Ash 12s and pulled back the bolt, loading a round into the chamber. They would load all the weapons, but they would be fired only when necessary. They needed to conserve ammo and reloading would be difficult while wearing spacesuit gloves. They'd wrapped their trigger fingers tightly with duct-tape, which made it possible to fire the weapons with their gloves on, but it was a challenge.

"Are we where we want to be?" Hawk asked. They had plotted a course to touch down as close to the light anomaly as possible. Their plan was to utilize the capsule as a base, and search the area.

"Think so. We were tossed pretty good, but we should be pretty close to our mark," Max said.

"We're dead here, Hawk, nothing but a trickle. Going short range suit-to-suit," said Svet, static filling the comm channel. "We got nothing left. All systems are down. The batteries must have been damaged. We've used up what little juice we had, so we're gonna have to pop the hatch manually."

Hawk nodded. Svet and Max collected their weapons and the three spacefarers fumbled around the cabin and each other. The spacesuits were difficult to maneuver in, especially in tight spaces, but thankfully their years of training had made functioning in them like riding a bike.

"Everyone ready?" Hawk asked.

Svet popped the hatch, and air rushed into the capsule.

# 3

Jungle sounds filtered into the capsule, a great braying and squawking and roaring. Something large and green circled in the clouds above the open hatch. Hawk breathed easy. His suit didn't show any warning lights, and he looked at each of his shipmates and smiled.

"As you can hear, we're entering an environment filled with unknowns. Heads on a swivel," Hawk said.

Svet inched through the hatch, then disappeared as something with coarse yellow skin darted across the hull and grabbed her like she was a ragdoll.

"SHIIIIIT," yelled Hawk. He thrust himself along the steel footholds until he was halfway through the hatch. The capsule leaned on an angle, one side crushed against a tree, and he used the metal ladder on the ship's side to get down.

Lush and abundant tropical jungle filled every empty space as the plants fought for access to sunlight. The spaceship had left a trail of broken trees and flattened vegetation where it tumbled, but the sea of green went on and on.

A horse-sized beast stood over Svet, slime dripping from its tooth-filled maw. The creature had a short neck and a long yellow and green striped head. Its tail shot out like an arrow as it bent over, and short arms pressed Svet to the ground as it prepared to take a bite out of her.

Hawk drew down and opened up with the Viking, peppering the creature with bullets. He cringed behind his tinted visor as he fired, the empty shells bouncing off his boots. Mindful of wasting ammo, he stopped firing after four headshots. The creature fell to the ground and Svet pulled herself out from under the animal, moving like a child who'd been bundled up by her mother so she could play in the snow.

Hawk ran to her, straining beneath the bulk of the spacesuit. Max followed, and in the space of a minute, the two astronauts were at Svet's side.

"Are you alright?" Max said.

"I think so." She was breathing hard, and her faceplate fogged as she sucked for air. "Just got… the air… knocked out."

"Easy," Max said.

A tree branch snapped. Hawk's head jerked toward the sound, but there was nothing there but a wall of green leaves and palm fronds. "Can you walk?" he said.

She nodded as Hawk helped her to her feet, and the two astronauts and one cosmonaut put their backs to the capsule and peered into the green gloom of the primordial jungle.

"That was close," said Svet. She turned to Hawk. "Thanks."

Hawk wondered if he'd done the woman a favor, or a disservice. "Don't thank me yet."

A lizard the size of a cat bolted through the foliage on its hind legs and hissed at them as it tore past. Insects hummed and buzzed, and the dense tropical canopy blotted out the sky except over their trail of destruction. There, a streak of blue cloud-filled sky cut through the greenery, revealing huge creatures with tent wings gliding in circles over their position. Rodents and small dog-like animals crawled from the jungle, and several ostrich beasts with dark gray leathery skin inched tentatively out of the underbrush, heads bobbing as they stared at the newcomers. Hawk felt like Bambi when the animals of the forest emerged to examine the new oddity. Pain danced down his back. Every creature for twenty clicks had seen where they landed.

"I think we should retreat into the ship. Re-evaluate," Hawk said.

"Da."

"We might have underestimated the wildlife," Max said.

"You think?" Svet said.

"Yes… I… Do," Max said, doing his best Chandler Bing impersonation and failing miserably.

Everything went still.

Hawk looked at his mates.

The insects had stopped trilling. There was no screeching, no grunts or whomps or clicks. Nothing pecked at wood. No birds fought. Only a gentle undercurrent of wind pushed through the forest, rustling large green leaves and rattling palm fronds. All living things had suddenly become one, and agreed to be silent.

The party kept their backs to the capsule and worked their way around to the metal ladder that led to the hatch. Max and Svet climbed aboard while Hawk covered them. Sweat inched down Hawk's back and his body itched beneath his spacesuit. Pain crept up his legs as his feet shriveled in his damp socks. When Svet and Max were inside he holstered the Viking and started to climb, each movement heavy and cumbersome in the spacesuit.

Hawk was half way up the ladder, his back to the jungle, when he felt vibration in the metal rungs. He paused, his instincts and training ahead of his thought process. If he stayed still the world might not see him and forget he was there. In the distance a sound like mortars exploding accompanied the trembling earth. It was growing stronger and steadier like a heartbeat.

Hawk rotated his head and looked over his shoulder, but saw only a wall of green. Beneath the shade of the thick canopy, Hawk lost his sense of direction. He pulled himself up the last few rungs and dropped into the capsule.

"What is it?" Max said.

"Don't know. Couldn't see. Probably the thing that tossed us."

"I think we were wrong. We should leave. Da?" Svet said.

Hawk's sigh echoed over the suit comm. Svet had a point. They needed to blend in, disappear, and staying in the capsule made them stand out like a cockroach on a baby's ass. But it did provide protection. "That reevaluation didn't take long," Hawk said.

"Make a bad decision, make another decision," Max said.

"Aye," Hawk said. "Grab what you can. We're gone in thirty seconds."

The earth trembled hard, branches cracked and the patch of blue cloud-filled-sky visible through the hatch was obscured by green and black striped skin. The spacefarers scrambled to gather their belongings, but a roar froze Hawk in place.

The capsule was knocked on its side, and Hawk, Svet and Max piled-up in the nosecone as the ship came to rest with a shuddering screech of metal. Another primal bellow of fury filled the world as fangs punctured the hull. Metal bent as the creature crushed the spacecraft, and the ship rolled and landed in loose mud. Dark brown dirt oozed in through the open hatch, filling the cabin.

"Let's go. Stay out of sight in the mud as much as you can. It'll hide you. Hurry now," Hawk said. He pushed Max toward the hatch and mud poured on the physicist as he wiggled out. Svet followed and dirt-sludge rose to Hawk's knees as he trailed after his mates. He was almost to the hatch when the hull jerked and he flew across the cabin, crashing into the control panel. The capsule rolled again and the inflow of mud stopped. Blue sky filled the hatch, and dust filtered sunlight streamed through rents in the hull.

Gunshots rang out. Hawk expected to get flicked like a booger at any moment. A guttural snarl echoed through the cabin as he sloshed through the mud, grabbing handholds and pulling himself through the shifting sludge. His faceplate was covered in grime and the jungle outside was cast in dripping sepia tone.

Hawk emerged from the capsule next to a huge claw.

He'd seen *Jurassic Park*, the new one and the original. He could pass Dinosaur 101. A three-story *tyrannosaurus rex*, or a closely related genus, stood over him, its long tail taut. Two fingered hands hung from stunted arms, and claw-like feet with razor sharp talons raked at the ground as if spoiling to run. Thick black legs supported a green, yellow and black streaked torso, and muscles heaved and pulled beneath the leathery skin. The dinosaur's thick neck pointed toward the jungle, its head lurching back and forth in spasmodic jerks as it listened for the source of the gunshots.

Hawk backed away, taking advantage of the diversion, eyes up, the T-Rex's torso undulating above him as it shifted its weight back and forth. A long scar ran along the beast's right leg, and bone poked through the darkened wound.

Hawk was exposed and had to move. If he could go unnoticed for a few more seconds he might slip into the jungle before the beast turned its attention back to the capsule. That plan lasted five seconds.

A flock of lizard-like beasts the size of chickens exploded from the foliage, yipping and puffing. They had gray feathers that appeared slick with water, and their red eyes were circled in rings of white. The T-Rex pulled its attention from the jungle and looked down at them with its dark eyes. The beast roared, and lifted a leg and stomped. The ground shook and Hawk staggered as the chicken-lizards scattered and disappeared back into the dense vegetation.

The T-Rex eased back with two thunderous steps and bent over, its jaws chomping and searching for Hawk. Teeth five feet long bit the air next to him. Hawk ran, not paying attention to his direction, what lay before him, or what might be waiting within the dark confines of the primeval jungle. The dinosaur bellowed again, and rose to its full height, whipping its tale in a wide arc that cracked against a tree as Hawk dove into the forest. Wood splintered, and trees fell around Hawk as he ran, leaves and branches falling like rain. The earth shook and the pounding of great footfalls filled the world. Vines and leaves ripped at his faceplate and spacesuit, and each step became more labored.

A gloved hand reached out and grabbed him, but Hawk instinctively pulled free.

"It's us. Here." Hiding within the cleft of a tree were Max and Svet.

"It's coming this way!" Hawk said, but the beast had already arrived.

The trees behind them parted and the dinosaur's head poked through the branches. It screamed in anger and whipped its tail, breaking the tree Max and Svet hid within. They ran blindly, pouring through the trees with reckless abandon, fear propelling them forward.

"Ahhhhh," Max yelled. He was down, clutching his knee.

Svet helped him up, but Max couldn't run, and as the two hobbled before the T-Rex, Hawk knew he had to do something or his companions would be lost.

Hawk did a one-eighty and bolted past his mates, between the T-Rex's legs, and under the beast as it pushed between two large trees. Branches fell, and the animal didn't appear to notice him, so Hawk yelled as he passed beneath the goliath.

The T-Rex cried out again, lifted a leg and tried to stomp Hawk as he passed. When it missed, the beast swung its massive tail, but Hawk pulled and juked, lumbering along as fast as his spacesuit would allow. He climbed over fallen trees as the beast tried to turn around in the tight forest and give chase. His suit fan was running full tilt, but Hawk was sweating profusely and struggling to breathe.

Hawk got back to the capsule, but there was no good place to hide so he dove into a mud puddle. The dinosaur shrieked, and when it couldn't find him it turned its attention back to the capsule. Its massive jaws crunched down on the spaceship, digging into the metal like meat. The T-Rex lifted its head and shook the capsule side to side, tearing at it with its massive teeth. The sound of ripping metal screeched and whined, and the dinosaur dropped the ship. It landed with a final crunch and looked like a flattened tin can.

Hawk crawled and slithered through the mud into the jungle, and he realized he still had one of the supply bags tied to a lanyard on his spacesuit. He hoped it was the one with the vodka in it.

# 4

They hadn't gone far before Hawk called a halt. They were about a mile from the destroyed capsule, and he and his team were exhausted, hungry and thirsty. A dark cotton sky rolled overhead, puffy nimbus clouds that looked ripe for rain. They'd followed animal paths through the dense jungle, and Hawk didn't like being confined. If they needed to move fast they'd get tangled in the underbrush, and with Max's knee hurt, that was a race Hawk didn't want to run.

Svet plunked down on a rotted log and let her helmet fall into her gloved hands, elbows on knees. Max went to pull free his storage bag and discovered it was gone.

"Shit, I lost my stuff."

"Da, me also," Svet said.

Hawk felt along his spacesuit and found his bag still dangling from its lanyard. He sat by Svet, his back to the log. He opened his bag and pulled out a ration of dried fruit and tore open the vacuum-packed bag, but when he went to pop a piece of pineapple in his mouth he realized he still had his helmet on. The suits were going to be a problem.

Svet was two steps ahead of him and she stood, feeling around the outer edge of her helmet, searching for the release clasps.

"What are you doing?" Max's voice was a static-filled whine.

"What does it matter? We can't live in these things forever." She unclamped the hasp on her helmet.

"But we don't know—"

"What? What don't we know? Wh—*static*—ee are. When we are," Svet said.

"What if the air is toxic?" Max said.

"Then we're dead anyway," Hawk said. "We won't know for sure tomorrow or the day after that. At some point we'll have to take the risk, why not now?"

"Da, and the animals. They are breathing fine, nyet?"

"Yeah, as hard as this is to wrap your noddle around I think we've somehow been thrown back in time. Way back, so the air quality should be better than what we're used to," Max said.

They'd discussed this back on the space station, but up in space surrounded by metal and technology the idea seemed beyond fantastical. Time travel wasn't possible, he knew that much, at least not the kind that jumped you from one time to another. Time dilation was a type of time travel, and maybe they'd moved so fast they hadn't had time to process it, but if that was the case they would have gone forward in time, not back. Was it possible this Earth was in the future and all their assumptions about the beacon were wrong? It seemed unlikely that the dinosaurs would get a second act and what about the land masses? Could they have circled the globe and come back together on the opposite side like a reverse Pangaea? Did any of it matter? They needed to survive, and from Hawk's perspective that appeared to be a 'death till you part' journey.

"Let me go first," Hawk said. He unclipped the hasp and lifted his helmet off, holding his breath. Slowly he exhaled and sucked in air. He smiled and took another deep breath.

They stripped out of their suits and their undergarments beneath were drenched through. The air smelt of shit and flowers, and it reminded Hawk of his grandmother's bathroom; rose air freshener laid over the underlying scent of crap and decay. Around them tall trees with round tops and small leaves towered over palms and tropical plants with large green and yellow leaves. The ground was covered in thick loam, and here and there bugs of various sizes and shapes trundled about their business, hoping to go unnoticed.

"What the hell?" Max said.

"Whoa," Hawk said.

They were both staring at Svet.

"What?"

The log Svet sat on was turning yellow, a moving ooze like honey slid over the log and onto Svet. Ants the size of a fingernail swarmed over the log, their antennas bobbing as they walked, dark eyes and mandibles standing out against the yellow. The bugs were coming out of a hole on the side of the log, and when Svet saw them she jumped up.

"Ah, one bit me," she said, rubbing her arm where a red welt had appeared. The area began to swell.

"Wish I hadn't lost the med supplies. I had a cream that could help with that and stop the itching," Max said.

"And burning," she said.

"That brings me to an uncomfortable topic. Max is hurt, and we need to hunker down and get settled so we can fix him up and get our bearings. But first, I think I need to go back to the capsule and see if I can find some of our supplies," Hawk said.

"Isn't that going to be dangerous with that animal around?" Max said. Then he seemed to realize the futility of his question and said, "I guess we need to get used to that, what with the things being everywhere."

They moved away from the ants and Hawk dumped his bag on the ground to take inventory. He had sixteen dried packs of rations, which they could split, so that would hold them for a few days until they figured what they could eat, and how to kill or gather it without being eaten themselves. There was twenty-five feet or so of thick cord, the bottle of vodka, four stainless-steel containers of water, and his small satchel of personals which contained pictures of his family, a copy of *The Martian* by Andy Weir, a flashlight, two pairs of socks, one pair of underwear, and a spare clip for the Viking with twenty rounds in it.

Finding the ammunition pushed another thought to the forefront. "Another reason I need to go back is your ammo. We need to save our bullets, because I don't see a sporting goods store around here."

"I stay and watch Max, and you go?" Svet said.

Hawk considered this. "Svet, I think I need you with me. We'll find a place for Max to hide until we get back."

Max said, "Yeah, what could you do? Shoot at the thing? I can do that myself."

"Da," Svet said.

They found a large bush that looked like a mangled *rhododendron* with large leaves and after a cursory check for ants and hazards, Max crawled beneath it with his gun. To be safe, they laid the spacesuits on the ground like a blanket and Max lay on top.

"You good?" Hawk asked.

"How will you know how to find me?"

Svet pulled her knife and said, "Mark trees."

Hawk nodded, and without another word, plunged back into the forest in the direction of the destroyed space capsule with Svet in tow. Huge ferns with green and red variegated leaves blocked their way, and as Hawk pushed through them smaller animals and insects fled before them, yipping and hissing their distaste at the newcomers.

Svet paused several times and carved large Xs into trees, marking their meandering path through the jungle. Going in a straight line was impossible with all the trees, plants and bushes clogging the forest. Forced to wear their spacesuit boots because they had nothing else, being stealthy was challenging. Hawk eyed every shadow, every clump of leaves. The confines of the jungle made it difficult to see what was ten feet away, and based on what Hawk had seen so far, the wildlife of this era was well camouflaged.

The air was sweet, and reminded Hawk of his home in Florida, but as they got closer to the wreck site it turned fowl. The scent of shit pervaded the air, and when they arrived at the crash site the cause of the rankness became clear.

A huge pile of crap, three feet tall, rested next to the remains of the capsule. Bones and other solid debris, such as bark and leaf matter, stuck from the pile like pins from a pincushion.

"Damn," Hawk said. He drew his Viking and panned it around the clearing in a wide arc, but there was no sign of their T-Rex friend or anything else big enough to cause them harm.

"Da," Svet said. She had her Ash 12 slung over a shoulder, and her knife was in its sheath on her right leg.

"Cover me while I look," Hawk said. He slipped the Viking back into its cradle and walked around the giant pile of dinosaur dung.

The capsule was a pile of metal, and food rations were scattered on the ground. Some were crushed and torn open, but Hawk collected them all and made a pile. Then he searched the area in a grid pattern, Svet watching with her cool gray eyes, her gun at the ready. The screech of an animal close by made Hawk pick up his pace, though the ground didn't shake. The buzz and hum of the jungle was loud, and every few moments there was a bark followed by a growl as the creatures of the day prepared to give up their claims to the beasts of the night.

It started to rain, small biting drops quickly turning into a spattering assault. The pile of dung began to run, and that's when Hawk saw the bag. It had been pushed under a pile of sticks and leaves, and Hawk was relieved to find it unopened and unbroken. It contained more food rations, a spare clip for an Ash 12 with twenty rounds, another flashlight, water, a knife, and Svet's purse containing her personal items, which thankfully included a small box of sanitary napkins. Hawk frowned. How would the creatures of this Earth respond to a human female's menstrual cycle?

Max's bag was nowhere to be found, and there wasn't much they could salvage from the capsule.

"Can you help me with this stuff?" Hawk said. He'd stuffed as many food rations as he could into the bag, but several didn't fit.

"Da," Svet said.

They followed the marked trees back to Max, their thick boot prints barely visible in the soft loam covered ground. They avoided several large birds that seemed intent on drawing every beast for ten miles to their location. They yelled and squawked, and dive-bombed them twice, but didn't attack. The rain picked up, and large drops fell through the dense tree canopy, slapping leaves in an odd rhythmic pattern that sounded like a jazzy drum solo. When they were close, Hawk called out to Max.

"Here," Max said.

"What now?" Svet said.

"It'll be dark soon and something tells me we don't want to be out in the open," Max said.

"We need to find shelter for the night and get out of this rain," Hawk said.

His companions nodded, but said nothing. They packed up the best they could, even bringing their spacesuits and helmets because Hawk explained they could serve as bedrolls and the material might be of use. They trudged through the thick vegetation, heads down, trying to make themselves as small as possible.

They'd walked about an hour when they found a fallen tree. It had uprooted, and had a large hollowed out hole beneath its labyrinth of dead roots. "This is it," Hawk said. "Svet, gather as many leaves and palm fronds as you can and we'll line the inside of the hole with them. Max, take a seat there and keep watch while I collect sticks."

Hawk checked the hollow beneath the tree to make sure there weren't already guests staying in this five-star hole, and found bugs and a few small lizards, but nothing of concern. He helped Max into their new shelter and he laid on the floor of green leaves and palm fronds Svet had laid. Hawk used the sticks and debris he'd collected to wall off the open side of the hole and hide them within and then covered everything with dirt to hide their scent. He thought about lighting a fire, then thought better of it. Best not to send up any smoke signals until they were prepared for what might come looking for them.

Hawk stripped off his gun holster and hung it from a tree root and plopped down next to Max.

"It's time to eat. I'm starving," Max said.

"And I need a drink," Svet said as she pulled free the bottle of vodka.

# 5

The two astronauts and one cosmonaut sat cross-legged in their makeshift shelter, the jungle outside a cacophony of life. Night had fallen, revealing a spectacular sky unblurred by light pollution or smog. The temperature fell precipitously, and Hawk estimated it was fifty degrees. Max and Svet draped their spacesuits over themselves as they passed around the bottle of vodka. Daggers of starlight stabbed the darkness as it penetrated through cracks and holes in Hawk's wall.

"Let me see that," Hawk said.

Svet laughed but didn't hand over the bottle.

"I'm not joking."

"Nor I."

"I know it's Russian vodka, but—"

Svet took a pull then dumped some of the alcohol on a piece of cloth torn from the inside of her spacesuit, and began dabbing her ant bite with it.

"Screw that," Max said. He smiled, swiped the bottle, and took a long swig.

"You think we should save some?" Hawk asked.

"For?" Svet said.

"Who knows. The future?"

"What future?"

"The map," Max said, his voice hesitant and slurred. He took another long pull and handed the bottle to Hawk.

Between them, hidden in the blackness, a map had been scratched into the dirt with a stick. Hawk and the others had drawn it, but without any landmarks it was hard to know exactly where they were. There was forest, mountains, the volcano, and the beacon, arranged from their recollections, nothing more.

"In the morning we'll find a clearing and see where the sun's at. That will tell us east and west," Max said.

"So? We don't know where we are on map," Svet said, pointing to the dark patch between them. The plan was to use a blank page from Hawk's book to transcribe the map and update it as they went.

"We'll reconnoiter the area, see if we can spot the mountain range," Hawk said. "That, along with the sun should give us a decent bearing and maybe we'll be able to see the beacon light as we get closer." Hawk had searched the night sky, but from his limited vantage point he didn't see it.

"Klevyy," Svet said.

"No, not cool," Max said. He flicked on the flashlight and trained it on the map. "This was derived from memory, and like Svet said we really don't know where we are. We could be on the other side of the mountains."

"Da, but we hit ocean," Svet said.

"Yeah, but then we need to come all the way back," Max said.

"We got nothing but time," Hawk said. "And I don't see another way. Do you?" He took a long pull of vodka and handed the bottle to Svet.

Max and Svet shook their heads, but said nothing.

"How's your knee?" Hawk said. Without ice and drugs there wasn't much they could do.

"A little better," Max said.

"In the morning I'll make a brace so it no bend. Be easier to walk," Svet said.

"I don't see myself going far for a few days. This has happened to me before and it takes a week or so for the swelling to go down, and that's with ice," Max countered. "It's an old football injury that rears its ugly head from time to time. Gretta used to say…"

No one spoke.

"Talking about her in the past tense when she hasn't been born yet feels strange."

"Makes sense, and you don't know if she's dead," Hawk said.

"Da."

"Michel," Max said. "We know he's dead, and that soon we'll be."

The hum of the forest filled the shelter.

Hawk tried not to think about his wife and kids, or Michel, and the idea that he'd never see them again, so he changed the subject. "You played football?" They'd been on the station for a year, but Hawk didn't know much about his shipmates beyond the basics. The routine aboard the International Space Station had been rigorous and time consuming, and there'd been little time for conversation of any kind, and when they did talk, it always veered toward the station and their work there.

"Not American football, but yeah, I was a backup at university. Got hurt at practice," Max said. "I played a little as a boy, but I was never very good. My father was proud, though."

"Football is a religion in Germany, no?" Hawk said.

"Yes, one my wife…" He trailed off again.

"Look we're going to have to get used to being here alone, without our families and friends. Not talking about them, or mentioning them, will dim our memories of them. I don't want that. I want to remember them all. Need to. Michel also," Hawk said.

"Da," Svet said.

"It's just, I can't bear thinking of them. It makes my chest ache," Max said.

"Tell us about them," Svet said. "You feel better." She handed the half full bottle of vodka to Max.

He took a pull, and said, "Gretta was my first girlfriend. We met in gymnasium and we both knew right away we were meant to be together. If it wasn't for her I wouldn't be here." He paused and cocked his head to the side. "You understand my meaning, ja?"

Hawk and Svet laughed.

"I do. Andrea and I were the same way, but we'd both dated several people before we met," Hawk said.

Outside, a great guttural shriek of anger pierced the night, then the wet sound of meat being torn from bone. Loud cracking echoed through the shelter, and the unmistakable horror of snapping bones made Hawk wince. Whatever was out there had been quiet before it attacked, because Hawk hadn't heard the animal's approach and by the sound of things the commotion wasn't far away.

Ignoring the chaos outside Svet said, "What of your little ones?"

Max started to answer, but paused. A beam of starlight illuminated a beetle-like insect with a dark carapace and yellow-streaked shell as it worked its way down one of the tree roots sticking from the dirt ceiling. It paused, turning its luminescent eyes on the three spacefarers, then continued its trek. When it got to the end of the root and could go no further its head swiveled, and it turned around and headed back up the root and disappeared into the darkness.

Max chuckled. “Having kids is like getting drunk for the first time. It’s cool, then it’s awesome, then it’s awful, then horrible. They capture your soul, take control of you, then break your heart,” he said. “Some say it all comes full circle, but my kids aren’t that old.”

Svet harrumphed, her teeth glowing in the darkness.

“He’s right. There’s no way you can understand.” Hawk was the biggest dipshit ever. He’d just reminded her that she would never have children. “I’m sorry. I’m an ass.”

“It’s A-OK. Really. My sister always said…”

There it was again. That past tense.

“What about you, Hawk? Did Jonah and Sally take away your control?” Max asked.

Hawk closed his eyes, trying to picture the night his children were born, but there was nothing but a blank canvas because he hadn’t been there. “No. I was always off fighting a war, or in some training. Andrea was the one who raised our kids.” His chest hurt. Now they were gone. “I always thought there’d be time.”

“Even with all the danger you lived through?” Svet said.

“Especially because of that. I’d cheated death so many times I started to take it for granted. I thought Andrea would always be there, and that I’d retire young and we’d spend the rest of our lives living and helping our children raise their own families. It was the life I chose, and the life Andrea agreed to. I guess we were too afraid to change.”

“Regrets?” Max said.

“I have a few.”

They chuckled, an odd sound beneath the screeching and hollering of the jungle outside.

"As the kids got older they had their own lives, and when they were young they'd drive me batshit because I wasn't used to being around them."

"Batshit?"

"Sorry, Svet. Crazy. Loony." Hawk searched for the Russian word. "Psikh."

"Daaaa. At least you both got to have kids. Vladimir and I planned to, but it was always after the next mission, the next war, the next opportunity we couldn't pass up." Svet hissed in the darkness. "Like a tour on the International Space Station. Not that we have much say."

With all the hoopla about how democratic Russia had become, when it came to serving the motherland your freedom was limited. This had always been evident on the station. While there was respect, there was an underlying wariness that separated Svet from her two crewmates. Despite history, the German and the American didn't share this distrust. This rare display of honesty by Svet swelled Hawk's worry wart.

Max took a long pull of vodka and gave Hawk the bottle.

"I'm gonna cap this," Hawk said.

A chorus of nein and nyet from Max and Svet.

"Listen." If a voice could stagger, Hawk's had. "I've seen *Gilligan's Island*, OK? I don't see myself building a still out of wood and using fruit to make booze anytime soon. And we might need for medicine… medical stuff."

"Were you always the buzzkill, or was it something you learned in officer training?" Max said.

Svet laughed, then burped. "We, how you say? Shit out luck?"

They all laughed, then fell silent.

"So, what do you guys think the light is?" Hawk said. The silence stretched out, the blackness got thicker, and the sound of animal chaos made Hawk's ears ring. "It was bright, so I'm having a hard time convincing myself it's natural."

"A mineral deposit of some kind?" Svet said. She yawned loudly.

"What mineral can retain and emanate light? Under the sun's rays maybe, but at night?"

The German physicist said, "All minerals reflect light. That's what makes them visible to the human eye. Some have an interesting physical property known as fluorescence. These minerals absorb a small amount of light and an instant later release this light on a different wavelength. This change in wavelength causes a temporary color change in the eye of the observer. The effect is most spectacular when minerals are illuminated in darkness by ultraviolet light, which we can't see, and they release visible light."

"So, Svet's right? It could be a pile of rocks?"

"I don't see how. The effects of fluorescence are short, and what we saw was a pulsating, strong beam of light."

"Could some light source from within the Earth be shining through minerals on the surface? Like a lava flow beneath an exposed vein of quartz?" Hawk asked.

"Possible. Hadn't thought of that," Max said. "But why would it pulse?" Max answered his own question, "There could be a random intermittent obstruction of some kind. I just don't know."

Hawk and Svet said nothing.

Hawk was sorry he'd thought of that. What little hope they had, and he wasn't fooling himself, they had very little, was in the light being a beacon. Something linked to intelligent life. Life that might be able to help them. If the light was nothing more than a natural phenomenon, there was no hope at all.

Svet's snore tore through the shelter.

"She's got the right idea," Max said. "What's the plan for tomorrow?"

"I'm gonna climb a tree."

"Logical," Max said. His Spock voice wasn't bad.

# 6

Morning in the jungle was a gray haze of twilight, dappled sunrays, and ethereal shadows. The creatures of the night slithered and crawled into their lairs, and the beasts of the sun rose to greet another day of survival. The sky was a distant memory, hidden by a thick ceiling of green life that sucked up every sunbeam. Vines and creepers fought with trees for supremacy, while giant ferns, mosses, and broad-leafed weeds shared the ground, which was perpetually drenched in a netherworld of dusk.

A hundred feet from their shelter, beneath the roots of a fallen tree, Hawk found the remains of the beast that was torn apart the prior night. Piles of knifelike shards of bone lay atop black stains on the jungle floor, and splatters of dark blood speckled the foliage including two large bent trees. The scent of rotting meat and earth stuck in Hawk's nose, and the maggots and insects that swarmed the picked-clean bones made his stomach gurgle. It was impossible to tell what type of creature it had been.

Hawk spent time fortifying the shelter, stacking more branches against the open end of their hole, and constructing a six-foot fence made of pointed sticks to keep out the smaller riffraff. Most critters stayed clear of them, but Svet found two spots where something had tried to dig into the shelter.

The cosmonaut worked on the interior of their accommodations, feathering the floor and walls with leaves and palm fronds. She tied the roots hanging from the ceiling into braids and twisted them into loops, from which they hung articles of clothing. She made a shelf for the food, flashlight, ammo, and their personals, and even dug a fire pit and created a chimney through the dirt ceiling in hopes of kindling a fire.

While they worked, Max rested with his leg elevated, his ankle suspended via a dried vine looped through a root-ring hanging from the ceiling. Hawk packed one of the bags with two food rations, their last bottle of water, and extra bullets. He strapped on the Viking and Svet grabbed her knife and shouldered an Ash 12.

"We need some light for tonight. The flashlight isn't going to last long," Max said.

"Da."

"Can we make candles?" Hawk said.

"Ja," Max said. "But we'll need a fire to do it. We need to get some animal fat and render it down. Find wick material."

"Da. Fire," Svet said.

"As I said last night, I don't think we should risk it until we better understand our surroundings," Hawk said. "The scent will carry for miles. The idea of sending the sweet aroma of cooking meat across the jungle doesn't fill me with comfort."

"Understood," Max said. "But we've only got enough food for a few weeks, and that's stretching it. We should try hunting, start experimenting with the plants, and save our rations for when we're in a real pinch."

"Da. Use dry wood. Keep smoke down," Svet said.

"We're almost out of water, Hawk. When we do find a source we'll need to boil it or take a big risk. I'd prefer to see animals drinking from the source, but that might not be possible. What we suck off leaves should be OK. It's probably all OK."

Svet and Hawk said nothing.

"Sorry. My scientist brain thinking out loud."

"No, please overthink. Overthink like a mother-fucker. You saw those piles of bones. That was a little one. If a big boy gets hold of us it's over," Hawk said.

His comrades said nothing.

"What about a test. Light a fire away from here. Watch from the shadows and see what happens," Hawk said.

"Da."

"Ja."

"Ria."

No laughs. Nothing.

"Get it? Diarrhea?"

"Shit?" Max said.

"Forget it." Hawk was determined to keep things light. He didn't want Michel's death and the loss of their families to be a constant weight.

"We need to conserve ammo so we need to make weapons," Max said.

"We can use shards of bone for arrowheads, spear points and knives. I can also make staves, a bolas, and maybe an incendiary device or two," Hawk said.

Svet chuckled. "You funny guy."

"I wasn't joking."

"Kakiye?"

"Hawk's right. We could make gunpowder," Max said. "In Arena, Kirk made gun powder from charcoal, sulfur, and potassium nitrate. All things found in nature."

"OK, MacGyver. Where the shit are we going to get sulfur and potassium nitrate?"

Svet said, "If you let me make fire I provide charcoal."

"Later. First we run our fire test and get a look from above," Hawk said.

Max's leg was getting better, but there was no reason he should stress his knee so Hawk and Svet trekked into the jungle without him. It was slow going. The underbrush was thick, and they were forced to change direction several times because massive conifer trees with widely spaced limbs and thick trunks blocked their way. Svet marked trees, but soon Hawk was having trouble maintaining a consistent direction.

They hadn't gone far when they came upon an open black patch. At the clearing's center a black pencil of a tree protruded from a blanket of green. Hawk figured a lightning bolt had hit the tree and torched the jungle, though much of the area had already been overtaken with creepers and underbrush.

Seeing the burnt tree brought hope. Fire wasn't anything new in these parts and perhaps the animals were used to the smell, they might even understand the danger and stay away. Fire might work better than any wall or hideout.

"Let's see if we can get that tree burning again. This is the perfect spot," Hawk said.

"Da. Want me to light it?"

"Naw, I got it." Hawk strode across the clearing until he stood before the blackened tree. It was nothing more than charcoal, and all it took was a few sparks from Svet's knife being tapped on a smooth stone to set it aflame. The fried tree caught, and black smoke as thick as night rolled over the clearing, lifting into the sky and covering the jungle in haze. There wasn't much left of the tree to burn, and tiny blue and yellow flames fought to stay alive.

With a pop and crack the tree came down with a crash, falling on the carpet of green. The fresh, moist vegetation smothered the flames, and the smoke got thicker and blacker. Hawk and Svet retreated to the tree break, waiting to see what their commotion would bring. Smoke billowed over the forest, sending nonsensical smoke signals through the gaps in the trees, reaching for the blue sky.

The smoke thinned and the smoldering flames winked out. Nothing came to investigate. The entire event had gone unnoticed. When he thought enough time had passed, Hawk said, "I guess that was much to do about nothing."

"Da. You surprised? With all volcanic activity the wildlife be used to fire."

"Still, I think we need to be cautious. The small fire pit you built in the shelter should be perfect. When we get back we'll gather some dry wood."

Svet lifted her Ash 12. "Hunt?"

"Not yet. And remember, we don't want to waste ammo, but for this first time I suppose we can waste a bullet or two until we get some primitive weapons constructed."

Svet smiled and nodded.

Test successfully completed, the pair plunged back into the thick jungle. Now their mission was to find a tall, climbable tree, preferably at the edge of the forest, yet said demarcation line appeared nowhere in sight. They hiked until Hawk estimated they'd traveled four miles, then stopped to rest and split a ration of dried beef stew.

Svet and Hawk passed the reflective pouch back and forth, taking small bites, savoring the dried beef and brown gravy. Hawk understood how they dried stew, and ice cream of all things, but he didn't know how NASA did it so well.

The section of jungle where they rested was comprised of tall, thick conifers with limbs widely spaced apart like the trees had grown very fast. Hawk thought he could climb any of them, but determining which one was tallest was impossible because the trees melted into a single canopy as they rose into the sky.

"Much further?" Svet said.

"Nope. I think I'm gonna climb this one right here." Hawk slapped the brown trunk of the tree he leaned against. Birds and insects chortled and squealed, and every few minutes a great roar or howl would rise above the tumult, but none of them sounded close.

Hawk got up and dusted himself off. "OK, see you in a few minutes."

"Da."

Hawk pulled the length of cord from his bag and put the loop on his shoulder. He jumped, grabbed the lowest branch and hoisted himself up. The branch was thick and had no problem supporting him, and he used it to ascend to the next branch. Limb by limb he climbed, and as he went things got tight, the tree's branches expanding into nearby trees. Insects dive bombed his face, and ants marched along the trunk.

When he was halfway up he realized the next tree over was taller, so he eased out on a branch and transferred himself to the larger tree and continued his ascent. Blue sky peeked through the canopy, and bright rays of sunlight worked their way through the dense leaves.

Hawk looked down, but he couldn't see Svet. He was two hundred feet up, and a nervous chill ran through him. He tossed an end of rope over the branch above him and tied the other end around his waist. This safety line would at least slow him down should he fall.

The branches got thinner as Hawk approached the top, and the tree swayed gently in the wind, easing back and forth with the additional weight like a clock pendulum. Breaks of blue cloud-filled sky were visible overhead, and Hawk flinched when a huge dragon-like *pterosaur* sailed feet above the tree canopy, blotting out the sun and drenching him in shadow.

When he could go no further, Hawk tied off his safety line and settled against the tree trunk. Many branches still obstructed his view, but he could see well enough.

The sun approached noon, and to the west the jungle thinned and opened into a massive savannah speckled with trees, bushes, and tall grass. To the south a blue lake shimmered in the sun, and beyond the savannah mountains and an erupting volcano cut across the horizon like a brown skid mark. Colored specks moved about on the plain, and flocks of birds and *pterosaurs* filled the sky. Two rivers ran from the mountains into the lake. To the east, jungle stretched as far as the eye could see.

They'd missed their mark and landed on the wrong side of the mountains. The beacon light was on the opposite side to the west. Hawk sighed. The mountains were a long way off. He judged at least two hundred miles. To get there they'd have a treacherous hike through the jungle, and then a trek across what appeared to be the local dinosaurs' main habitat.

He took a mental snapshot in his mind, and was relieved to see how close it was to their rough map. When he transcribed it into the book he'd space things correctly.

Thanks to gravity going down was easier than the climb up. Hawk climbed limb-to-limb, no longer using the safety rope, confident in his abilities as he worked his way back to the ground. When he dropped next to Svet, the Russian cosmonaut handed him the last of their water.

"Thanks."

Svet pulled the slide on the Ash 12, and said, "Ready?"

"Da," Hawk said. They'd seen small furry marsupials and lizards, but they didn't appear to have much meat on them, so they'd have to take a few and the Ash would blow most of the tiny things apart. "No gun. Time to make some spears."

Svet frowned.

# 7

Five days later Max's knee was doing better and it was time to make a difficult decision. Should they split up, with Hawk and Svet going on recon and exploration missions, while Max stayed close to basecamp, not stressing his knee and gathering firewood, working on long term food supply challenges, and expanding the shelter and its defenses? Or, should they pull up stakes and start their trek to the mountains before Max was at full strength?

"The question is, would you be able to go far, in this jungle with all the obstructions and climbing we'll need to do?" Hawk said.

Max rubbed his chin, and stoked the small fire in the corner of the shelter. Three squirrel–like animals were skinned and roasting over the flames on the end of sticks. The aroma, while not exactly the sweet smell of steaks on a barbeque, was close enough to get Hawk's mouth watering. Space rations were food and did the job, but in much the same way a cake without icing was still a cake.

Max said, "I think if I push it now I might have a setback. So, no, I think I need another week or two. What's the rush, anyway?"

Hawk nodded.

"So? We stay?" Svet said.

"For now. I'm going to try and find a path to that lake in the meantime," Hawk said.

"That certainly won't be a path less traveled. More like the autobahn," Max said.

With that settled Hawk took their dinner off the fire and pulled the charred creatures off their roasting sticks. They were cooked well to ensure any dangerous microbes or diseases would be thoroughly destroyed. Svet had collected some leaves, and Max made a passable dressing from the guts of a blue fruit similar to grapefruit.

Water was a problem, which was another reason they needed to search the area. It hadn't rained since they'd first arrived, and there were no puddles or large leaves filled with water. The supply they brought from the station was gone, and the coconut-like fruit of the palms only supplied minimal water, less than its modern relative.

Gray smoke filtered through the roof vent, nothing more than a narrow hole in the dirt ceiling that Svet had lined with small stones. They'd managed not to attract attention from the locals, but Max said it was only a matter of time before a huge *ankylosaurus* or *dravidosaurus* found their hiding place, whatever the shit they were.

Hawk dozed off and had dreams of home; his wife, kids, all sitting around the base of the Christmas tree, smiling and laughing, opening gifts. He wasn't there, but his family didn't appear to notice. Depression had kicked in the last two days and the monotony of their plight settled in like a relative who just wouldn't leave. He hid his despair from his mates—he was still the leader, and it was important to appear in control and strong, even when he felt anything but. Michel's dead face tormented his dreams, a constant reminder that Svet or Max could stray down the same path. He kept his white pill in a pocket, encased in its plastic vile. He fingered it several times a day, the idea of ending it all and resting growing in him like a cancer.

Hawk left the next morning. Svet would work closer to camp, spiraling out and back, mapping the area and collecting greens and information, while hunting with their newly made spears. Max was to start building weapons. His first task would be finding a piece of wood to make a bow, and then spinning enough sinew from one of their small kills to make the bowstring. They'd collected shards of bone from the carcass they'd found, and two round four inch rocks that he'd use to make a bolas.

Hawk struck out in a new direction on a virgin path, working his way under tree branches, through wide ferns, and over ant and insect infested mounds that were larger than any anthills he'd ever seen. He saw several small dinosaurs, but Max was the scientist, and Hawk was clueless when it came to identifying these less recognizable geniuses.

His bag of supplies hung from his waist on a vine belt he'd made, and he'd cut holes in his spacesuit boots, turning them into ugly sandals of a kind. He planned to travel two days before he turned around and headed back to camp, which meant he'd be gone three nights. Hawk hoped to make twenty miles in that time, though he had no idea where he'd sleep. He considered climbing a tree and securing himself to a bow with his rope, but then he remembered that wouldn't provide any safety unless he went real high, and he wouldn't be comfortable sleeping that far up with nothing firmly holding him in place.

The first day ended with a splash of rain, and Hawk was grateful for it. He was able to fill his water bottle by directing the runoff of a large leaf, while also drinking his fill as the water drops fell from the drenched tree canopy long after the short downpour ended. His neck hurt from catching drops in his mouth, but he felt better than he had in days.

No shelter like the fallen tree presented itself, so Hawk collected some dried branches and kindling and sparked a fire beneath the boughs of a thick conifer using dried leaves. He'd sleep with his back to the tree, and try and keep the fire going all night. He ate half a space ration, overloaded the fire, and settled against the trunk. Stars blinked through tiny gaps in the tree canopy, and the sound of the jungle's roar was steady and mind numbing.

Hawk closed his eyes, but had trouble falling asleep. The night dragged on, the darkness so complete he couldn't see anything beyond the ring of his firelight. He dozed several times only to be woken by a primal yelp or wail. The Viking rested in his lap, and each time he woke he grabbed it, panning it around like a flashlight, but there was nothing to be seen except the glowing orange eyes of the mouse-like creatures that came, discovered there was no food for the taking, and disappeared back into the jungle.

"Screeeeeeeeee. Screeeeeeeeeeeeee."

Hawk's eyes snapped open and he grabbed for the Viking, which had fallen off his lap and lay in the dirt. He snatched it up and rubbed the sleep from his eyes. Above, perched on a branch, a large yellow and red hawk-like bird the size of a pit bull with a long hooked beak and sharp black talons stared down at him with white-rimmed eyes. It flapped its wings in protest of his presence, and let loose with another, "Screeeeeeeeee."

"Easy. I got nothing," Hawk said to the bird.

"Screeeeeeeeee."

"Quiet, before you bring every creature in the jungle."

"Screeeeeee. Screeeeeeeeeee." Louder this time, as if the animal understood him and was saying screw you.

Hawk lifted his gun and trained it on the bird, but it stared back with its glassy eyes. Hawk got up, and that movement was enough to propel the bird into flight. It climbed upward, its wings pounding as it navigated the close confines of the forest.

He kicked dirt on his coals, ate the rest of the ration he'd opened the prior night, and plunged back into the jungle.

He looked back and the metallic pouch that had contained his food was on the forest floor. He was the first litterbug in history. He went back and stuffed the wrapper in his pocket. That piece of trash made him think of the coke bottle that fell from the sky in *The Gods Must Be Crazy*, and then his mind skipped to the Bradbury story, *The Sound of Thunder*. Could what he and his shipmates did change the future? He didn't think so. Earth was headed toward an extinction event, and Hawk didn't think anything they did here would survive that, let alone a hundred million years. Hawk reminded himself that it didn't really matter. If they wanted to survive they had to interact with their environment, because there was no shiny path that let them move about without touching anything.

It was midday when a clearing in the trees appeared ahead. He checked the Viking, and inched forward, gun before him, scanning the forest. He found the glade so out of place within the lush jungle that Hawk marveled at its existence. There were no signs of fire, or lightning, and as he scanned the area his heart leapt in his throat.

Nine round polyhedron shapes spanned the clearing. Hawk looked side to side in disbelief. The edges of the multisided objects were sharp and clearly cut. Someone had made them, even from thirty feet away that was obvious. Viking held before him, Hawk made his way across the odd clearing. The ground was hardpan and hard as rock.

The nine polyhedrons appeared to be made of stone, but closer inspection revealed they were made of a plastic-like material

Hawk had never seen before. They were smooth to the touch, and had no discernable markings. Each different shades of slate-gray, the objects ranged in size from a golf ball to an elephant, and were arranged in a line with a tip that pointed north-east, the largest piece being at the south-western end.

Hawk examined the markers. He'd already decided that's what they were. They weren't natural formations, and their spacing and the existence of the clearing were evidence. But who had put them here? And when? What was their purpose and what did they point to?

The sun was past noon, and the sky was a clear blue, not a cloud in the sky. A flock of birds circled overhead, but nothing predatory, and Hawk flashed back to the huge dragon-thing with sail wings they'd seen when they'd crash landed. Insects chirped and buzzed so loudly it sounded like the hum of a small motor. Hawk took a pull of water and wiped his forehead with the back of his hand.

The markers were in a perfect line, arranged to look like an arrow. Three half size markers formed a triangle on the north-east end. He'd thought the arrow pointed in the direction of the light beacon, but now it was clear it didn't. Still, hope swelled in him. Was the clearing a landing marker? If the ground hadn't been free of plant life, the markers would've been consumed by the jungle long ago, but something kept that from happening and Hawk had a feeling it was more than hard packed dirt.

He took out his copy of *The Martian* and added the location to the map as accurately as he could. If he was right, they'd probably find more markers and perhaps the others would reveal more. He repacked his bag, and ran his hands over each marker, looking for notches or indentations he might have missed. In his wildest fantasy he'd find an activation switch that, when initiated, would show some sign of technological advancement, but he found no such thing.

There was a rustle of branches and Hawk looked up to see a gap opening in the leaves of a massive fern. A horse-like head covered with brown scales and feathers poked through the leaves, its thin snout filled with razer teeth, its eyes yellow pits of aggression. The beast howled, and pushed through the trees into the clearing. It stood a foot taller than Hawk, and reminded him of the fictional raptors in the first *Jurassic Park*.

Hawk hid behind the largest marker and drew the Viking. He fired once into the air and the beast stopped short, its head bobbing as wet eyes focused on him. The surrounding trees exploded as every creature capable of flight burst from the canopy like a cloud of gnats, and fled squawking, tittering and screeching.

Hawk used the distraction to make a run for the tree break, knowing the sudden movement might spur the beast forward. When he'd almost reached the trees, he looked over his shoulder. The dinosaur hadn't moved, but it tracked him, seemingly uncertain if this creature without much meat on its bones was worth the effort.

The dinosaur decided he was and bounded forward.

# 8

Hawk pivoted and pointed the Viking, firing three shots in fast succession, each striking the raptor-like beast in the chest. The dinosaur came on, its large glassy eyes bulging from their deep sockets, jaws open, blood spurting from the wounds. The animal was almost on Hawk when it slowed, stopped, and fell on its side with a crash and a puff of dirt.

Hawk leaned against a tree and slid to the ground. His heart pounded in his head, his stomach a pit of ice. The jungle had gone quiet, the gunshots as foreign in these parts as a Starbucks. The fallen dinosaur spasmed, and Hawk jumped and smacked the back of his head on the tree trunk. The ground shook slightly, and Hawk got to his feet.

*Rumble.*

*Rumble.*

Hawk didn't know how he was going to survive in this version of Earth. It seemed like every step he took there was something waiting to bite, stab, or crush him for food. The ground stopped trembling, and Hawk pulled his knife.

"Time for you to learn about the food chain, bitch," he said to himself. He went to the fallen dinosaur and examined the corpse. The legs were all muscle, and the short arms were skin and bones. A thin layer of muscle and fat covered the beast's back, and it looked like the breast area might provide some quality meat.

He plunged the knife into the creature's chest, and red-brown blood pulsed from the wound and the stream caught Hawk in the face. The astronaut fell back and dropped the knife. A bird squawked, and to Hawk it sounded a little too much like laughter. He got up and wiped the blood from his eyes with the back of his hand, got the knife, and went to work cutting himself a steak. The sinew beneath the skin was thick and tough and would be perfect for making bow strings. The scent of raw meat filled his nostrils and he stepped back, jerking his head side to side. The carcass would bring others.

He wrapped the meat in a giant leaf and stowed it. As he traversed trees and knifed through huge ferns he wondered how dangerous the meat might be to his system. So far, nothing he'd eaten had affected him. If he cooked his kill well he'd probably be fine. He had to get used to the idea that there'd always be the possibility of microbes that could prove problematic and potentially fatal. As with the terrestrial water, they didn't have much choice.

Then there was the primal urge to eat the beast that had tried to kill him.

The jungle thinned, the trees becoming more spaced out, giant ferns covering the forest floor and filling most gaps. He was starving, so when he judged he was far enough away from his kill, he kindled a fire and cooked the fresh meat. It smelled delicious. The steak was thin, and only took a few minutes to be charred brown all the way through.

Hawk ate greedily, fat dripping down his face, which was already caked with the animal's blood from his butchering job. He was licking his fingers and pushing dirt on the fire when he saw the large mound of leaves.

Sunlight filled the jungle, the tree canopy not as close and tight as it had been. The pile stood three feet high, and looked like a landscaper had raked the area and went off on break before the ritual bagging. A gentle breeze floated through the jungle, pushing around leaves both alive and dead. There was no cleft in the land, the pile wasn't against a tree or other natural gathering point. It stood alone in a small clearing drenched in sunlight.

Hawk wiped his hands on his pants and went to the pile. It reeked of rotting vegetation and all the leaves had turned a deep shade of brown. If it wasn't for their coarse texture, Hawk might have mistaken the pile for dinosaur scat.

He picked up a stick and stirred the leaves, probing for anything hidden within. He paused, his mind warning him there could be giant ants, snakes, an entire animal kingdom could be hiding beneath the leaves and stirring them to life might not be the smartest thing. Then again, Hawk knew he wasn't the smartest person. He resumed prodding the pile. The stick knocked on something hollow and he cleared away the remaining leaves.

Six eggs the size of squashed basketballs sat mounded within the nest of leaves. They were brown with streaks of yellow and black, and had coarse shells that looked like sandpaper. He picked one up, turning it in his hands and holding it up to the sun. It was warm to the touch and as the sunlight shone through the egg he saw the baby dinosaur within.

Hawk smiled, caressing the egg. Then remembering where he was he put it back down on the pile and backed away. Where there were eggs, there were mommies, and judging by the size of these eggs, mommy and daddy would be big. Unfortunately for Hawk, that thought was late in coming.

A *triceratops* poked its armored head through the ferns, thick horns curved to the sky, its eyes dark baseballs. The three curved horns were the size of a man's arm and protruded from the dark green shield that surrounded its head. Thick legs supported the huge torso, and the beast towered over Hawk.

Mommy.

This time Hawk didn't panic. He stayed still, making no erratic moves. The dinosaur shrieked, the piggish sound ending in a high-pitched wail that sounded like a horse whinnying. The beast jerked its head up and down, stomping its right foot as if preparing to charge. It roared again, inched forward, and threw its head in the air and snorted.

To Hawk's left the trees got thicker, and the massive dinosaur wouldn't be able to fit through the filter of tree trunks. He bolted, heading for a thick section of tall, full conifers. The *triceratops* hesitated, stomping its feet and kicking up dust. Hawk was in the trees before it gave chase and a cacophony of cracking wood and exploding earth passed over him like a gust of wind as the creature slammed into the woods.

Hawk looked over his shoulder and saw the *triceratops*' massive shield was stuck between two thick tree trunks. The beast churned forward like a machine, digging into the wood and tearing up the ground. The conifer bent and swayed, but didn't break.

Another *triceratops* blocked Hawk's way as he ran, this one dark red with streaks of black. It was smaller than mommy, but had bigger horns and large battle scars on its shield.

Daddy.

Hawk juked left into a stand of stunted palms, fronds lashing his face and arms, causing small paper cut-like gashes that leaked blood. The thunder of the *triceratops* faded, and the ferns thinned as he ran blindly through the underbrush. The land opened into a large path that appeared to be the main animal trail he'd seen to the east of the lake. Claw prints large and small marked the packed dirt, and several smaller animals paused in their journey as Hawk burst out onto the natural thoroughfare.

The was no sign of his pursuers. Hawk figured daddy had gone to see what mommy was screaming about, and upon finding the eggs undamaged decided pursuing him wasn't worth the effort. He panted and sucked for air, his chest heaving, sweat dripping down his back and forehead.

He slipped back into the tree break and followed the path. He didn't want to draw attention to himself, and strolling down the regions equivalent of I-95 wouldn't be the best way to accomplish that. *Pterosaurs* soared overhead, their sail-like wings snapping in the wind like tent flaps, their shrill cries drawing his attention. Something big circled above the flock of *pterosaurs*, a massive thing that looked three times the size of the rest, but it disappeared into the oncoming clouds.

He hiked the remainder of the day, and as the sun reached for the horizon he could just make out the lake across a thin savannah pocked with trees that ran around the dark blue water. Hawk climbed a tree and searched the plain, looking for a safe path, but animals of all sizes and shapes covered the savannah.

To the north two massive *tyrannosaurs* fought over a decayed carcass, and smaller beasts covered in feathers and scales chased each other about while birds fled from flying reptiles that plucked the birds from the sky. Everything roared, chirped, or brayed, and the odd sounds created an eerie tune that sounded like grunge metal without the thumping bass. There was no way he could get to the lake's shore. It was too dangerous.

With no safe place to hunker down for the night, Hawk decided to start back. He walked until dark, then went without a fire and lay beneath a fern with low hanging branches and covered himself with leaves to hide his scent. He slept undisturbed and was famished when he awoke. He ate some breadfruit, and drank the last of his water. If he hiked the entire day, only stopping for short rests, he should make it back to camp by nightfall. Hopefully Max and Svet had stockpiled some chow.

Back in the thick jungle the temperature dropped, and a chill ran though Hawk. He was weak, his lack of food and water taking its toll. The insects were back in full force, and they buzzed his head and bit any exposed skin. The black gnats were the worst. They flew into his nose and eyes, and their bites left little red itchy welts. They were impossible to see, and Hawk smacked himself in the face more than once as he swatted at the things.

He encountered no dinosaurs or other large beasts, but he heard them. Cracking wood and crunching vegetation, braying, shrieking, and growling provided a constant reminder of the dangers that lurked around every curve in the path. Ants and insects seemed to rule the world, and more than once Hawk had come upon a shifting pile as ants devoured something unrecognizable.

The smaller lizards and marsupials appeared content to leave Hawk alone. Most spied him with curious eyes before disappearing back into the camouflage of the jungle. Large flying beetles dive bombed him, but Hawk had gotten adept at swatting them before they landed on him. The mosquitoes were particularly large and harsh, and Hawk worried about the diseases they might carry. In his time the little vampires were the number one cause of disease proliferation, and if there was a harmful virus prowling this version of Earth, the mosquitoes were the most likely delivery service.

A wave of sadness washed over him when a mouse-like creature that resembled his daughter's hamster scuttled onto the path before him, stopped and looked him up and down, then bolted into the jungle. His daughter loved the little vermin more than she did her brother, and she took it everywhere. It rode shotgun in her breast pocket, and Hawk smiled as he recalled his wife telling him she'd gotten called to the school when Sally's teacher had found a gnawed carrot in the child's desk, and when questioned, discovered the furry creature in her hoody.

The daggers of sunlight piercing the tree canopy faded when Hawk broke free of the jungle and saw the fence around their shelter. Hawk whistled, and Svet and Max came out to greet him. Svet and Hawk hugged, and Max patted him on the back.

“You made it,” Max said.

“Barely. Anything new here?”

“You won’t believe what I find,” Svet said.

# 9

The markers were the same as the ones Hawk found. They formed an arrow in a clearing that shouldn't exist about three miles from camp. Nine polyhedrons arranged largest to smallest, with a triangle tip pointing west. The sun was still in the east, having just risen above the rim of the world. It was hot, and Hawk wiped sweat from his brow.

He held *The Martian* open to the map he'd drawn on the blank spread at the back of the book. He penciled in the location of the new markers as best he could, and drew dotted lines from the tips in the direction that point and they intersected.

"You make anything of it?" Hawk asked Max. He handed him the open book and the physicist examined it, brow furrowed, face stoic.

"I think if this is truly an intersection point, then there should be more markers. Perhaps one here," Max said. He pointed to a blank area northwest of their position.

"One here also, da?" Svet said.

Max drew in the two proposed marker locations. Max's site appeared to be a full day's trek, assuming no delays. "If we find a marker there, the question becomes what's at the intersect location? Another marker?"

"Leading to yet another?" Hawk said. They had no clues. Like the first grouping he'd found, there were no markings on the polyhedrons, no signs or writing that would explain their purpose, or if they had a purpose at all.

"I don't know," Max said.

"That worries me more than anything else. Max unsure," Hawk said.

The German chuckled. "I can see how you might be frustrated, like when Google goes down."

"What do you think, Svet?"

The cosmonaut ran her fingers through her greasy blonde hair. None of them had bathed in some time, and they'd have to remedy that before their stank brought unwelcomed guests. "I no understand. Maybe very old? Part of civilization long gone?"

Max said, "Possible. What concerns me is the lack of vegetation in the clearing. It's like a permanent dosage of poison covers the area. Even hardpan will soften in time as rain and sun perpetually stress the hard-packed dirt. Even with regular maintenance I don't see how these areas can be free of plant life and creepers."

"Da," Svet said. She bent and ran her hands over the concrete-like dirt. She rubbed her fingers together and sniffed her hand. "No smell anything. Nothing can be seen."

Max nodded.

"Must be a reason?" Hawk said.

"Agreed. I believe these markers were created as signposts," Max said.

"Da. Why?" asked Svet.

Hawk and Max said nothing.

That was the kicker, wasn't it? According to Earth's historical record there hadn't been any civilizations on Earth during this era. If they were right about their time estimation, that is. Max had said they were roughly fifty to seventy-five million years in the past judging by the position of the land masses, the flora and fauna they'd seen, and the local animal life. T-Rex's, for example, lived right up until the massive extinction, and weren't prevalent in the Jurassic period as many portrayed them. Hawk also knew all the estimates were based on dating techniques that had inherent flaws, and their estimations could be off by millions of years, as could their assumption about prior lifeforms and what they may have left behind.

"It doesn't make sense, but the scientists of our time qualified all their findings going back this far," Max said. "Perhaps there was a thriving civilization here and all signs of it were destroyed in the coming cataclysm that wipes out almost all life on Earth."

Hawk said nothing. The other possibilities were impossible to believe, yet they brought some hope. None of them said it aloud, but was it possible off-worlders had visited Earth, and placed the markers?

"We're going to find marker, ja?" Max said.

“Da. See for sure.”

Hawk closed his book and slipped it in a pocket. He looked up at the sun as it crept across the sky, and a warm breeze redolent of earth and shit pushed across the clearing. Swarms of gnats, flying beetles and mosquitoes hung around his head like a cloud, and he constantly swatted at them.

“I think we need to check it out, or at least one of us does,” Hawk said. What choice did they have? They had nothing but time and the markers might provide clues to finding the light beacon, if in fact that was what the markers pointed to.

“Nyet. We all go,” Svet said.

Hawk started to speak, but Max beat him.

“I agree with Svet. We shouldn’t split up again. If we get separated we’ll never find each other in the thick jungle.”

“I don’t see why we all should be at risk,” Hawk said, but even as the words left his mouth he didn’t really believe them. Risk? Was he joking? Leaving the shelter in the morning to take a piss was a risk. Squatting under a fern to take a shit was a risk. Hunting. Risk. Drinking. Risk. Eating. Risk. He’d have to get used to the idea that risk management was a thing of the past. It was about survival.

Svet and Max said nothing as they waited for him to work it out on his own. They both stared at him, eyes wide and patient. They’d been together long enough to know that he had to come to decisions in his own way, on his own terms.

“Shit. You’re right. Staying in one place is dangerous. Wc need to move around. If we settled in the creatures we need to stay away from will surely find us.”

“Da.”

“Ja.”

He spared them the shit joke this time.

They left the next morning, and sealed up the shelter, leaving behind anything they felt they didn’t need. Svet and Max dismantled the fence Hawk had built, and used the thick sticks to close off their entrance. Max had argued that if they didn’t mothball their shelter, they were likely to find animals living in it if they returned.

Using the sun as a guide, they headed northwest, doing their best to stay on line to where they expected to find another set of markers. They brought three days of food, and the last of their water. Searching would take time because they didn't have the exact location, nor were they certain of the exact direction. There was also the possibility that they might be wrong, and had miscalculated entirely and there was no new signpost to find.

They camped that night within the hollow of a massive dead tree that hadn't had the courtesy to fall. It smelled of root and dirt, and Svet worried the thing might fall with them inside, to which Max pointed out from their position they'd be fine. They ate a meal of breadfruit and dinosaur jerky Svet had made from one of her kills. They were still using guns to hunt the big game, as none of them had mastered the construction of a bow and arrows, let alone mastered its use. The other weapons couldn't take down large game. Svet had discovered several types of edible leaves, and many roots and fruits that weren't poisonous, but tasted like cardboard.

"We should be close," Hawk said when they set out the next day. They had no way of knowing if they'd gone too far, and in the thick jungle, visibility was limited. They fanned out, separating themselves by a quarter mile or so, and combed the jungle, walking slowly, keeping in touch every few minutes with a yell.

This went on for the better part of the day before they found the third clearing, and the arrow there pointed southeast. They added it to the map, and when a third dotted line was added a clear intersection point stood out like a *stegosaurus* at a dance party.

"So that's it then," Max said.

"Da."

"Do we head straight there? Or head back to camp first?" Max said.

Hawk weighed this as he examined the map, Svet and Max looking over his shoulder. "It looks roughly the same distance. I say we go see what's there. We've got enough food."

"Ja," Max said.

They set out at once, following the line of the arrow through the thinning jungle. They hadn't seen any animals bigger than a dog since leaving camp, but ahead in the jungle there was a loud ruckus; cracking tree limbs, grunts and wails of aggression and pain.

*Crack. Crack. Crack.*

It sounded like two rocks were being smashed together. Hawk escaped a thick tangle of ferns and two dinosaurs knocking heads and swinging club-like tails fought before him.

Max inched out of the ferns behind him and said, "*Ankylosaurs*."

The beasts looked like living tanks; armored heads and tails the color of honey, and flecked with blood. The dinosaurs had black flanks and they swung their long powerful black tails, each of which had a knob-like club at its end. The beasts didn't appear to notice them, and the threesome slipped by the scene, the pounding of cracking tails and the hiss and growls of battle fading as they trekked deeper into the jungle.

It was mid-morning on the third day out when the large clearing appeared like a mirage. It was lined with thick palm trees that looked like they'd been planted in neat rows at the clearing's edge. But instead of finding nine polyhedrons arranged as an arrow, they found something more interesting.

Five polyhedrons fifteen feet tall stood at the center of the clearing. They were multi-sided, and each flat surface contained a hieroglyph. The markers were arranged in a similar fashion, and Hawk's best guess was the arrow pointed in the direction of the light beacon.

"Good God," Max said.

They entered the clearing with caution, guns at the ready, but everything was quiet.

The hieroglyphs showed a series of scenes depicting stick figures that looked vaguely humanoid, and there was writing, but it was gibberish.

"Look at this one," Hawk said. He examined the head polyhedron that depicted several pictures of what looked like the Earth, but it had thin lines drawn from a large wound on the surface of the planet depicting an explosion, and several adjacent cells showed primitive drawings of destruction. Panels displayed drawings of objects that looked eerily like a modern cellphone, with numeric key pads, but instead of numbers there were odd shapes.

"Is that what it looks like?" Max said.

"What does it look like?" Svet said.

Hawk jumped in before he could answer. "I think that thing in the lower quadrant is the beacon. The lines coming from it portray fire and destruction."

"Da. One here shows hole in that spot," Svet said.

"Oh, boy," Max said.

"What is it?" Hawk asked.

"Not yet, let me take a closer look," Max said.

Svet and Hawk watched as Max examined each hieroglyph, even the duplicates. When he was done, he said, "I can't be sure, and I'll need more time to study these things. I suggest we use your book and copy all the pictures as best we can for future reference."

"Care to hazard a guess?" Hawk said.

"Da?"

"This is wild speculation at this point," Max said. He sighed. "I think this here," he pointed to the drawing of the bare spot in the middle of a drawing of some simple woods. Stick trees surrounded the empty area, and it had lines shooting from it. "This could be energy. An explosion. Who knows." He paused and wiped the sweat from his face.

"And?" Svet said, the impatience sharp in her tone.

"And, I think the light beacon might not be a beacon after all," Max said.

"What the hell is it then?" Hawk said.

"A monitoring device to record the event that killed off the dinosaurs."

# 10

They set out for the beacon the following morning, using the towering tree on the horizon as a guidepost. Max's revelation about the purpose of the light beacon hadn't changed Hawk's mind, if anything the speculation fueled his desire to find whatever they'd seen. If Max was right, and Hawk wasn't certain he was, whoever had planted the device would want the data it created, and that implied some type of communication.

They moved through a forest of trees even Max couldn't identify. They had long broad leaves and large basketball-sized fruit hanging from thick limbs. Svet scaled one of the trees and they ate the fruit, and for the first time they all felt nauseous. Perhaps there was a reason the trees weren't picked clean like most of the other fruit trees they'd seen.

The party drank water from a thin stream and rested beneath a great fern. The jungle erupted with life around them: insects, birds, small dinosaurs and reptiles, each with a distinct color and manner, flitted around the two astronauts and one cosmonaut. They held their guns at the ready, but Hawk felt no danger, though he thought he'd never feel comfortable or at ease again.

"So, now that I've digested what you said, I'm thinking it might be a stretch. I mean, if an alien society placed the monitor, why not just be here when the event takes place? Watch it with their own eyes, or whatever they use to see?" Hawk said.

Max chuckled. "We're talking about thousands of years here, Hawk. Even an advanced race might not know exactly when the extinction event occurred."

"Possibly dangerous, da?" Svet said.

"Ja," Max said. The scientist rubbed his forehead. "Hadn't thought of that. Whatever caused the extinction event will be dangerous to any life forms on the surface, and waiting thousands of years in space wouldn't be advantageous to anyone, even if the race had a life span well beyond ours."

Satisfied, Hawk said, "So you think the device can communicate?"

"I would think the data would have to be received somewhere, otherwise what's the point, eh?" Max said. Then his eyes grew wide as Hawk's meaning dawned on him, and he said, "Maybe we can send a message?"

"I realize it's an extreme long shot, and even if we could there is no guarantee the message would be received. Even if it was it could take hundreds of years to get to its destination, and the race that received the message could be hundreds of light years away."

Max's face fell and he looked away.

Svet said, "So? What we do? I say we still go? What else is there?"

Max and Hawk said nothing.

"Maybe we find more clues? More… how you say, hero-glyphons?"

"Hieroglyphs. Maybe," Max said. "Whoever built and placed the markers obviously wanted them to be found and went through great efforts to make sure anyone who might stumble across them would know what they were."

"A warning? To other space travelers of the danger?" Svet said.

"Maybe," Max said.

That was the hitch, wasn't it? Hawk had done his best to keep the morale of his mates up, but with each passing hour their plight became more resolute. They were trapped here, and they were never going home. Even if the best possible scenario occurred, and aliens came to fetch them, unless they had a time machine, which hitherto wasn't possible, they were stuck in this time. His stomach ached, and he was frustrated, angry, and tired, and he didn't feel like doing much of anything.

When the sun had passed noon, he said, "Let's get moving." Grunts and moans from Max and Svet, but they got up. "Chins up, this is the witching hour."

They'd found that the bigger dinosaurs liked to hunt in the morning and afternoon when it wasn't so hot. This cycle was typical of lizards, and Hawk recalled an iguana he'd named Siggy that lived in a tree outside his bedroom window back in Florida.

You could set your watch by the creature's daily routine, and he was finding dinosaurs to be equally predictable, which was useful since they were doing everything they could to avoid the beasts.

Hawk followed an animal trail that let around an odd assortment of rocks that was out of place and looked like they might have once been some type of structure or monument. Huge centipedes five feet long scuttled and slithered into the jungle as they examined the stones, but when they found no markings, Hawk put the location on their map and moved on.

By nightfall they'd made a lean-to shelter with palm fronds and laid in some food and went in search of water. While they were gone something had tried to obtain access to their shelter. A pile of scat the size of a large cat stood in front of the shelter's blocked entrance, as if the offending animal understood exactly where it was crapping.

Hawk cleared it away with disgust, and pulled away the sticks that secured the opening. In their absence worms, beetles, and what looked like snakes with legs had burrowed through the dirt and infested their new home.

Together they cleaned their sleeping areas, but Svet and Hawk climbed into the spacesuits, even though that meant sweating all night. Max laughed at them. "They're only bugs," he jested. "They can't eat you."

At that moment one of the bugs he claimed couldn't eat him gave it a try, and bit him on the arm. He screamed, a red welt rising on his flesh. He scratched at it. Svet had found what she believed to be some type of aloe plant, and she broke one of her leaves and rubbed the translucent jelly onto her friend's arm, and it improved.

The party woke the next day to water pouring through the ceiling of their shelter, and this hastened their exit. A torrential rain fell; thick, cold and biting. Mud slid through the jungle and soon everyone and everything was soaked through. Each carrying a bag containing their meager supplies, the party hastened into a thick stand of saw palmetto where the tree canopy blocked the fierceness of the weather.

As the day waned, a clearing appeared in the forest ahead, so they stopped and ate a meal of space rations. They were out of dino-jerky, and there were no fruit trees around except the ones with the large bulbous stuff that made them sick.

Hawk estimated their huge guide-tree was forty or fifty miles away, and they were bound to be knocked off course by the deep forest. The solution to that dilemma was Hawk, the expert tree climber.

Four days passed as the party fought their way through the jungle, stopping several times for Hawk to climb. Each time, they'd changed course because the forest impediments had forced them off their path. They saw no large predators, but were constantly tested by the smaller breeds, who peeked from within the trees, watching and examining everything they did.

What they heard was another story. Beasts great and small screeched, bellowed and screamed as they fought with each other in their daily struggle of survival. It had been truly lucky that their capsule had landed in a heavily forested area, because if it hadn't been for the thick cover of trees, they'd be dead.

As the party approached their tree marker, Hawk counseled caution, so they slowed their pace and crept silently through the ferns and scrub palmetto. Ants dominated the ground, and more than once they'd seen swarms devouring carcasses that were no longer recognizable, and were careful to give them a wide berth.

The forest thinned out as they approached the huge tree, and the thick trunk came into view. It was so black one might walk into it during the deep primordial night. Max said he didn't know what type of tree it was, for its size was beyond any tree he'd ever seen, including the great redwoods of California. Its leaves were the color of blood, and thin yellow veins ran through them. Thick branches reached out at odd angles all along the trunk, and on many of them horrific creatures rested.

"Those are *pterosaurs* of some kind. I'm sure of it. But what species I couldn't tell you," Max said.

Svet's eyes bulged from her head, and Hawk's stomach went cold.

The tree was filled with the beasts, their leathery wings folded, teeth sticking out from powerful black beaks. A fowl puddle of yellow brackish water was at the tree's base, and several baby dragons tossed about in the nasty water. Above, the males stood still as stone, their yellow bulbous eyes scanning the area while the smaller females tended and kept track of the young.

"Be very quiet," Max said. "There are hundreds of them. Looks like the tree serves as a rookery."

From their position within the ferns they observed what had never been seen by human eyes. There was a carcass the size of a dog next to the puddle, and the females tore pieces of meat from the fallen animal and tossed them into the beaks of their young, who whined the second they'd consumed the treat. Hawk was reminded of the bird house in his backyard at home. Every year a bird would lay eggs in it and for a month all that could be heard from his deck was the screeching cry for food, and the momma bird's answering wails of impatience. His chest grew hot. When he thought of his family a deep, all-encompassing sadness overtook him, and his mind returned to the unavoidable fact that he would never see them again. Hawk didn't think that feeling would ever go away, and he wasn't sure he wanted it to. He thought of Michel, and that crazy laugh he had. How it sucked you in and made you smile, its echoes filling the station.

"I'd like to get a closer look," Max said.

"Nyet," said Svet, but Max ignored her.

Before Hawk could protest, Max inched into the underbrush. He moved through the groundcover and ferns, advancing cautiously, his focus never leaving the tree of flying killers.

Hawk held his breath, and sweat dripped down his forehead into his eyes.

Max was halfway to the edge of the clearing the tree towered over when he stepped on a stick and a loud *snap* reverberated over the jungle. Every pair of *pterosaur* eyes turned their way. Max dropped to the ground out of sight, and Hawk pulled his head back within the cover of the fern, but it was too late. The males leapt from the tree, their sail-like wings snapping and fluttering as they charged. The flock squawked and chirped as it came, filling the air like a cloud of gnats, coming straight for them.

# 11

Hawk stood frozen for an instant, the fog of *pterosaurs* filling the air like raindrops. "Run!" he screamed, but Svet was way ahead of him. When Hawk turned tail, the Russian was in front of him, weaving in and out of trees like a running back cutting through a secondary. His heart pounded in his chest as he trailed after. The shrill cries of the beasts sounded like dying seagulls, and they blocked all other sound as they came on in their fury.

It was then that Hawk remembered Max. He looked over his shoulder, but couldn't find his mate.

*Smack.*

Hawk ran headlong into a tree, bounced off the trunk, and landed on the forest floor in a heap. Blood ran from a gash in his forehead, dripping into his eyes and momentarily blinding him. He wiped the blood away with the back of his hand and saw Max. He hid beneath the cover of a fern fifty yards away, but the flying menaces weren't fooled. The leader of the pack landed atop the fern and bit at the physicist. Max rolled side to side, avoiding the snapping jaws filled with a double row of small sharp teeth.

Remembering his gun, Hawk drew the Viking and fired. The bullet struck the *pterosaur* in its gangly midsection, and the force of the bullet knocked the flying reptile off his friend as if a great gust of wind had torn it away.

The shot must have reminded Svet that she too had a gun, because the Ash 12 rattled to life and *pterosaurs* fell from the sky, their death cries terrible. Hawk ran, searching for cover, but there was nothing thick enough. The flying carpets didn't slow, cutting in and out of trees like missiles, their sail-like wings folding and spreading with such precision Hawk was impressed by their agility.

Hawk came upon Svet, hiding behind two large trees that formed an alcove where a person could hide. She laid cover for him as he ran past her, and he holstered the Viking. Blood ran into his eyes again, and pain rocked his back as his arms and legs pumped as hard as he could move them.

"Watch out," Svet yelled.

Hawk was struck from behind and two claws grasped at his shoulders. He threw himself into a roll, pulling free and twisting round to face his attacker. The beast crash landed and

stood before him, its beak open, eyes gleaming. It snapped its beak and hissed as it came forward.

Hawk pulled the Viking, and as the creature jerked its head preparing to strike, he put a bullet between its eyes. The *pterosaur's* head exploded with a spray of blood and bone, and the animal fell over, its bony legs coming to rest on top of him.

The beasts filled the sky and Hawk rolled, avoiding another attack as he vaulted to his feet and dove under a large bush with tiny prickers. The flying reptiles settled on the bush like a cloud of smoke and ripped the vegetation apart attempting to get at him. Hawk emptied the Viking, hitting several of the animals, but the gunshots didn't scare the dragons and they came on with the furious determination of hunters desperate to get at their prey.

The *pterosaurs* stopped screeching as one, like a light switch had been flipped and all their energy had been drained. The ground shook, and the dragons scattered.

The ground trembled again, and a great cry split the day. Bile crept up Hawk's throat as he contemplated flight or fight. He chuckled to himself amidst the chaos. Fight. That was funny shit.

He burst from his hiding place and headed back toward Max and Svet. The cosmonaut still hid within the trees, but as Hawk ran past she fell in behind him. The *pterosaurs* fled in every direction, their cries filling Hawk's head as he ran through the underbrush, leaves whipping at his arms and face, blood once again dripping into his eyes.

Max still hid beneath the fern, and it took a little coaxing to get him to come out. The ground trembled harder, as whatever great beast had come to investigate the turmoil got closer.

"Come on. We gots to go. And fast," Hawk yelled.

"Ja," Max said, and emerged from his cover.

They were surrounded by a glade of trees, and it was difficult to see beyond their immediate surroundings. *Pterosaurs* filled the air like a tangle of seagulls, circling out of reach, waiting for the show to start.

"Which way?" Max asked.

Hawk closed his eyes and listened hard, blocking out the screeching reptiles, the push of the wind, and the constant chirp and buzz of insects. The rumble was getting closer, and sounded like it was approaching from the north. They needed a better hiding place, but Hawk saw nothing that would serve. The trees and underbrush provided little cover. Max trained his Ash 12 on the flying reptiles, but the guns were useless against the bigger dinosaurs, and seemed only to irritate the beasts. Svet's gun was empty, and she was reaching into her bag for more shells when a colossal roar froze them in place.

Hawk had come to fear the moments of complete silence in the jungle. The anti-alarm only lasted a few seconds, but when it came one heeded it or died. There was no other motivator more effective in bringing together life, both human and animal.

A great head like that of a bird with no feathers burst through the trees to their right, and Hawk pulled the Viking, only to remember it was empty.

"Don't move," Max said. The three companions stood still as stone as the great beast's head rotated on a thin neck, its eyes the size of basketballs shifting side to side. "It looks to be some genus of *stegosaurus*. Perhaps a *dravidosaurus* or *dacentrurus*."

"Ssssh," Svet hissed.

The dinosaur turned, revealing its short dull teeth, and blue eyes. Bony plates and spikes guarded the creature's back, neck, and tail. The beast reared up on its hind legs, and whined, but it didn't sound very threatening to Hawk. Its blue eyes looked almost kind, and the creature's gray and black leathery hide looked smooth and wet.

"No worries," Max said. The phrase sounded comical coming with his German lilt.

"No worry, nyet?" Svet said.

"These guys are plant eaters, though I don't doubt it would stomp us to death if it felt threatened. More likely it will run."

"Let's see," Hawk said. He raised his hands and yelled, stepping toward the beast.

The *stegosaurus* whined again, but this time it stepped forward and stomped its front paws.

"That no work. We…"

Svet was cut off as the beast charged them and Hawk and his mates turned tail and bolted into the jungle. Daggers of sunlight sliced across their path, which was barely an animal trail. The shrill echoes of the insects accompanied the pounding of his heart, and Hawk gasped, sucking for air as he threw himself forward, using trees and underbrush as cover. He zigzagged right and left, making it difficult for the large animal to maneuver through the trees.

The forest thickened, and the sounds of pursuit lessened as they ran, but Hawk was in a frenzy, and he wouldn't stop until the thing was a mile behind. The bag of supplies tied to his belt smacked his leg as it hit tree trunks and got caught on ferns and underbrush. His forearms were filled with gashes from pushing aside the sharp palm fronds of the saw palmetto and dwarf palms. His thigh muscles were tight as rope.

The ground gave way beneath Hawk's feet, and he cartwheeled, arms spinning in circles as he tried to stay upright. He went down hard, landing face down with a *splat*.

In their haste, Svet and Max fell on top of him, and the trio sank beneath a black-dirt substance that sucked them into the earth. Hawk recalled hearing that pits of quicksand and tar dotted the prehistoric landscape, and as he sank deeper into the shifting mud he felt the urge to let go. To slip beneath the surface and let everything come to a merciful end like Michel had done. He thought of the pill in his pocket, asked himself again why he hadn't taken it.

He held his breath, and he was under the Caribbean Sea, blue and yellow fish all around him, his wife Andrea and the kids swimming beside him. Dappled sunrays cut through the water and green plants danced and swayed with the roll of the sea. Andrea looked at him and smiled. She beckoned to him to come see something she pointed at below her, a great void of blackness with a monstrous dinosaur head sticking from it.

Svet and Max struggled on top of Hawk, pushing him further into the muck, jarring him from his reverie. He sucked in sludge as he sank within the shifting sands, his arms and legs finding no purchase as he struggled to right himself and get his head above the mud.

Svet rolled to one side and Max the other, and the pressure driving him downward eased. He jerked his head free, treading in place and keeping his head above the muck, but the shifting sludge sucked him under.

His shipmates beside him were also inexorably being drawn down into the pit. They all struggled to stay above the sand flow, but it was Svet who kept her wits about her and was attempting to work her way toward the side. Several creepers hung from trees, and if she could get hold of one they might pull themselves out.

Max's head slipped under the surface, and with a great effort Hawk freed his arm and grabbed the German's collar. The fabric tore, but he held on, though he was sinking faster with the additional weight. His pumped his legs, but in the thick sand he was tiring quickly.

Svet had almost reached the edge, and with one last massive lunge she pushed herself forward, coming up just short of a creeper that trailed to the edge of the quicksand pit. She rolled and heaved like a dying fish, disappearing beneath the sand and reappearing as she butterfly-stroked through the muck.

Hawk's chin dipped below the surface, and he was losing his grip on Max. Could it really end this way? He'd been to war, and sat on the end of a missile that carried him to space. He'd survived every danger that had ever come his way, and now he was going to die like a crab beneath the sand.

Hawk closed his eyes as his head went under.

A hand gripped his shoulder, and his head was jerked free of the muck. He tugged on Max, and found that he had leverage. Max came up sputtering and coughing, and he and Hawk clung to each other like newborns to their mother.

Svet held Hawk with one hand and clutched a creeper in the other. The thin green vine twisted and strained as it held the weight of all three of them. Using Svet's body, Hawk pulled himself over the Russian and managed to get a hand on the creeper. Max yelled and sank like a rock, but grabbed Svet's legs before they disappeared in the sand.

"Swim god damn it. Swim!" Hawk yelled.

Svet breached, flailing wildly, her hand finding the end of the creeper. Hand over hand, Svet and Hawk pulled themselves to the edge of the pit and crawled out, the sand sucking at them the entire time. Before he got up, Hawk tossed the creeper end to Max, but the physicist was nowhere to be seen.

Large bubbles popped on the surface, but the German was gone.

# 12

Glops of wet brown sludge burst from the pit as Max pushed to the surface with one last effort to stay above the shifting sands. Hawk tossed the end of a creeper to him, but he couldn't grab hold of it. After three tries Max managed to get a hand on the vine, then two, and Hawk and Svet pulled the exhausted physicist from the quicksand.

The three companions lay spent at the pit's edge, sucking air and rubbing at cuts, bumps, and bruises. Hawk felt like he'd run through a thicket of torn bushes: trickles of blood ran down his face and hands, and his jumpsuit was ripped in many places. The jungle buzzed, and Hawk rolled on his side and threw up.

Getting cleaned up would have to wait. The day was waning and they needed to find shelter for the night. Hawk's stomach kicked him, asking for food, but nausea threw a counter punch, and his muscles were stones. "I say we build something in the bows of that conifer there," he said, pointing across the glade. "The animals probably stay away from this area."

"Might be water around. We're in a depression," Max said.

"We have two full bottles," Svet said. "Little food."

That settled it. They rested and then built a crude platform ten feet off the ground in the branches of the conifer. They found a nasty puddle, stripped down, and rinsed off. They also washed off their clothes. Hawk slept like a baby, falling off as he stared up at the stars through the gaps in the trees. Falling asleep in the jungle was like trying to nod-off while laying on a sidewalk in mid-town Manhattan on Wednesday afternoon, and it amazed him how used to the terrible night sounds he'd become.

Braying, grunting, tittering, and shrill wails were background to the lead track of crashing trees, cracking bones, and the sloppy-wet sound of meat being torn and devoured. The land itself trembled, vibrating the trees and everything that touched them. It was a chorus of pops, chirps, screeches, and snarls, all of which blended into a loud buzz that made Hawk's ears ring.

Despite this, Hawk woke refreshed, and climbed his home tree to get their bearing.

Their marker, the huge *pterosaur* rookery, was to the northwest, and the lake he'd seen was to the southwest. A great savannah dotted with patches of jungle stretched to the base of the mountains in-between. Large dots moved around on the open plain and great clouds of dust rose into the blue sky as herds ran and scattered and the larger beasts fought for supremacy.

When he'd climbed back down to the sleep platform, Max and Svet were awake.

"Anything new up there?" Max asked.

"No." Hawk drank some water and sat, stretching his back and legs. He was sore all over, several of his cuts had swelled with infection, and his feet cramped every time he moved them.

"Nyet?" Svet said. Her blue eyes blazed, and red blotches covered her face and neck where insects had taken a bite.

Hawk sighed. "I don't think we can cross the plain, it looks like *The Road Warrior* out there."

Svet laughed.

"No roads?" Max said.

"He not that Max," Svet said.

It was Hawk's turn to laugh. "Famous Australian film. They never mentioned it on *Friends* or *Star Trek*."

"So, what you think?" Svet said. "We go around?"

Hawk sighed louder and harder. "I think we have to. It's way out of the way, but we can follow the outskirts of thc savannah around to the mountains."

"How far?" Max said. He still appeared agitated about being on the outside of the joke. His normally slack face was tight, his bright eyes narrowed.

"I'd say about a hundred miles instead of fifty, but once we get up on those mountains we'll get a much better view," Hawk said.

"See light?" Svet asked.

"I sure hope so," Hawk said.

"And we need to stay as far south of the volcano as possible," Max said.

Having set their goal for the foreseeable future, the party packed their meager belongings. Hawk felt like a million pounds had been lifted from his back. There were no decisions to be made for a long time, and it would take total ineptitude at this point to get lost. It was a *Dora the Explorer* trail: go to the savannah's edge, which was due west. Follow the edge of the plain to the north, and around to the tallest mountain that was on a rough line with the tree marker and the giant arrow.

The day was a long, dreary, miserable trek, and so were the next twenty. The party was tired most of the time, and when they weren't hiking they were sleeping or hunting. They still used their guns because they hadn't had time to perfect their primitive weapons, let alone learn to use them. The harsh terrain made traveling slow, monotonous, and frustrating. The jungle was thick and rich with small game and insects, and they didn't happen across many larger dinosaurs. It was agreed that Hawk must have misjudged the distance to the savannah, because they still hadn't reached the great plain and there were no signs of it being near.

On their morning march, the company traversed a thick section of conifers packed so tight it was hard to push through them. The weather turned nasty, and a light rain coated everything with a layer of moisture. They broke free of the forest and were confronted by an impenetrable stand of bamboo that stretched into the distance to the north and south. It was impossible to hack through the stuff with only knives, and they were forced to go north, which took them miles off course.

The sun arced toward noon when they came across an opening in the wall of bamboo. A five-foot wide path disappeared on a wandering trail into the thick green patch of bamboo that was so lush it had canes eighty-feet tall.

"What you think?" Svet said.

"I think if there's a path it goes someplace. Probably through this shit."

"Agreed," Max said. "This animal trail is most likely very old, and was in use when the bamboo swarmed over the land. The heavy traffic would have killed the tender young shoots."

"We had this stuff back home. Horrific shit. A shoot can grow a foot in a day, and it will spread ten feet in every direction in one season if given the proper light and water," Hawk said.

"We no have much in Russia."

Max said, "I worry about the traffic we'll meet. Going around would be safer. And…"

He didn't say it because they were trying to help each other keep their minds off their situation, but Hawk knew what Max intended to say. "What's the rush?" He didn't because there was no rush. There was nothing at all except their blind quest to nowhere.

"I say we try it," Hawk said.

"Da," Svet said.

Max sighed. "That's it then." He stormed off into the bamboo and Hawk and Svet trailed after.

It didn't take long to lose all sense of direction in the green maze. The trail narrowed to three feet across, and took many twists and turns. When they reached a clearing, and found a pile of bones, they hurried on, taking the wider of two paths that appeared to head west.

Thick green canes whispered and sighed in the breeze, and bamboo leaves rattled like water rushing over stones. They were forced to choose a path three more times as the tangled maze of trails crossed over one another and the party unintentionally backtracked several times. When it became clear they were lost and going in circles, tempers flared.

"Mudak," Svet spat.

"Hey—don't bring mothers into this," Hawk said.

"You wanted to try," Max said. "What did you say?"

"You mother fucks," Svet said.

Hawk laughed. He laughed harder than he had since he'd left his family in Florida to live in a tin can. "Motherfucker," he corrected.

Max laughed, and Svet joined in, and for a few seconds they weren't totally screwed.

"Max, you think you can get us back to the beginning?"

"Same odds as getting us to the other side," he said. "But I think I remember several of the paths. We try a new way. Ja?"

"Da," Hawk said.

Svet smiled.

Max led them back down familiar trails, tried new byways, and things seemed to be going well until the bamboo ended and they stood in a large clearing where many paths intersected.

"The center of the maze," Hawk said. "Shit. Max, I could have done that."

"Nyet," Svet said.

Piles of bones, white as clouds, dotted the clearing, and the scent of decay and rotting flesh permeated the air. The ground was black with blood, and dried skin, mounds of fat, and piles of scat littered the area. *Pterosaurs* and birds as black as night circled above, carrion beasts looking to get their share.

"I think we should—"

A sharp growl stopped Max midsentence. The sound was low and melodious, but it grew as something untold moved through the bamboo. Cracking canes, and the gurgle and pop of a massive beast moving through the maze made Hawk's stomach go cold.

"Back the way we came," Hawk said. He spun on his heel and started for the path when he was met by a creature he didn't have a chance of classifying.

It wasn't dinosaur, lizard or mammal. A forgotten beast whose fossil remains had escaped the prying searches of anthropologists stood ten feet away, its green eyes narrowed as it examined Hawk. Curved white fangs stuck from an extended jaw, and blood caked around the animal's mouth. Its tight fur was dark yellow and it walked like a human, except with wide sweeping steps that made the thing look like it was going to fall over every time it lurched forward. Each appendage ended in a four-fingered paw, which sported a long curved talon that looked sharp as a knife. Perhaps this was a distant relative of a bear, but the beast had no ears and its arms and legs appeared too short for its massive torso.

The creature chuffed and snot flew from its nose as it bounded forward with a roar. Hawk ran, and the maze twisted and turned before him. He heard Svet and Max chugging behind him. The growl-bark of the creature in pursuit was close, but he ran blindly, taking random turns, and the sound of commotion died away.

Row upon row of green bamboo shoots created a wall on both sides of the path and none of it looked familiar. There was no place to hide, and if they met anything coming from the opposite direction they were screwed. A cramp stiffened Hawk's right leg, but he ran on, the pain causing him to limp as he shuffled forward, desperation propelling him onward.

The trail widened into a dead patch of bamboo he hadn't seen prior. It was as if some poison had been spilled in the area, killing everything. Then he remembered the clearings where the markers had been placed, and how nothing grew there. Hawk was getting tired, and he heard his companions sucking air behind him. The sounds of pursuit faded and all he heard was the wind pushing through the canes and a distant rumbling.

Hawk reached the end of the path and tripped on a bamboo root that looped from the jungle floor like a handle designed to catch his foot. He sprawled to the ground, kicking up a cloud of dust. Then Svet tripped over him and fell, followed by Max. The spacefarers lay in a tangled heap, panting and staring back into the maze. The maw of the maze entrance was dark and quiet, the yellow bear-thing having given up.

They were right back where they'd started.

# 13

Hawk lost track of time and had no idea what day of the week it was. He'd given up counting the days, but he knew it had been at least a month since they escaped the bamboo maze. Max had been keeping track of the number of days since landfall, but he admitted his count could be off by as much as five days. Hawk and Max had full beards, and even Svet had grown hair in spots not traditional to females. All three of them were dirty, greasy and hadn't bathed at all in days.

Trapping and hunting food was difficult, as their passage through the prehistoric jungle was unavoidably loud, and most animals cleared out of their way as the party stomped through the forest like T-Rex larva. Gathering food caused numerous delays, and they'd spent four days in a treehouse they'd constructed, while they built up their strength and supplies.

Max managed to make two bows and a stack of arrows, but firing the weapons with any semblance of accuracy was difficult. They practiced hitting targets scratched into trees from ten feet away, then fifteen, and all three of the travelers were proficient from that range, but anything farther was next to impossible. The bows weren't very strong, and the tree branches they'd used to make arrows didn't have enough weight to fly true. When they did hit something, the arrows didn't have enough force and would bounce off a dinosaur hide without leaving a mark. Goal one was to construct a better bow and better arrows.

Their spears and Hawk's bolas were another matter. Using shards of bone as tips, they'd constructed serviceable throwing javelins that flew true and did major damage. Svet managed to take down a mid-sized raptor-thing, and that had supplied them with a good amount of meat, which they cooked, smoked, and dried into jerky. Hawk was getting accurate with his bolas, which he'd made from bark rope and two round weighted stones. He managed to snag several birds, and five ground animals that looked like squirrels on steroids. The flesh of the large rodents was tough, but it had a sweet taste that reminded Hawk of duck.

They'd also learned much about the flora and fauna. They identified edible fruits and lettuces by watching the habits of the beasts. The larger dinosaurs moved slowly, and had trouble changing direction or squeezing through tight spaces, and this made them easy to avoid.

They'd found no new markers, and the jungle was a monotonous trudge that changed very little. They were starting to despair that they'd gone in a circle when they hit the edge of the savannah, and saw they were much farther north than they'd expected. The bamboo patch, several ravens and cliffs, as well as thick stands of trees had driven them off course. Hawk figured they were only a few miles from the plains northernmost edge, and that meant soon they'd be able to turn southwest and make a direct line to the mountains having avoided the chaos of the open plain.

The up-close view of the savannah confirmed Hawk had made the right decision. All manner of creatures big and small roamed the plain, kicking up clouds of dirt and trampling any vegetation that had the guts to stick its head above ground. The northern end of the lake wasn't visible from where he stood, but he could imagine a line of animals waiting their turn to drink, a nice orderly line with no fighting or disagreements.

Hawk chuckled.

"What funny?" Svet said. She tore off a chunk of jerky she was munching on.

"Nothing. Just wondering what's going on down at the town waterhole."

Max said. "You see that there? In the middle of the plain? What do you make of that?"

What Hawk would have given for a set of cheap field glasses, but he had nothing. Not even a piece of paper to roll up to make a tube.

At home in Florida, people collect trash along the beach and mound it into a single pile, propping up sticks, and hanging shells and other items from them. The garbage piles became a form of art, and some of the sculptures got big before they were cleaned up and destroyed. This marvel in the center of the plain looked like such a piece of folk-art.

Tree branches and bamboo of various sizes made a tepee structure that rose into the sky thirty feet or more. All about it leaves, creepers, and mud filled in holes making it look like a solid structure. To Hawk it looked manmade, and even though he knew that was impossible, the thought teased his brain.

Reading Hawk's mind, Max said, "You think whoever placed the markers is still here?"

"Nyet," Svet said, but Hawk wasn't so certain.

"Should we check it out?" Max said.

A chorus of "Nyet and no."

They stayed within the tree break as they worked around the savannah and were forced to trek deep into the jungle twice to avoid a *stegosaurus* fight and a large dinosaur that looked like a baby T-Rex tearing apart the carcass of an unknown beast. Knowing the dinosaur's habits helped the company avoid them, and out of sight was truly out of mind. The prehistoric creatures didn't seem to smell them, or have much space awareness. When they saw food they gave chase, but a human could be standing right next to a dinosaur and if it didn't see the person, the beast would have no idea anyone was there.

Hawk was on point when he hit a strange glade of tall pricker bushes with tiny purple leaves and white spidery trunks. They grew close together like a hedge, and the party gave up fighting through the tough plants and went around. Again.

They walked the rest of the day, and made camp by a river with clear cold water. After drinking until bloated, they filled the water bottles and proceeded to take a bath. Svet went first, then Max and Hawk. Svet said she didn't care if they saw her naked, but Hawk wasn't comfortable with it.

That night they slept on a platform built in the trees. This had become their preferred method of shelter, and except for ants, which crawled and burrowed everywhere, being off the ground served them well. When the quest was over and they knew for sure they were stuck in this time, Hawk envisioned a treehouse that rivaled Swiss Family Robinson's famous abode.

Sometimes Hawk believed he could be happy living with nature, enjoying the fresh air and crystal-clear water. Then Michel's face would fill his mind, and sorrow would wash over him anew. Despite this, he couldn't help but think about the future. What came next? It was hardwired into his brain.

The next morning dawned bright and clear, and so did the next eighteen days as they traversed the northern edge of the plain and headed toward the mountains. The tallest peak rose in the distance and was occasionally visible through the tree break. Further north, sticking from a large cleft in the mountains, was the erupting volcano. Hawk figured it was the one they'd seen from the space station. If it was, they were on the right track. The huge cone belched thick clouds of black smoke that darkened the sky. The air smelled of sulfur as the smoke thinned and crept across the jungle like fog. Dark lava spilled over the side of the crater and down the sides of the massive cone, where it cooled, releasing white smoke and steam that disappeared into the black smoke above.

"We may want to cross a bit further south than we intended," Max said.

"Too close to lava flow?" Svet said.

"Ja," Max said. "Don't see why we should chance it. What's a few more days?"

A loud buzzing sound rose above the normal daylight cacophony, a stone steady vibrating static that got louder as they got closer to the foot of the mountains. It made Hawk flashback to home, and the hum of powerlines and transformers.

The hive they discovered was ten feet around, and it hung from a thick branch beneath deep green leaves the size of manhole covers. The air around the hive was black with insects, but Hawk was too far away to tell what type they were.

"Bees?" Svet said.

"Ja, I think so," Max said. "The insect fossil records dating to the Cretaceous are sparse, but with the emergence of flowering plants I'd think the pollination machines would be on the rise."

The fellowship traversed the hive and found themselves staring down the face of a tall cliff. It appeared out of the jungle like a mirage, and Hawk estimated its height at one hundred feet.

Creepers clung to the cliff face, and bushes and small trees protruded from every outcrop of stone.

On the horizon, the mountains stood out like a scar on the land, massive gray-brown stone with ragged peaks and sheer sloops. Hawk didn't see an easy way up, nor did he see a way down the cliff face. The rock wall extended to the north and south, cutting the team off from the final part of their journey.

"We have a hundred feet of line. You think it's enough?" Max said.

Hawk went to the edge of the cliff and stared down at the deep green jungle canopy. "Maybe. Even if we come up a little short at least we'll be closer to the ground."

"Da," Svet said. She pulled the rope off her shoulder and ran it through her hands, making sure there weren't any knots. When the rope lay in a pile before her, she said, "You hold?"

"I'd like to tie off on a tree, but the closest one is twenty feet from the cliff edge, and we can't afford the rope," Hawk said.

"Let's see how far our rope will get us," Max said. He fed the line over the edge, letting the end slide down the face of the cliff. It got caught in the vegetation several times, and Max lost his measurement count, which he made using the length of his arms spread wide as he dispensed the rope. When the end hit bottom they still had ten feet of rope, so they tied the line off on the nearest tree.

Hawk said, "We can use the creepers to climb to the ground. Svet's a good climber and when Max and I are down she'll untether the rope and work her way down tying off as she goes."

One by one the two astronauts and one cosmonaut inched down the cliff, clutching the rope like it was a lifeboat and they were alone on a turbulent sea. Birds, bugs, and small rodents bit, cawed, and screeched at them as they disturbed the equilibrium of the cliff face. When the party reached the ground they were tired, dirty, and hungry, so Hawk called a halt and they made camp and settled in for the night.

They stayed with the cliff to their backs for four days, stocking up on dino-jerky, water, and adding to the rope using dried vines. Hawk felt the ascent into the mountains would be difficult without climbing gear, but there was nothing for it. The mountains had to be crossed.

Max estimated that seventy-five days had passed since they'd crash landed, and on the seventy-sixth day the jungle thinned and they arrived at the base of the mountains. Off to the north the volcano spewed lava and smoke, and the stench of it filled Hawk's nostrils. Rivers of orange fire burned rock lava beds into dark stone, and every few minutes a massive explosion shook the ground. Ash fell like rain.

The three companions camped in the jungle and saw and heard nothing unusual. When they woke, they ate, broke camp, and headed for a thin mountain cleft that rose into the blue sky.

# 14

Smoke mixed with steam snaked through the jungle, making it difficult to see more than ten feet ahead. Hawk was on point, one of the Ash 12s held before him. The forest grew thin, and no animals frolicked and crawled within the underbrush. The sounds of rending and cracking stone, the ripping of fire, and the languid push of the wind created an eerie melody that made Hawk uneasy, the erupting volcano only forty miles or so from their position.

Lava and sulfur vents appeared in the jungle, releasing heat and toxic fumes. The land was still forming, and every few moments the ground trembled as the immense geological upheaval that formed the continents of this time continued. For all Hawk knew, he could be standing in what would become his backyard millions of years in the future.

The future. There it was again, staring at him like an unblinking eye, always evaluating and measuring, making him feel like he wasn't doing enough, wasn't trying hard enough. These doubts had driven him his entire life, but somehow the fear of failure no longer motivated him. Sometimes he thought he suffered from some type of PTSD. He'd certainly been in enough battles, but they'd never affected him, or so he'd thought. He was able to fight, kill, and move on, not something a normal person should be able to do. Was he normal? What type of person left their family alone so they could go kill? It was Viking-like, and the reason for the killings, all the war, was so buried in his past he hardly remembered them. He'd come to understand that there was no valid reason. Killing another person was a crime against nature, and he'd done it for reasons he thought he'd understood, but now knew were nothing but justifications to do his master's bidding. Now helplessness was his new fear, and one he couldn't control or abate.

His nose stung from the heat of the smoke, but the steam felt good. Stray beams of sunlight fought through the thinning canopy and smoke, ethereal rays that looked to be from Heaven. Heaven.

If God presided over this lost world of the past he'd showed no sign to Hawk. On the contrary; Hawk felt abandoned and alone, despite his two companions that followed dutifully behind.

The mountains loomed up before them, and as the jungle gave way to the underbrush covered mountain slopes, Hawk saw for the first time the full difficulty of their ascent. Sheer rock faces provided no clear path, and the valleys and depressions had no clear entry points. The climbing would be hard, but Hawk didn't doubt their ability to summit the peak that was their destination.

Max was a problem. Svet was an experienced free climber, and she regularly risked her life on some of the most difficult climbs, and all with no ropes or safety lines. Hawk wasn't so adventurous. He climbed a few times, but always with a harness and a guide rope, which was much different than what would be required to get over these mountains. They had rope, and that was good, and Hawk figured he could tether himself and help the scientist when needed.

The jungle ended at a rock wall, and the party headed south, away from the volcano and its spewing lava. They discovered a thin cleft in the rockface where they could start their ascent, and thus turned upward. They ate a light meal of fruit and dino-jerky, with a salad of yellowed leaves from a lush plant that yielded romaine-like lettuce. Svet had made a dressing from rendered animal fat and the citrus juice of a hard-brown fruit that looked like a coconut. It had none of the nourishing flesh, but twice the juice. Though bitter, the fruit served as a source of water, and when Hawk used his imagination he could almost fool himself into thinking the stuff tasted like lemonade.

Refreshed, the party began their trek into the mountains. The cleft was bordered on both sides by sheer rock walls that rose two hundred feet, and there appeared to be no outlet.

"An old lava bed?" Hawk asked.

"Most likely. Doesn't look like it's been used for a long time. These rocks show no signs of current stress. Those dark lines and the porousness of the stone are indicative of dried lava, but the color is odd."

"Da. No black?"

"Svet's right. Normal hardened lava takes on a blackish hue," Max said.

"Different chemical makeup?" Hawk said.

"Most likely. I think—"

A loud explosion froze the three companions in place. The ground trembled, then fell still.

"I wish we could see what was happening," Hawk said. From within the hallway of stone the activity of the volcano wasn't visible.

The pathway plunged through a thick section of rock and emerged on a broad plain devoid of life. Hardened lava had claimed the area, and the remains of blackened trees stuck from the stone like rusty nails. To the north, the top of the volcano was obscured by thick black smoke, and it looked to Hawk like a secondary cone had formed because lava poured from the main cone's side in a new direction.

The spacefarers pushed on, using the rope several times to traverse difficult spots, and by lunch they'd worked their way high above the jungle. Hawk climbed atop a huge boulder while Max and Svet rested, and from his new vantage point he saw the land from which they'd come; the lake, savannah, and the vast, never ending jungle beyond.

They traveled through a patch of stunted trees covered in black ash, and came upon volcanic vent with thick fumes pouring from it like a smoke stack. The plants closest to the vent were brown and dried from the intense heat. Several smooth caves of varying sizes pocked the mountainside, lava tubes formed when the mountains sprang from the ground.

"You think we should head further south?" Max asked.

"Nyet," Svet said. She motioned to the south where several unclimbable walls of stone blocked the way. To the north, a thin valley cut through the stone and it was clear it had once been a lava bed, so unless they wanted to get closer to the geological monster, the forward path was the only one available to them.

The party pushed upward into the clouds, trekking west over jagged boulders as the explosions of the eruption grew closer. The path grew tighter, and the sheer rock walls taller. Hawk choked from the smoke, his eyes stung, and he rubbed them until his vision blurred. Max had one of his socks pulled across his face, and Svet wore a breathing mask she'd made from a leaf and some moss, but nothing stopped the smoke from penetrating, or the steam from drenching everything through.

The cut in the stone the party walked through narrowed and made a right turn, heading north. Small bushes and tall flowers with firework tops grew in every crag, or patch of dirt, but there were no trees or other long-established vegetation. The sky was overcast, and ash fell like the faintest of snow showers. Thick black clouds blanketed the horizon like a menacing storm.

The path ended at a steep wall of stone that rose two hundred feet or more. A wide groove had been formed at the upper edge of the wall, and it was clear a lava falls had once spilled over the precipice.

Thick raindrops fell, and Hawk called a halt. "I'm concerned about a flashflood. If water starts running in here we're trapped with nowhere to go."

Svet and Max said nothing, but Hawk knew what they were thinking. What if the flood wasn't of water, but of molten lava?

Fissures appeared along the path, great rents in the earth that released steam and smoke, and clouded the area. Vents were becoming more frequent as the newly risen mountain range took shape. This led to a warning from Max. "Maybe we should back off."

"What do you suggest? Turning around?" Hawk said.

"The land here is still transforming, still being molded by the shifting continents and the further away we can get from the lava the better."

Svet shook her head no, but said nothing.

Hawk looked back the way they'd come, then up at the rain drenched cliff face, then down the narrow path that no longer went toward the summit, but north toward the volcano. "I don't know. I feel confined here, but it'll be difficult climbing these faces. We either climb, head back, or take the path north and risk the lava trail."

Another explosion shook the ground, and a rock tumbled over the cliff's edge and sent Hawk and his companions running for cover. The boulder landed with a crash, broke apart, and dust rose around the stones.

Hawk took that to be a sign. "Yeah, I guess we should be safe rather than sorry."

Svet didn't like the idea of going back at all. "How you know another way is not worse?"

"I don't, but the further we are from the spewing lava the better off we are. Nyet?"

Svet shrugged and Hawk waited for Max's vote. Not that their party was a democracy, but at this point calling him the leader meant something entirely different than it had up in space.

"I say we climb. We're not close to the volcano, and going back would be a guaranteed hardship."

"OK then."

They climbed steadily for the rest of the day, and once they got up the cliff face they were only forced to use the ropes twice. Once on a steep, slippery incline, and the second time the rope served as a railing as the party moved along the edge of a ravine with black bubbling molten lava flowing in its basin.

Large birds and *pterosaurs* circled above, and an occasional rodent darted between the rocks, but that was the only wildlife. The animals knew to stay away from danger, unlike humans.

A large lava vent pushed through the greenery, and as the party passed it, a section of ground adjacent to the vent collapsed, sending the trail behind them plummeting into the earth. The party pushed on, and soon found themselves overlooking a river of lava that flowed deep within a channel of rock. The black magma bubbled and churned, orange glowing cracks released heat and steam.

There was no way forward, and no way back.

The plateau the spacefarers stood on was roughly five hundred feet wide, and a hundred feet across. Large boulders, weeds, and an occasional flower fought for survival on the barren ledge, but there appeared to be no way down.

An explosion lit the fading day, and it was close. Spatters of lava crested the mountain on the opposite side of the channel, and the flow of magma below doubled as it rose toward the ledge where the party stood.

Hawk backtracked to see if he'd missed an outflow, or another way up the side of the mountain, but the vent they'd passed had collapsed, and getting back down using the path was no longer possible.

The lava continued to rise, and Hawk's stomach went cold, even as the intense heat made him sweat. He rubbed smoke addled eyes, and sat on the ground and let his head fall in his hands.

"What we do?" Svet asked.

Hawk was despondent, but Max jumped in. "Let's look around, maybe there's another way."

A large chunk of the precipice on which they stood cracked with a deafening screech of rock being cleaved, and it fell into the lava below and disappeared. The ground shook, and black smoke rolled over the precipice. Hawk lost sight of Max and Svet as they searched.

A trickle of molten rock leaked from the rock face, and Hawk watched the new tunnel form.

"Here!" yelled Max.

Hawk couldn't see his friend through the thick smoke and steam, but he went toward Max's voice and found him staring up at a cave mouth twenty feet from the ground. The tunnel's dark maw beckoned, but Hawk hesitated. It reminded him of the dwarf caves in *The Lord of the Rings*, and how the party had no choice but to go beneath mountains.

We cannot get out. We cannot get out.

They are coming.

The trickle of lava spewing from the cliff face doubled, and rock came raining down, the pitch burning Hawk's clothes and arms. He spun around and almost fell, panic filling him with doubt, sweat rolling into his eyes, his skin scorched with heat.

There was only one way they could go.

Moria.

# 15

Hawk had only gone ten feet into the cave when he halted. It was so dark he couldn't see his hand in front of his face. The batteries in the flashlights had long since gone dead, so Max had made torches, the tips of which were wrapped with dried vines and dipped in tar, but they had no means of lighting the brands. Dripping water and the tilt of the wind echoed in the confined space, Hawk's pounding heart filling his head. In the darkness he was alone, despite his companions, and he had an urge to sit down and give up.

"What to do?" Svet said, the whites of her eyes next to Max's.

"I know," Hawk said. "Give me one of those torches."

"But how—"

"Just give me one, fast."

A shuffling and scraping in the dark as Max put down his bag and rummaged through it. Seconds later a stick was pressed into Hawk's hand.

"Wait here," he said.

He inched back toward the cave mouth, his hand running along the smooth wall. Fire and daylight lit the opening. Flames and brimstone, dark smoke, steam, falling rocks—all greeted the astronaut as he exited the cave. The drip of lava that pushed through the cliff face was now a torrent, and soon the precipice on which they'd stood would be consumed by fire. Black lava bubbled and hardened as it dripped over the rocks, and Hawk thrust the end of the torch into the nearest conglomeration.

The torch caught and blazed to life. Hawk ran back into the cave, the fire from his brand throwing dancing yellow light about the lava tube.

"That's better," Max said.

"Da."

"We'll see how long it lasts. How many more do we have?" Hawk asked.

"Three. I only brought them in case we needed to move about at night. I didn't plan for extended use."

"We'll have to use them sparingly."

"If we can," Max said.

Hawk played the torchlight around the tunnel. Black striations marked the smooth walls, and the path ahead looked like a rollercoaster track as it twisted and rose. Bugs like giant cockroaches scuttled on the cave walls and in several spots water dripped from an unseen supply.

"Argggg," Max yelled.

Hawk spun around and shone the light in Max's direction.

An animal that looked like a small chicken stripped of all its feathers moved languorously up the wall, the roach-bugs clearing a path for the creature. The odd albino beast had two sturdy legs and two forearms, and short black antennas flopped over its head. The creature turned and round globular eyes that were too large for the beast's head stared at him. Its front claws clicked against the volcanic stone, and it whistled and squeaked as it worked its way up the wall and disappeared into a hole.

The ceiling was full of fine stalactites that looked like rain that had frozen before it reached the ground. Piles of stones blocked the way, and the party was forced to climb over. There were no other passages, and as the tunnel twisted and turned upward, Hawk felt the temperature rise. He didn't voice what his companions were surely thinking: if this was once a lava tube, couldn't it be one again?

The tunnel gave way to a natural chamber much larger than the lava tube. Hawk tripped over a stone and almost fell. The darkness was thick, the scent of dirty moisture saturating the air. Their shadows disappeared into darkness as the path widened, but there was still only one path.

"What is that?" It was Svet, and she pointed up at the ceiling.

Dark figures the size of large birds were wedged within the stalactites. Hundreds of them. Maybe thousands. They didn't move, or make a sound, but as Hawk lifted the torch to get a better look, the beasts were disturbed.

As if the creatures had a single brain, their wings opened as one, and a dark cloud dropped from the cave roof. Pounding wings and high-pitched screeching filled the cave, and before Hawk could react, the flying beasts were among them.

They looked like baby dragons, a cross between a *pterosaur* and a bat. A single row of sharp teeth gleamed in pelican-like beaks, and tent flap wings pounded the air, their red eyes glowing in the darkness.

Hawk ran up the tunnel, which narrowed as he went, becoming no more than ten feet side to side. The echoes of the pursuing dragons pushed down the cave, and he heard Max and Svet behind him. Even with the torchlight seeing what lay ahead was difficult. There were many dips in the floor, and the twists and rises of the tube were unpredictable, and Hawk almost took a tumble several times.

One of the bat-things grabbed Hawk's shoulder and he used the torch to knock it off. The beast shrieked, but didn't attack again. The creature was on fire, and as it took to the air it collided with several of its friends and set them ablaze.

Hawk ran on, not heeding the dark or the possible pitfalls and dangers. The air reeked of rot and burning flesh, and he gagged. The torch went out and he put his hands out, feeling in the darkness for obstructions. The sounds of pursuit eased, and Hawk slowed and ran his hands over his shoulder, ensuring he wasn't wounded. His shoulder hurt from where the dragon had grabbed him, but no blood trickled from the area.

Max and Svet came even with him, and Hawk slowed to a jog. The howling and chirping of the batsaurs faded.

"Guess they didn't like fried bat," Hawk said.

"Those things weren't bats. I don't know what they were, but they weren't bats. Bats have rodent-like bodies. No, those things we saw had elongated bone structure, and their torsos were thin."

The three companions halted and stood in the darkness panting, the glow of the extinguished torch providing little light. Hawk blew on the torch, lightly at first, then harder, and soon the brand was ablaze again and the tunnel filled with orange flickering light. They took a break and rested, ate some food, and plunged on. They hiked an hour or so when the torch sputtered, and Hawk was forced to use it to light a new one.

"What we do with no light?" Svet said.

"We crawl if we have to," Max said.

"Da," she said. "I remember such a thing when I was on missile duty."

Hawk and Max looked at each other with squinted eyes.

"You know. The rockets that will get New York, Los Angeles. I used to man a silo, and every few days the power would cut out and I'd sit in the pitch-black for hours, hoping command wasn't trying to contact me."

"How is that possible?" Max said. "Typically those systems have redundant power."

"It no work."

"Did you have fire control during the outage? Did the outages affect the entire system?" Hawk asked.

Svet laughed and didn't respond.

They were millions of years in the past with no hope of getting home, but national security was national security.

An hour passed and the second torch went out. Hawk halted. This time when he blew on the orange embers nothing happened. "Should we try and go on in the dark? Save our light?" Hawk asked.

"How would we light a new one if we had to?" Max said.

"Da."

"Good point. Using the knife to spark a flame might take a while. Give me another torch," Hawk said.

Max rummaged through his bag and drew out another torch and unwrapped the leaf that protected the tar-covered tip. He pressed the head of the old torch to the new, and black smoke filled the passage, but the new torch didn't catch. Hawk blew harder, the smoke stinging his eyes and throat.

The new torch blazed and Hawk jumped backward into Svet and they both fell to the ground in a tangle.

The new light revealed a giant centipede. It was ten feet long and a foot around, and had two large antennae atop its head. Red eyes scanned right and left as the giant arthropod wiggled down the wall onto the floor. It squealed, a low pitched wail that rose in strength. Another centipede appeared on the wall above the first.

"Umm," Max said. "I think we should go."

Two more of the slippery creatures snaked into view and joined their friends. The creature's legs twitched in an odd wave-like pattern as it rolled along. It looked like the wall moved, as the centipedes came at them, unintimidated by the torchlight. They were white, except for the pinpricks of red that were their eyes, and the dark red tips of their fangs.

"We should go," Max said again. "Don't want to let them get those teeth into you."

"They're bugs. Big bugs, but just bugs," Hawk said.

"They're not just big bugs. Centipedes are predominantly carnivorous," Max said. "They are known to be highly venomous, and often inject paralyzing venom."

One of the beasts reared-up and spat at them. The venom missed, but it kickstarted Hawk's engine and he ran into the darkness of the lava tube.

Between pulling breaths Max said, "Funny fact. Centipedes can have a varying number of legs, ranging from thirty to three hundred fifty-four, but they always have an odd number of pairs of legs. So no centipede has exactly a hundred legs."

Hawk didn't think it was funny at all.

Svet tripped over a stone and went down hard, the thud of bone hitting rock making Hawk flinch in the darkness. The scuttling of a million feet clicking and tapping on stone was getting closer, and soon the party would be overtaken. Max helped Svet up. The woman was a machine.

Hawk puffed in and out, losing his breath. "Max," he said. "Can you get the last torch out while you run?"

"I'll try."

Snapping and drumming and scurrying echoed through the cave, a million crabs coming for dinner.

"Here," Max said. He thrust the torch toward Hawk who grabbed it, lit it with his torch, and handed his to Max.

"Keep going. Don't wait for me, no matter what," Hawk said.

"Nyet," Svet said.

"Go. Go now. I'll be right behind you."

Hawk skidded to a stop and rubbed the end of his torch on the cave wall. Tar came off on the stone and set the cave wall ablaze.

He did this until there was no tar left on the torch and a ribbon of fire circled the tunnel.

Hawk caught up with his friends, and they ran by the light of the last torch. The lava tube ahead filled with gray light, and for an instant euphoria pulsed through Hawk. He broke into a trot. Max held the flickering torch up high like an Olympic runner. A circle of light appeared ahead, the tunnel turning upward on a thirty-degree incline.

Hawk slowed as he approached the light, his astronaut trained mind screaming for caution. The cave walls were filled with moss and flowers. Light darted through cracks in the ceiling, and as Hawk inched from the tunnel he took a deep breath of air.

"Der'mo," Svet said.

The party stood on an outcrop of stone overlooking a valley enclosed on all four sides by the curved stone walls of an ancient lava bubble. Tropical vegetation and trees grew within the bowl of the basin, and sunlight streamed through a large opening formed by the collapsed mountainside.

"What is that?" Svet said, pointing.

In the center of the jungle below, a giant white dragon rested atop a nest of dead vegetation and branches, its giant wings folded at its side, head resting on three large eggs.

# 16

Hawk paced across the precipice, stopping every other lap to stare into the cave mouth. There were no signs of their pursuers, but based on what he'd seen when he'd lit the first torch, there was only one way to go.

"We try and sneak around?" Max said.

"Da."

Hawk smiled. Andrea could read his mind also. It was uncanny. He'd be floating around in space, thinking of something that needed to be done around the house, and he'd get a message from her that it had been handled. Or when sadness would wash over him because of their separation, and he'd get an unexpected message or find a support note she'd hidden. This was proof there were paranormal abnormalities that science couldn't explain. Hawk and Andrea were connected by an unseen tether that stretched thousands of miles, but it couldn't cross time.

The dragon slept on the valley floor, and nothing stirred in the jungle.

"What do you make of that, Max? Looks straight out of *Game of Thrones*," Hawk said.

Max stared at him with a vacant expression, eyes wide, mouth open a crack.

"A dragon. You know of dragons in Germany, ja?" Hawk said.

Svet shook her head.

"It is most certainly a species of *pterosaur*, which the adventure writers of the day refer to as a *pterodactyl*," Max said. "There are fossil records of these beasts with forty-foot wingspans, so the size of this beast is no surprise. What is odd is the creature's head. If you noticed when we've met these congenial creatures in the past—" Max paused to allow for laughs, and when none came, he continued. "You'll remember the *pterosaurs* we've seen so far have thin torsos with stunted front arms, and an elongated skull and jaw. Our friend below looks more like a flying T-Rex, with its thick midsection, clawed appendages, and bird-like head. The spikes down its spine are truly unique, and remind me of *stegosaurs* or *scelidosaurs*. Its light pigmentation is an indication of a cave dwelling animal, like the albino centipedes."

"So I should assume it will attack?" Hawk said.

"Most certainly."

"Plus the babies, nyet?" Svet said.

"Ja, plus the babies, which means dad is around."

Hawk stopped pacing. He hadn't thought about dad. "He's gonna be one big bitch," he said.

"Probably off hunting," Svet said.

Max said, "*Pterosaurs* can fly at speeds up to seventy-five miles-per-hour and can cover hundreds of miles in a single day. This is the perfect nesting area. Secluded and unreachable by the larger predators. These monsters have probably called this place home for a long time. Look there on the far side opposite us."

Across the valley on the far wall two wide tunnel mouths opened into caverns twice as large as the lava tube they'd just traversed. "At least there might be a way out, but even Svet couldn't scale those curved walls without gear."

"Nyet," she said, looking up at the rockface above them.

"We'll work our way around the outer-edge, giving the dragon as much space as possible. Stay out of sight. Run silent, and maybe we can slip by."

Hawk was considering the dilemma of which tunnel to take when Svet said, "Which one?"

Hawk and Max said nothing.

Getting down to the valley floor proved difficult, and the party was forced to leave behind the length of rope that had gotten them out of several binds. When they got to the bottom after several minutes of difficult belaying, Hawk stared up at the rope, thinking of when Frodo and Sam had the same dilemma. Unfortunately for the spacefarers, there was no elfin word or magic in the rope that would untie the knot that held it fast to a stone.

With more than one backward glance, Hawk and his companions abandoned their rope and picked their way through the field of boulders and saw palmetto at the base of the cliff's edge. Purple flowers bloomed in patches of heather, and small animals darted amidst the low grass covering the forest floor.

Animal trails let into the woods, and a small lake sat nestled against the cliff, a thin waterfall streaming from a crack in the stone. Rays of sunlight sparkled through water as it gushed from the mountainside.

"This would be a perfect place to call home if it wasn't for the current residents," Hawk said. "Protected and sheltered from the chaotic weather and predators. Fresh water, we could cultivate crops on the plain at the center."

Svet and Max said nothing. The idea of never going home, of putting down roots in this place still too new and absurd. Hawk knew that feeling would never fully go away, and as if on cue, sorrow engulfed him and his stomach turned to ice.

He'd always wanted to put down roots, but he was a leaf. He created roots, the trunk and its branches, then separated, floating on the wind to die. He'd never have the chance to be roots. Michel was the one who used the tree analogy to explain his life. They'd discussed whether the leaf got to choose its path and concluded no part of the tree had much choice. Roots dug for water, trunks supported weight, and branches grew leaves. That's how it always was, and always would be.

"Sorry," he muttered.

"Nyet. You are right," Svet said. "If we get out of here alive we should mark the location. Things no work out we come back."

"And what of our friends?" Max said.

"We drive them out," Hawk said.

To that Max had nothing to say.

The companions spent the better part of the afternoon slinking around rocks, cutting through stands of oversized ferns, and dodging insects of the crawling and flying variety. A large scorpion-like insect shot venom at them and Max screamed like a child. Hawk didn't blame him. The thing was five inches long with a stinger that looked like it could do massive damage.

Dusk fell over the jungle as the sun moved past noon and no longer shined through the opening above. Ambient light filtered through the hole, and it was just enough.

They collected sticks to make new torches with as they went. There was no tar available, but they chose resinous branches from a tree that dripped a syrupy fluid that was like a tasteless honey. The two astronauts and one cosmonaut hunkered down for the night behind a large boulder and ate some dino-jerky and drank the last of their water. They refilled the containers from the waterfall, and bathed quietly in the clear water. As darkness fell they slept, taking turns on watch, but nothing bigger than a group of monitor-type lizards observed them, and they heard nothing from the dragon.

The next morning the party searched for fruit in the thick jungle. They found some nuts, and a tree with berries that looked like oranges with an apple-like flesh but no sweetness. It filled them up and didn't make them sick, so they picked a bunch and stowed them for the future.

After hiking most of the morning, they reached a bare patch where there was little cover. To get to the tunnels on the opposite wall they had to work their way behind the resting dragon, which hadn't woken or moved since they'd first seen it.

"Let's do this fast. Go as quietly as you can, and try not to kick up any dirt. I'll go first. When I reach the cover of those rocks on the far side follow me," Hawk said. "Got it?"

A chorus of da and ja.

Hawk inched from his cover within a fern and headed for the pile of stones, his gaze drifting to the giant *pterosaur* as it rested in its nest. So it was that his attention wasn't focused on the ground before him and he tripped over a rock and went sprawling onto the ground with a shriek.

The dragon unfurled its giant wings and flapped them hard, kicking-up a gale of dust and debris.

"Screeeee. Screeeeeeeeeeeeeeeeeeeeee." The beast's tooth filled beak was pointed up, and it wailed and screamed as if Hawk had stolen one of its eggs.

A great shadow fell across the opening in the mountainside and daddy made an appearance.

The creature was larger than mommy, and as it descended into the valley its massive wingspan blotted out the sunlight. The beast's leathery hide was yellow with streaks of black, and large bulbous eyes rolled and focused on him. Daddy dragon cried, an earsplitting wail that left Hawk's ears ringing. The *pterosaur* filled the sky as it descended.

Hawk vaulted to his feet, arms and legs pumping as fast as they could. He considered pulling the Viking, but even if he could manage to hit the thing while running he doubted bullets would do much against this goliath. Both dragons yelled, and Hawk felt the beast was almost upon him when he dove for cover beneath a spreading fern at the edge of the clearing. He saw Svet and Max peek from their hiding place behind a stone. Smartly they hadn't followed him.

Daddy chomped on the fern Hawk hid beneath. The top of the plant disappeared and Hawk was exposed. The beast threw the treetop aside and Hawk got up and ran, the *pterosaur's* jaws chomping air where he'd stood.

He bolted into the jungle, searching for a place to hide, but there was nothing but ferns, palmetto, and trees. The beating of the dragon's wings was like a hurricane, and the forest swayed. Leaves were torn from branches, and palm fronds rattled and stung him as he ran. Hawk wove through the trees, watching the ground. Every cut and bump he had ached. He was hungry, tired, and uncomfortable from sunburn, bug bites, and lack of sleep.

Hawk looked over his shoulder, searching for Svet and Max, but saw nothing but a giant yellow carpet coming at him with a mouth full of tiny sharp teeth.

The forest was getting thicker, and he hid behind a thick tree, peering around its girth, panting and sucking for air. The dragon had halted its pursuit, and sat atop a tree, searching the jungle. It cawed every few seconds in frustration, but finally gave up and flew back to its mate, settling beside the giant nest.

As if daddy hadn't been fast enough, or watching close enough, mommy chirped and spat at the bigger dragon, pawing at him with her front claw and pushing him away. Hawk chuckled. Some things never change, no matter what.

Hawk waited behind the tree for several minutes, listening for his companions, but Svet and Max didn't come. He wasn't worried. They were most likely playing it safe, and they knew where Hawk was going, what they intended to do, so he decided to head to the caves and wait for his friends there.

The jungle was difficult to get through. The ferns and weeds were thick, and the conifer trees grew close together, their trunks forming walls that caused Hawk to travel far out of his way.

The *pterosaurs* had grown quiet, but he had no doubts the beasts would be on their guard. He climbed up a steep hillock that looked to be a pile of stone from the fallout that created the caves. It was covered with soil and tiny green plants with blue flowers, and to Hawk it looked like an old fashioned funeral mound.

He reached the top of the pile, but as he shifted his weight to look back the way he'd come, a rock dislodged and tumbled down the hill. Hawk fell ass over teakettle down the side of the rock pile and landed in a mass of white sticky webbing that covered the entire area. He thrashed, trying to free himself, but the thick webbing held him fast.

A dark cloud of spiders, each the size of a man's hand, advanced on him like a swarm of flies.

# 17

Hawk screamed for help. He knew it might bring unwanted attention, but he didn't know what else to do. The spiders pressed toward him, spreading out as they circled their prey. Hawk bucked and heaved, unable to break the webbing, but the movement launched several of the arachnids into the jungle.

Hawk reached for the Viking, but couldn't get to it. He rolled and turned, but the thick silk cordage held him fast. He struggled and pulled against the webbing, and managed to free a shoulder. He drew the Viking and squeezed off two shaky shots. The weapon turned in his sweaty hand with the force of the recoil and the gun slipped from his grasp, landing on a sticky patch of web ten feet below.

Those two ill-sighted shots saved Hawk's life. The mass of spiders paused as one, their wet eyes rolling above sharp fangs.

"You there!"

It was Max.

Hawk's mates appeared atop the pile of rocks he'd fallen from. Svet opened up with her Ash 12, bullets striking the webbing around Hawk. The taught lines of silk twanged and snapped and Hawk fell. Spiders flew in every direction as he plummeted, and he landed on a fern covered in webbing and rolled to the ground.

In the distance one of the dragons wailed, and the spiders scuttled into hiding like a dark wave receding from the shore.

Hawk landed atop an anthill, and within seconds small red ants were crawling all over him, biting and leaving red welts. He slapped and brushed at them as he got up, and then Svet was next to him, brushing him off and pulling strands of sticky spider web from his hair.

"Screeeeeeeeeeee."

The dragon was close. Max joined Hawk and Svet and they slipped behind a rock and waited for the *pterosaur* to move on. It screeched several more times, and landed atop the pile of rocks, jaws snapping. After several minutes of prodding with its beak, but finding nothing, the beast flew off. The pounding of its wings created a gale that sent spiders, alive and dead, tumbling through the air.

Insects buzzed and chirped, animals scampered through the underbrush, reptiles bleated, and a large monkey-like beast with short arms and long legs bounced around the tree canopy, staring at them and yelling, as if the creature was trying to tell the dragon where they were.

"This way," Svet said.

The party snuck back into the jungle, taking care not to make noise. The *pterosaurs* were on guard now, and Hawk doubted daddy would be leaving anytime soon. He scratched at his ant bites, and seeing this, Svet reached into her bag and dug out her special aloe cream.

"Here, rub this on. Stop swelling and itching."

"Thank you," Hawk said. He did as he was told and felt better.

The forest was tight, and it took two hours to get to the cliff face. Several hundred feet above the ground two large cave mouths looked over the valley like giant eyes.

"How're we going to get up there?" Max asked.

"Da," Svet said. "Which one?"

Hawk sat on a stone and took a long pull of water. The cave entrances looked very similar, and without a closer look it was impossible to tell if the tunnels turned upward, or if they dove deeper. "We have to get up there and take a closer look."

Svet harrumphed. "How we do that? Things will see, nyet?"

"Ja," Max said.

The sun passed noon and the gray of dusk settled over the valley like a coverlet. "I think we wait until it gets a bit darker, then we climb up there. Hopefully in the failing light the things won't see us."

"Climb that face? In dark?" Svet said.

"We'll do most of it at dusk, but yeah, unless you've got a better way?"

"Sure would be nice to have some rope," Max said.

They rested then foraged for food and found brown nuts that looked like almonds but tasted like rotten meat. Their explorations revealed an easier way to ascend to the caves—not a path, but a gradual face that had few impediments. At Max's direction, the party found as many creepers as they could, and weaving them together made thirty feet of cordage.

They needed it. The climb proved sketchy, as there was a layer of sand beneath the lava pebbles, and they constantly fell and slipped backward. Svet had gotten good at climbing as hard as she could and as soon as she hit a loose patch and started to slip, she'd dodge to the side and prop herself against a stone. Twice the stones hadn't been large enough to support her weight and she'd rolled down the mountainside. She wasn't hurt, but didn't appreciate Hawk humming Like A Rolling Stone when she managed to climb back to where he and Max waited.

The darkness was tunnel-like in the hollow. Moonlight seeped through the hole in the stone ceiling, casting errant rays that fell upon jungle scenes like spotlights on a Broadway stage. Small *pterosaurs* flew circles around the columns of light, and clouds of insects darkened the sky.

After an hour of hard climbing they reached a vertical section that required Svet's skill. The lithe Russian worked her way up the rock face like a spider, and when she reached the top she dropped down one end of the vine rope. She tethered the other end to a stone, and helped the boys up.

When they finally reached the cave entrances darkness had overtaken the world, and the companions entered one of the cave mouths and started a fire. They'd agreed to spend the night, and make their decision as to which tunnel to follow under the light of day.

Hawk couldn't sleep. The buzz of insects and the scuttling of animals echoed off the rounded valley walls, causing a maddening stereo effect. Hawk passed around some dino-jerky and pulled free the vodka they'd saved. Hawk took a long pull, and passed the bottle to Max, who eyed it warily.

"What if something happens tonight?" he said.

Hawk laughed a little too loudly, and he covered his mouth. The party sat in silence for several minutes, waiting to see if the outburst had woken the dragons. If it had, they showed no sign and Hawk said, "Drink up, Max. What the hell else can happen to us?"

"If you no drink, pass," Svet said.

Max took a pull from the bottle and passed to it Svet, who drank deeply. The bottle got passed around, and the three spacefarers who had become family drank the last few drops of Russian vodka, the likes of which wouldn't be seen in these parts again for millions of years.

Svet had fallen asleep when Hawk held the bottle up to the fire and tilted it. "One mouthful left. You want it, Max. I want you to have it." Hawk burped.

Max cackled. "Don't lie, commander, it doesn't suit you."

Hawk upended the bottle and his mouth filled with the sharp bite of alcohol. He rolled the vodka around his mouth, letting his mouth go numb. The hint of wheat and potato was refreshing. The burn as the vodka slid down his throat made Hawk smile. He capped the empty bottle and put it in his bag. It could be used to carry water, and perhaps one day he'd make a primitive liquor or beer.

Max said, "So, what do you think? Which one?"

"Not sure. I need more light, but based on what I've seen so far, this one we're in. It looks to head upward, while the other passage bends down. That could change, however, fifty feet in, so we'll want to reconnoiter both tomorrow as far as we dare. Also, this one smells much less foul than the other."

"Indeed. For me, that's the biggest indicator," Max said.

"Nyet, Vladimir. Nyet," Svet was arguing with her husband in her dreams.

Hawk leaned back against the tunnel wall. Dreams. That was all they had of their families now, random synapses in their brains conjuring images and memories that might not be true. Hawk didn't care. He loved dreaming of Andrea. It made him feel like she was still with him somehow, even though she hadn't been born.

"Do you dream of your wife?" Hawk asked.

Max looked pensive, and said, "Hawk, I don't think I remember what she looks like. It's been so long she's slipping from my mind, as if she never was. Scares the hell out of me."

"I understand," Hawk said. "When I start to feel that way I picture Andrea in mind for a long time. I take a mental snapshot, and look at the picture every day. When we're hiking, preparing for sleep. That way she's always fresh in my mind."

"I wish I had a real picture," Max said. Svet was the only one lucky enough to have a picture of her husband. Max's family picture was lost on the space station and Hawk's had been chewed into tiny pieces when their first shelter was ransacked.

"Better get some sleep. We've got a long one tomorrow."

"Ja," Max said.

"Visualize the dream you want to have as you fall asleep, and sometimes you're rewarded with a facsimile of your fantasy. Might help," Hawk said.

"Ja, I try," Max said. He laid down atop his spacesuit, and was asleep in moments.

Hawk was up all night thinking about the past, his family, and Michel. He still saw his friend's dead face in his mind's eye every night, those haunting gray eyes asking Hawk why? Hawk didn't have any answer, and wasn't sure why Michel would be asking. Hawk fingered the plastic vile in his pocket that held his suicide pill. He hadn't thought about taking it in a long time, but thinking of his family, and Michel, made him want to end it all and join them. What were they doing? Their quest was a joke, and deep down he knew it.

When the basin filled with light he woke his companions. As was the plan, they delved into both lava tubes and confirmed what Hawk had deduced in the dark: the left tunnel smelled better, and twisted upward.

Svet kindled a fire by throwing sparks into dried moss with her knife. Once the fire was smoldering, they lit their torches and plunged into the darkness.

White bugs of all sizes and shapes fled into the blackness. The party kicked-up dust as they went, making it hard to see inside the tunnel, even with two blazing torches. Hawk had the feeling there were always bigger, more dangerous creatures just beyond the circle of torchlight, watching, waiting for the flames to go out. That wouldn't happen anytime soon, because Max had prepared fourteen fire brands in total, and if they weren't out of the caves by the time they were used up that would be the least of their problems.

After walking for almost three hours the tunnel turned sharply up, so much so that Hawk slipped and fell twice on the incline. Max went down five times. The striations of the cave walls were much different here than in the first section of tunnel. Here there were veins of a different color lava.

The party came to a halt across from two branch tunnels, but both were narrower and plunged downward, so the party stayed the course. The air got hotter as they walked and their burdens heavier. They stopped briefly to drink some water and rest then pushed on. They'd been walking for two hours when a bright oblong patch of light marked the end of the lava tube.

"Hurrah," Svet said.

They started to run, laughing as they went, their cares forgotten for a time, the euphoria of having beaten the odds filling them with ignorant hope. The cave mouth exited onto a vast plateau, and Hawk skidded to a stop. The blue sky was clear, and a gentle breeze pushed warm air from the volcano over the mountains.

"We're over. We made it," Hawk said.

"Da," Svet said.

Max sat on the ground and let his head fall into his hands. It was hot, and sweat inched down Hawk's back and across his forehead.

Below, stretching to the horizon, was a vast sea of blue water; beyond lay a massive twisted jungle.

# 18

Hawk decided it was best for them to make camp on the precipice and spend the night. Up with the clouds, away from the hazards that roamed the ground, the party would await nightfall, and hopefully they'd see the beacon light and their path would be verified and their quest validated.

"What do you make of the sea below?" Hawk asked Max.

"It's shallow, and we should be able to cross it. See that patch of water reeds in the center? I don't think the sea is more than five feet deep there, and judging by the coloration of the water from up here, that appears to be the deepest section."

The inland sea stretched as far as the eye could see to the south, and terminated in jungle to the north and west. A thin ribbon of beach marked the shoreline below, and the thick forest to the west and north encroached into the sea.

"Is it still growing?" Hawk muttered.

Max said, "As the landmass Pangaea pulled apart scientists believed great rents in the land would have been exposed to the sea, and they believed many shallow seas covered land that will be above sea level in our time. The fossil records support the hypothesis in many locations."

"We go around?" Svet asked. She knelt on the ground making a fire ring of stones in the cave mouth.

Hawk sighed. The inland sea was large, and going around to the north would take them way out their way, and expose them to all the dangers that lurked in the woods. Hawk said, "Let's see what night brings. If we see the beacon light, we'll know exactly where we need to go. If the light is to the north, then perhaps going around might make sense."

"Ja," Max said. "But do you think we can cross that?" He pointed at the blue shimmering sea. "I think we can."

"Me too."

With that settled the companions fell into their normal routine. Max collected wood while Svet busied herself making a fire.

Hawk moved all their belongings into the cave, as the lava tube would be their quarters for the evening. Then he went hunting with a bow and arrow, but came back an hour later with nothing. Svet and Max sat by the fire, drinking water and talking.

When Hawk arrived, Svet took her hand off Max's leg. "No luck?" she said.

"Nothing. Didn't even see anything." If either of them noticed Hawk's double entendre

they didn't let on.

"We've got two pieces of jerky left and some of those nasty nuts we found," Max said.

"That'll have to do. Tomorrow we can see about getting some fish," Hawk said.

"It should be easy enough to make a pole, but what of hooks?" said Max.

"We shall see."

They ate and drank in silence, and each snuck off to a private area to go to the bathroom and prepare for sleep. Hawk hid behind a bush, where he managed to pee and squeeze out a thin little piece of shit which smelled like a dead body. Most likely the remnants of the nuts. He wiped himself with a leaf, then used some precious water to rinse his face. Refreshed, he returned to camp to find Svet and Max hard at work.

Max used Svet's knife to whittle a branch into a fishing pole. He'd gotten the wood from a bush that could be found everywhere in this prehistoric time, and it reminded Hawk of a *forsythia* bush, with its small yellow flowers and thin, flexible branches. Except these specimens were three times the size of the plants Hawk had known.

Svet worked on something less critical. She was making string from animal sinew, and next to her lay a body for a ukulele she'd made from the shell of the large bulbous fruit they'd found, and over it she'd mounted a deck made of thick bark, a knothole serving as the sound hole. Once she carved a neck and mounted the strings, she would have a relative of the guitar and mandolin. She'd been working on it for weeks, and Hawk and Max were looking forward to her first concert.

The instrument was a constant reminder to Hawk of what they'd lost. He and his companions spent so much time surviving, trying to reach the beacon, that they no longer lived. There was no leisure, no fun, and Hawk resolved to change that.

"Either of you play chess, or checkers?" Hawk asked.

"Da," Svet said. "I was a chess champion in school. What is checkers?"

"A weak version of chess," Max said. "I'll make the board when I'm done here and then we can carve pieces from wood, and use pebbles as pawns."

"Excellent. Look out for material as we go," Hawk said. It felt good to make plans that didn't involve finding food, water, and shelter. It would be a welcome diversion from their situation, which constantly reminded them how screwed they were.

The sun slipped below the horizon, leaving only a bruised sky. In the half-light of dusk the three friends sat motionless, not speaking, staring at the western horizon as if everything in their lives depended on seeing the beacon. To some extent it did. They hadn't discussed what they'd do if the western sky remained dark and forlorn and they didn't see the light.

A nervous energy ran through camp as the darkness deepened. Hawk busied himself cleaning the guns and counting the ammunition. There were fourteen rounds left for the Viking, and thirty-two for the Ash 12s. Still a decent amount, but they'd used more than half their supply since crash landing. They'd have to be more careful, or the guns would become nothing more than metal clubs.

As the stars appeared so did a glow to the west.

"There!" Max shouted, and Svet and Hawk leapt to their feet, following the scientist's finger as he pointed southwest.

A pulsing pillar of light cut through the darkness, ascending into the sky like a rocket trail, its odd rhythm blinking and shuddering. It was far off, much farther than Hawk had imagined, and though seeing the beacon brought comfort and hope, the fact that they were so far from their goal tempered the excitement.

"Further south than we thought," Svet said.

"Ja."

"At least it's there," Hawk said. They had a long way to go, but at least they knew they were going in the right direction. In the distance the column of flickering white light rose to the heavens, its presence a validation of every decision Hawk had made since the day of the cloud's passage. He felt vindicated, from what he didn't know, but a weight had been lifted from him. A weight that defined him. With the beacon visible, there was only one thing left to do, and it would seal their fate.

The next morning, they packed up and scaled the cliff that led down to a steep incline, terminating at a large pile of boulders. Beyond, stretched a flat section of rock that sloped gently down to a jagged crag where they hoped to descend the rest of the way to the seashore. The sound of small waves breaking on the beach below, and the salty-shit scent of sea air was a welcomed change from the wet nastiness of the caves. The breeze was fresh and temperate, and Hawk and Max took off their shirts.

Svet whistled. "Beef cake, eh?"

Max laughed nervously, and looked at the ground.

Hawk smiled. He was aware that Svet and Max had developed a close relationship, and perhaps even a romantic one. They went to great lengths to keep this from him. Why, he wasn't sure, but Hawk knew the simple math. Two men, one woman, and unless they got funky, either he or Max was guaranteed a lifetime of self-gratification. That idea dredged up another thought: what if Svet were to become pregnant? If they were having sex, were they using protection? He didn't see how they could be, beyond the ineffective pullout method, which worked about as often as a coin landing on heads.

"You with us?" Max asked.

"Yeah, just…"

They'd almost reached the base of the mountains.

"Screeeeeeeeee. Screeeeeeeeeeeeeeeeeeeeeeeee."

"Hide. Hurry." Hawk darted behind a large stone, followed by Max and Svet.

A dark shadow slid over the land, blotting out the sun.

"Screeeeeeee."

A dragon with yellow and black skin flew overhead, its giant canvas wings outstretched as it glided on an air current. It was their friend from the caves, his markings unmistakable. The beast didn't see them, and banked hard to the north, heading for the jungle. The party stayed hidden for several minutes until the dragon was nothing more than a speck on the northern horizon.

They reached seaside by midday, and gentle fifteen-inch waves broke on a rock beach. There was a series of large boulders and the party hunkered down between two of the huge stones and drank some water and rested.

"Do you think we should head north now? Get under the cover of the forest? Build a platform?" Hawk thought going to the jungle was best, but he was committed to making this a group effort here on out. Their escape from the caves and volcano had given him a new perspective. One of acceptance. As if some God protested his moment of Zen, an explosion sounded off as the volcano erupted. The ground shook and rocks tumbled toward the sea.

"Build platform," Svet said.

"Ja."

They gathered their things and hiked up the beach, a gentle breeze pushing sand and seaweed along the shore of the shallow sea. The sun was going down when they entered the trees, and got to work building a platform. They were old dogs at the process, and within an hour a six-foot by six-foot platform was ten-feet off the ground in the bows of a tree with thick branches and tiny oval green leaves.

They found the usual produce and fruit in the jungle, having learned long ago what was good to eat and what wasn't. The large coconut-like fruit was everywhere, and they still had two bottles of water. They ate jerky and fruit, and by the time the sun was a smudge on the horizon they sat around a fire at the base of their tree.

"Did I show you what I found on the beach?" Max said.

"Nyet."

"Look." He unrolled a leaf and within was the rotten skeletal remains of a fish.

"Dead fish?" Svet said.

"I think I know what he's thinking. Fish bones can be used to make hooks," Hawk said. "I'm wondering about our bigger problem."

"That," Svet said, pointing at the inland sea.

"I'm thinking we need to build a raft. At least one big enough to carry our supplies and guns," Hawk said.

"It's a long way, and there could be some nasties in there," Max said.

The creatures of the sea in the Cretaceous were no less formidable than those that walked on land. Even Hawk knew that. Megalodon and the like. "Max, the big bastards can't swim in water that shallow, right?"

"No, but…" Max cut himself off.

No need to dwell on the possibilities. Hawk and his partners had agreed not to focus on the negatives. By all accounts they all should be dino-chow by now, or burnt to a crisp, or pecked to death by Smaug's bastard father, or being slowly eaten alive by ants. All these pleasures had left their marks, but they were still here.

# 19

The next morning found the three companions sitting on the rocky beach, the cool inland sea lapping on the shore. Svet had her spacesuit boots off, and she sat with her feet in the weak undertow, her head thrown back, blonde hair flowing behind her. She looked beautiful, and he noticed that Max was also watching the Russian, and when he saw Hawk looking his way, Max diverted his eyes.

Hawk smiled. Max and Svet had taken a walk along the beach the prior night, which he had warned against citing unknown creepers in the sea, but they didn't heed his warnings. When they came back smelling of sex he couldn't help but be amused by their audacity. A myriad of beasts could be living in the sea, and Hawk was wary of sitting on the banks of the shallow ocean, especially in the dark.

So it was that while Max fished and Svet sat at leisure, he stood guard with one of the Ash 12s, his eyes scanning the crystal-clear sea for lurkers. He saw fish, several of which nudged Max's bait, but didn't take it. The scientist had dug for worms, but found none, so instead settled on a beetle, which he skewered on a hook made of fish bone.

"I think I need better bait."

"Da."

"Maybe one of those purple caterpillar-like things? Have you seen any?" Max said.

"Not recently. They hide in the cracks of bark on the conifers, and there are plenty of them around. Let me go look for you," Hawk said. "Svet, can you keep an eye out while I'm gone? Shouldn't be more than fifteen minutes."

Svet smiled and glanced sidelong at Max. Hawk couldn't help but laugh to himself. "Maybe more like a half-hour," he said. He handed Svet the Ash 12, and disappeared into the forest. Once within the tree break he paused, hiding behind a tree and observing his companions. They didn't wait long. Within minutes of Hawk leaving, the two lovers were rolling around on the beach entwined like rope. Hawk faded into the jungle and left them alone.

Alone in the jungle doubt crept in, the sorrow and worry. He saw Michel's foggy eyes, and his family sitting around the Christmas tree without him. Flipping through his mental photo album just wasn't doing the trick. He took the plastic pill holder from his pocket and held it up to the sun. He didn't know if Max and Svet still had theirs, but he imagined they did. Would they even care if he was gone? Were third wheels ever missed?

He cracked open the container and spilled the small white pill into his hand. Death within twenty seconds. Hawk didn't remember what was in it.

A dinosaur roared, and he put the pill away. There may come a time when he couldn't carry on, keep the sorrow and loss at bay, but that day wasn't today.

He took his time, walking slow, scanning the trees for game and bait. He found several of the purple slugs pilled together beneath a large section of bark, and he peeled them off and rolled them into a leaf. He'd only been gone ten minutes, so he sat with his back to a tree, resting, and giving his friends privacy.

Svet and Max were married, but given their situation, were they doing wrong? Were they betraying people who hadn't even been born yet? Hawk was willing to give them a pass. Despite the fact that the spacefarers had done an admirable job surviving in this harsh environment, if Svet and Max found comfort in each other, so be it. He wouldn't stand in the way. In fact, when he got back to the shore he'd inform his friends he was aware of their relationship, and once acknowledged there'd be no need to hide any longer. If by some amazing chance of fate they found themselves back in their time, they'd deal with it.

Hawk yawned. He hadn't slept that well, and his eyelids drooped. He yawned again as a gentle breeze pushed through the trees. Insects sang, lizards bleated, and in the distance a great animal roared its dissatisfaction at something. When they'd first arrived the sounds of the giant beasts had sent a shiver through him, but now they were no more than background noise. He closed his eyes, and promptly dozed off.

Andrea rolled over, her long brown silky hair falling over Hawk's face as he lay next to her in bed. He inhaled, sucking in her intoxicating scent and the smell of her flowery shampoo. Sun shone through the bedroom window, and the sound of children's laughter carried on the breeze. He brushed the hair from his face and stared at his wife. She breathed gently, her chest rising and falling in a slow, steady rhythm.

Hawk felt the urge to wake her, to tell her how much he missed her, how much he loved her, how he would do anything to be with her again, but as he reached out to touch her she slid away from him, falling away into the sheets and disappearing into the bed.

"No!" he yelled, but she was gone and Hawk lay alone, staring at the ceiling, his chest heaving, tears leaking from his eyes.

Then she was there again, as if brought by his grief.

"Do not despair, my love," she said. She smiled, and looked so peaceful Hawk stopped weeping and threw his arms around her, pulling her close. But there was nothing there, and he fell forward into blackness, screaming and grasping for his wife as she receded into the distance.

"Fear not. You are free. Don't mourn for me, my love. Live, and perhaps we'll meet again."

Hawk woke with a start, his face hot from a stray sunbeam that cut through the tree canopy and landed on his face. Sweat rolled down his back, and he rubbed his eyes. The leaf containing the bait had fallen from his hand, and the purple caterpillar-things were inching away in every direction. Hawk scooped them up, and wrapped them in the leaf once more.

He got up and stretched, then made his way back to his friends. Svet was asleep on the beach, the Ash 12 laying across her chest. Max stood knee deep in the sea, his line cast out into the depths.

"Ah, you're back," Max said.

"I wanted to give you guys some alone time."

Max jerked back as if struck.

"Look, I know about you guys. It's fine, you don't have to hide."

"We thought we were being so careful."

"Lovers always do."

"How do you feel about it?"

"I don't."

"What about the adultery?"

"I think our situation requires an extreme exception to most rules. I know you love your wife, shit, I just…"

"Just what?"

"Never mind. Let's get this new bait on your line."

Max jerked his line free and Hawk went about the task of pulling off the beetle and hooking a purple caterpillar.

"Hope this works better," Max said. He drew back the pole and cast his line out into the clear water. He'd tied a pebble to the end of the line to act as a weight, and the bait sank to the bottom as soon as it struck the surface.

Hawk took the gun from Svet, who still napped peacefully.

"Jaaaaaaaaa," Max screamed. "Look at that big one."

A large fish with yellow and blue scales glided past the hook, then turned in a wide arc as it picked up speed. As it passed the bait again it pecked at the bug, but didn't take the bait. The fish had teeth because a red and black goo seeped from the slug, its insides clouding the water. When the fish got no resistance, it turned again and this time chomped on the bait.

Max heaved the pole, and the fish jerked and spasmed as he hauled it to the surface. Silver gills sparkled in the sunlight as the fishing pole bent and the line tightened and stretched.

"Get it on land before the line breaks." Hawk knew a little about fishing, but not enough to be giving advice. But he was hungry.

Max braced himself, then threw himself backward, yanking the pole as he fell. The fish flew from the water and Hawk saw the flash of white teeth as the beast flew past, then snapped at the end of the line and landed on the beach. It flopped around, trying to get back to the sea, but Hawk stepped forward and smacked it on the head with a rock, and it fell still.

The commotion had woken Svet, and she said, "Do you know how to clean?"

"A little. You?" Max said.

"Da." Svet came forward and freed the dead fish from the hook and pulled her knife. "Go get some dry wood, da? I clean?"

"OK," Max said. He walked into the jungle.

"Dig hole?"

"Sure." Hawk knelt and dug with his hands, pulling sand between his legs the way he did when he built sandcastles with the kids. His stomach went to ice. Who would teach his son how to be a man? What it means to have responsibility? The thought made him feel like dying.

Svet used the knife to remove the fish's scales, then she gutted the animal, cutting it up into two nice fillets. Max returned with wood, and before long the fish was roasting over an open fire, and the companions drank water, watching the sea.

"So, he knows," Max said to Svet.

Hawk had never seen Svet embarrassed, and in many ways he knew her better than he did his wife. You get to know people when you're locked together in a tin can two hundred miles above Earth. But there's a first time for everything, as Svet's face turned red as a cherry.

Hawk let her off the hook. "No worries. It's cool. Better that I know so I can give you some space."

"Nyet. We all together," Svet said.

"Yes, but I really am OK with you guys having a relationship. No need to worry about me."

As the two astronauts and one cosmonaut experienced their first awkward silence, the sea breeze gusted, bringing the scent of rotting fish and fire. A light ash fell like snow, covering everything in a gray blanket. Hawk held out his hand, the ash covering his palm. The wind gusted hard off the sea and the ash was gone as fast as it appeared, and palm fronds rattled and clicked.

"That last eruption must have been a big one," Hawk said.

"Ja. I was worried."

"What you mean?" Svet said.

Max rubbed his face.

"Tell me, da?"

"That volcano was busting apart. We may have gotten very lucky. I think the slope we climbed is under lava right now."

No one spoke, and the snap and rumble of the tiny waves soothed Hawk's mind. It reminded him of Andrea's relaxation CD, the way…

"Hawk, it is long way across sea," Svet said.

Hawk breathed deep, wishing he had just one mouthful of whiskey. "Can you play us something to take our minds off that?"

"Da." Svet went to fetch her ukulele.

"You're sure you're OK with this? Me and Svet I mean?" Max asked.

"Yeah. Sure."

"I think tomorrow I'm going to build us our own platform. That OK?"

"A O."

Again, they had nothing else to say. A wall was already between them, a separation that Hawk would never be able to bring together. Suddenly the idea that he'd always be alone washed waves of sadness over him, his thoughts his worst enemy.

Out on the inland sea a surge of white water broke the surface about a hundred yards out. Small white rapids appeared from nowhere, as if a school of lazy fish had suddenly been disturbed.

The roar of a giant snapped Hawk's head around, and he searched the jungle. He rolled onto his belly, staring into the trees, waiting for a snout with a gaping maw of teeth to press through the vegetation.

Instead, Svet stepped from the trees with her instrument and she paused when Hawk and Max stared at her. "What is it?"

"Just missed you," Max said.

Svet smiled, but looked away as she came forward and sat on the beach between them. She plucked the strings of her ukulele, which she'd completed the prior night by attaching her bamboo neck via a glue she'd made from tree amber heated and recast. She rolled her shoulders and strummed the small guitar, playing a quant Hawaiian melody.

Hawk's muscles eased, and he leaned back, soaking in the music and staring up at the fading blue sky.

Water splashed on the placid sea and a massive knot of water pushed toward the shore, cresting in a wave filled with teeth.

# 20

The giant fist of water surged from the sea, revealing a beast that resembled an alligator. It was fifteen feet long and its tail had a swim fin at its tip. The creature's black eyes sat above a massive jaw lined with crooked teeth. Hawk tried to get a bead on the thing with the Ash 12 as it burst from the water, shooting like a missile toward Max who stood holding his fishing pole, eyes wide, mouth hanging open.

Hawk fired, but the beast came on, absorbing the bullets and wriggling across the beach. The beast's black hide was scarred white in spots, its short legs ending in webbed claws.

Max screamed and ran, but it was too late. The dino-gator missed the scientist with its first bite, but as it lunged past the physicist, its tail whipped, catching Max on the backs of his legs and cutting him down. He face-planted, his head smacking hard on the rock-strewn beach.

Hawk fired again, opening up with the machine gun and peppering the beast with bullets. When the gun clicked empty Hawk ran toward the melee, but skidded to a stop when the lizard turned its oblong head in his direction.

This bought time, and Svet used it to help her man. She threw a baseball sized rock at the beast, and it connected on the animal's head. The giant gator flipped and spun around, turning its dark eyes on the blonde. She turned and ran hard, heading for the forest.

Momentarily unsure which castaway to attack, the prehistoric animal paused, and this allowed Max to put some space between himself and the beast. It didn't help much, however, because the animal was incredibly fast for its size. The creature returned its attention to Max, and zigzagged across the stones after him.

Svet had reached the trees, and Hawk knew she was most likely heading to camp to get weapons, but would she have enough time? The creature was almost on Max and Hawk yelled, "Watch out!"

Max dodged left, and the creature barely missed catching him in its snapping jaws. It reacquired its target and shot at Max again, who had no place to hide. The forest was still twenty feet away and there was no way he was going to make it.

The report of the Viking sent birds spraying from the trees. Svet stood just within the tree break, the pistol held before her, her face twisted in a hideous grin as she pulled the trigger.

The two head shots at close range slowed the beast. It stopped, its gaze ranging side to side, blood dripping from its skull. The lizard's eyes rolled closed, its legs gave out, and the beast collapsed on the beach.

Max stopped running and watched the animal take its final breath.

"Don't get to—"

Hawk didn't finish because the prehistoric gator wasn't dead after all. As Max neared the beast it jerked and heaved itself forward, jaws wide, and it got Max's leg. He screamed, going to the ground as he clawed at the beast's jaws clamped on his leg, blood spurting through his fingers.

Before anyone could react, the beast's legs gave out again, and its jaws went slack, releasing Max's leg. The scientist crab walked backward, putting as much space between himself and the animal as he could.

Svet put a bullet in the gator's head, and any life the creature still possessed fled from its limp body.

"Max, you alright?" Hawk said as he ran to his friend's side. "Oh no," he said when he saw Max's leg.

Max's jumpsuit was torn and a wide gash and several large puncture wounds marked his lower thigh. Blood leaked from the wound as Max covered it with his hands.

Svet knelt next to him and kissed his forehead, then examined the wound. "Not that bad. You were lucky."

"Yeah, good thing the beast was half dead or your leg would be gone. Svet, get that fire raging and heat some water. We need to staunch that wound, and bandage it up before it gets infected."

"Da," she said. The fire still smoldered and smoked as the fish cooked. She took the food off and threw on more wood, stoking the flames. She placed one of the stainless steel water bottles next to the blaze, and went to Max and gave him some fish. "Eat. Make you feel better."

Max did as he was told as the water heated. Steam pushed from the top of the bottle like smoke from a chimney, and Hawk cut several strips from Max's spacesuit, which was starting to look like giant moths had been feasting on it. Using a leaf as a potholder, Svet took the bottle away from the flame.

"This hurt, da?" Svet said.

Hawk had his bandages and some thin vines at the ready and as soon as Svet cleaned the wound he'd bandage it up.

"Ready?" Svet said.

Max nodded, but said nothing.

She carefully pulled away the ripped fabric around the wound and poured the hot water over the gash. Max howled, and clenched his teeth as he leaned back, staring at the sky. When the water was gone, Max was panting like a dog, his face red, eyes bulging from his head.

Hawk smeared some of Svet's aloe lotion over the gash and covered it with a leaf. Then he wrapped the spacesuit fabric around the area and secured it all using the vines. "How do you feel?"

"Stupid," he said.

"Don't. It could have happened to any of us," Hawk told him. "We've become lax because we're getting too comfortable in the jungle. We must be more cautious and vigilant from now on."

"He be all right," Svet said.

"Yup, he should be fine. The wound isn't that deep, but we're not going anywhere for a while," Hawk said. What he didn't say was he worried about an infection. There were bound to be an array of unknown pathogens lurking everywhere. If the wound was to become infected, there would be nothing Hawk or Svet could do for him, aside from amputating the leg. With no drugs or medical equipment, Hawk didn't even want to think about how that could be achieved, or what the chances of Max's survival were. They'd keep the wound clean and change the dressing twice daily, and hopefully that would suffice.

First order of business was to get Max someplace safe where he could rest. This proved to be complicated. Their platform was ten feet in the air, and the only way to get Max up to it was to use their length of creeper cordage and pull him up, but that could injure him more, and Hawk wasn't sure their vine-rope would hold.

It was decided to make a long ladder that would lean against the platform to create a ramp, one that could be hauled up into the tree to stop inquisitive beasts from checking out their home. Hawk and Svet commenced the work of constructing the ladder, which was difficult without any tools. Hawk used a hatchet made from a flat rock he'd rubbed against another stone to sharpen it. He'd placed the sharpened stone at the end of the split stick and used vine to tie it in place.

They made a stretcher from vines, branches and woven palm fronds. Max was tired, but he held onto the litter so tight his knuckles were white. Slowly, rail by rail, they pulled the stretcher up the ramp created by their ladder, and by nightfall Max was asleep on the platform.

The days that followed were uneventful but busy. Hawk and Svet searched the surrounding forest for materials, both for the raft and the treehouse they were constructing. Max's first injury had healed quickly, but Hawk feared this time he'd be laid up for a couple of months. The shallow inland sea could wait, and in the meantime laying in food supplies, finding water and material were the main goals. They cut up the dead alligator, and roasted, smoked, and cured the meat with salt they made from evaporating sea water within a stone bowl they'd found in a nearby rock.

The treehouse house wasn't exactly what Hawk had in mind when he'd envisioned his Swiss Family Robinson house, but it was better than any shelter they'd had thus far. There were three platforms, each surrounded by walls of woven vines accessible via tree limbs that had been rigged with vine guiderails. The tree canopy served as the house's main roof, but Svet and Hawk laid layers of palm fronds for extra protection. The largest central platform served as the main living space while the other two served as sleeping quarters.

Max rested on a bed of dried moss and leaves, covered by his spacesuit. Svet tended him regularly, changing his dressing and cleaning the wound, which had closed but was still purple and swollen. There appeared to be no sign of infection, though the gash was a little red around the edges. Svet used salt water she'd made to cauterize the wound, and this helped.

They hunted with bow and arrows, by spear and bolas, and Svet and Hawk were able to restock their supply of jerky. Hawk found a large puddle fed by a thin stream and constructed a water purifier from a thick piece of bamboo he'd made into a large cylinder open on one end. He made a small hole in the bottom, then filled the bamboo beaker with sand and small pebbles. Once the dirty water was passed through this purifier, it had only a slight cloud with an earthy taste. Hawk drank first and didn't get sick, but they boiled everything they drank just to be safe.

For building the raft, bamboo was the preferred material, but the nearest patch was several miles away so it was decided Hawk would trek there alone while Svet looked after Max.

Hawk stopped by the treehouse after getting his first load for a drink of water, and Max said, "Are we sure we want to cross that sea? What if there are more of those things?"

"Da," Svet said. She wiped Max's forehead with a wet rag.

"We haven't seen another gator, and I'm concerned about the dangers in the forest. Crossing the sea is the safest way," Hawk said.

"You say," Svet said.

Ok, if that's how it's going to be, Hawk thought. The couple were supporting each other. Now he felt more like a third wheel than he ever had. Hawk said, "You think we should go around, Svet?"

She looked at Max, doubt spreading over her face, but she said, "Da."

Anger rose in Hawk, the old commander in him reestablishing itself. "Well, I'm in charge, and we're crossing the damn sea." Hawk stalked off and Svet and Max said nothing.

Hawk headed back for more bamboo. He saw no larger dinosaurs, but several of the smaller species hid within the forest, content to stay away from the travelers. Hawk watched them as he would squirrels.

The ammunition was dwindling. They'd fired a total of fourteen rounds at the prehistoric gator. That left them eleven rounds for the Viking and twenty-one for the Ash 12s. Hawk didn't know if they'd be able to get by without the weapons. He considered for the thousandth time the crazy twist of fate that made Vladimir send guns to the station. If he hadn't, the spacefarers would most likely be dead.

It took Hawk ten days to tie together the raft, and he busied himself making a mast and weaving a palm frond sail. It wasn't big, but any momentum they could get would help them cross the inland sea faster. Max and Svet were giving him the silent treatment after his outburst, but he didn't care. He knew he was right, and that feeling had driven every decision he'd ever made.

As the days passed, all chores done, Hawk wandered the forest alone, searching for guide stones or anything except the never-ending jungle. But he didn't stray far. Things were becoming normal, and that was hard to accept. He was dirty, hungry, was never going to see his family again, or his friends, or eat a lamb chop or drink a martini. His new reality was becoming normal, complete with fighting with friends.

There were flowers everywhere and the air was scented with pollen. His stomach grumbled. Time to cook some seafood stew down on the beach. They set large beacon fires at the edge of the sea every night to keep away any lurkers. Sitting on the rock beach wasn't so bad, but it was no Cocoa Beach.

# 21

The travelers lived at the edge of the inland sea for a long time, probing, and living comfortably on fish and game as Max healed. There were sixty-eight slashes in the trunk of the tree they lived in, and though Hawk and his mates knew they'd missed a few days, it was close. Max's leg felt good, and he was ready to move on. So was Hawk.

Leaving the treehouse was bittersweet, but it hadn't been time wasted. The next one would be better. He'd learn from his mistakes. Deciding what to leave behind was hard, and in the end the party abandoned anything they could make again, like many of the tools and other comfort items like cups and bowls they'd made from bamboo and large nut shells.

Svet and Max were back to normal, and anger they'd felt toward him dissipated. They had the same argument about crossing the sea, but this time it was more civil and Hawk explained why he felt the way he did—again—and Max reluctantly agreed, but things had changed. It was Hawk verses Max and Svet here on out, and he needed to remember that going forward.

The weather turned nasty the morning they were to leave, and there was a brief debate as to whether they should postpone their departure. It was decided to press on. Even with the wind gusting there was barely a ripple on the inland sea, and it wasn't that far across. Hawk estimated the reeds in the center were no more than five miles away. With a little luck, they'd be on the other side and on dry land by nightfall.

Hawk had updated the map in the back of *The Martian* to include the western side of the mountains, the inland sea, and the surrounding jungle. He put an X on the far left, marking the beacon's location. There was a lot of jungle between the sea and the X, but as the party got closer the light would mark their way.

The tide was coming in, and the sand beneath the raft was damp. They lashed their bags, food supplies, weapons and ammunition to the boat, and Hawk hoisted the mast and flew his palm frond sail, which was eight feet at its base and worked to a point. Wind tugged at the craft as the sail went up, jerking it toward the sea. After two months of monitoring they'd learned the wind came out of the east in the morning most days, but usually flipped midday. They'd have to take the sail down at some point.

They made poles to push and steer, and since the water was shallow they could wade next to the raft if need be. A variety of fish and reptiles swam along the shore, but they'd seen no crabs, sea urchins, or any signs of alligators or other dangerous beasties.

Ready to cast off, the spacefarers dragged the boat to the sea, and hopped aboard as the wind grabbed the sail and inched the craft forward. Hawk poled from the rear, with Svet on the port side, Max the starboard. The plan was to pass well south of the center marshland because it was likely to contain predators.

The raft floated well, though it creaked and moaned like it might fall apart. Wind chirped and squeaked through the gaps in the palm frond sail like a mistuned orchestra, and the slap and pop of the raft cresting the small waves eased Hawk's nerves. The sea breeze felt good, and his skin tightened as a thin sheen of salt covered his face. Waves lapped over the bamboo deck, but their supplies and weapons remained dry. The raft cut through the water like a brick, sending ripples over the rolling sea. Grass and rocks on the bottom hid fish large and small, but the abundance of sea life wasn't surprising. The inland water would be calm compared to the ocean. Small shiners leapt from the sea in waves, creating miniaturc rapids.

"Oh scheisse," Max said.

Mouths filled with needle teeth chomped two and three of the shiners with each bite as a school of larger fish fed on another.

"Those look big," Hawk said.

The large fish were breaching from the water, jaws snapping on shiners. The commotion attracted *pterosaurs*, and they circled in the sky like vultures, their mournful cries rising above the splashing water.

Hawk picked up his spear and held it at the ready. The water went calm, and beneath the clear water dark shapes surged around the raft. Fish launched from the water, their rows of teeth white as bone, their scales flashing in thc sunlight.

"Down!" Hawk yelled.

The three travelers dropped to the bamboo deck, covering their heads as fish sprang from the water, mouths biting at air. A fish landed on the deck, flipping and tossing itself in a frantic dance to get back to the water. Its teeth caught hold of a gear bag and it shook its head, tearing the fabric like a shark.

Svet kicked the beast, and it flew into the water. More of the killer fish arced across the raft in a cloud of teeth. Hawk hammered them away and one caught his boot and another his arm. He screamed, shook off the fish and ripped his forearm open in the process, but it didn't stop him. Hawk was possessed, and he kicked and swung at the creatures, fighting them off.

The school passed, the water calmed, and Hawk fell to the deck exhausted. "Everyone OK?"

"Da."

"Ja, you?" Max said. "You are bleeding."

Hawk looked at his shoulder as if seeing the wound for the first time. "I'm alright," he said. Hawk rolled on his side and ladled sea water over the gash with a cupped hand. He winced, but the arc of tooth punctures felt better.

Svet was at Hawk's side, cleaning the wound and bandaging it with the red stained rags used for Max's dressings. "You fine. Scratch."

Hawk laughed. "A scratch? You Russians are tough." He forced a smile and fell back on the deck, staring up at the blue sky. To the west, dark clouds marched across the horizon, and by nightfall there'd be heavy rain.

Hawk looked at Max, but the German didn't say what Hawk knew he was thinking: told you so. "Let's get moving," he said. The clear water revealed no threats, but the *pterosaurs* still circled above, awaiting round two and hoping for spoils.

The world left them alone, and Max and Svet poled across the shallow water while Hawk rested. The bleeding had stopped and he was no longer in pain. He'd been lucky. Again. How many times was fate going to spare him? How many monsters would miss their mark? He couldn't shake the feeling that his time was almost up, and he didn't like the feeling.

The sun marched past noon and the sea became a desert; heat rolling across the water like waves of fire. The horizon to the west was a wall of dark clouds that looked like a sandstorm, but Svet still poled the boat forward. Max had collapsed from the heat, and they were running out of water.

They ate a little, rested, and pushed on.

Birds sprayed from the ominous water reeds at the center of the inland sea as something big thrashed within. Hawk thought this was the resting place of the dino-crocs, and he and Svet stood at the front of the raft, guns at the ready, as they slid past the reeds.

Hawk felt better as the reeds faded, and the far shore lay before them. Nothing stood between the companions and their goal. The wind shifted, as predicted, and they took the sail down. Their progress slowed considerably, but they were still moving at a pace that would get them to the cover of the jungle by nightfall.

Hawk was hurting, and the thought of being stuck out on the open water in the dark made him think bad thoughts. They'd have no protection, and if a big critter decided to have an evening snack they'd make a dainty morsel.

The sun went behind a cloud, covering the raft in a rolling shade. Hawk took a deep breath. It felt good to be out of the sun.

"Screeeeeeeeeeeeeeeeeee. Screeeeee."

It wasn't a cloud that had blocked the sun, but their friend from the caves. The beast descended with wings spread, beak pointed at the raft like an arrow, mouth open, teeth gleaming in the sunlight.

Hawk brought up the Ash 12 and opened up, screaming like a madman as the machine gun rattled his arms. Bullets peppered the dragon as it veered right, taking itself out of the line of fire. Its black skin looked wet, its yellow streaks covered with brown mud. It circled, wings snapping in the wind like a flag, its dark rolling eyes settling on the raft again as it straightened and came in for another attack run.

"Into water," Svet said. Then she hesitated, her eyes scanning the sea for killer fish. She looked at Hawk, then up at the *pterosaur* as it knifed toward them, and jumped in. Max followed, and both of Hawk's mates stood in the sea, their guns above the water and trained at the beast.

Hawk fired again, but this time the creature wasn't put off. Tiny holes leaked brown-blue blood across the dragon's chest, but it came on. Hawk's Ash 12 clicked empty and he tossed it onto the raft and dove underwater. The beast tore into the boat, and bamboo cracked and split. All the gear, and the Ash 12 Hawk had used, slipped into the sea as the raft broke apart.

Hawk surfaced and scrambled to grab the machine gun before it fell into the water, but he couldn't get it and the gun sank to the bottom. Their supply bags floated listlessly on the surface and Max and Svet moved away from the remains of the raft as it broke apart. Each still held a weapon, Svet an Ash 12 and Max the Viking.

Their bags of food, water, and ammunition floated away as the dragon turned in a wide arc and came at them again with a piercing cry that sent pain firing down Hawk's back. He dove beneath the sea again as the beast streaked into a hail of bullets as Svet and Max fired at the dragon.

Hawk surfaced, sucking air. The sea was settling, and to the east the dragon fled back to its home in the mountains where mommy and eggs waited. What the female *pterosaur* would think when her mate arrived dripping blood on her nest, he could only imagine, but part of him wished he'd be there to see daddy get chewed out.

"You alright?" Max said.

"Think so," Svet said. The Russian collected their supplies, most of which still floated on the rolling sea. The commotion had driven all the creatures away, and the three companions stood alone, waist deep in the sea, exhausted and wondering what more could happen to them on this horrible day.

"If anything, this proves we were right to stay off the savannah. Whenever we're exposed, we get hit," Max said.

"Da," Svet said. "Stupid thing probably saw from its perch atop the mountains."

Max looked up and searched the sky, as if waiting for every flying creature within a hundred clicks to be eyeballing them.

"That was our boy, Smug from the caves," Max said.

"You mean Smaug? From The Hobbit?" Hawk said.

"No, I mean that thing is smug. It came after us like we were rats."

"I hope it's the last we see of him," Hawk said.

"Da," Svet said, but she didn't sound convinced. Like Max, her gaze strayed to the sky. Again, neither Max or Svet reminded Hawk of his decision to cross the inland sea. Had they gone around, Smaug wouldn't have seen them.

The raft was in four pieces and they salvaged a portion that was still afloat to transport their gear while they walked in the four-foot-deep water. One of the Ash 12s was lost, and they only had six bullets left for the Viking and eleven for the other Ash 12. The water was up to Svet's chest, and she swam more than walked. Hawk's wound throbbed.

The sun dropped below the rim of the world when the party entered the flooded jungle, and it started to rain.

# 22

A pounding rain fell, obscuring the sky and sending all the wildlife into hiding. Hawk, Svet and Max waded through the ghostly trees, the light of the fading day creating odd shadows within the deluge. Hawk was sure he'd seen someone hiding behind a tree, but when he investigated he found nothing.

Rain tapped on leaves, a million miniature soldiers marching across tinfoil, a static that grated nerves and tightened necks. Head down, Hawk put one foot in front of the other, fears of what might be below the surface of the water long gone.

The water got shallower with each step, and it was clear this section of the inland sea was newly formed. Weeds, grasses, and flowers still stuck from the earth, apparently unware they'd been covered with water. They swayed gently back and forth with the roll of the sea, and each step Hawk took kicked up a cloud of silt.

The sea diminished, and the party worked through knee-deep mud, the *cluck* and *plop* of feet pulling free rising above the pouring rain. The jungle formed around them, the trees becoming closer together, the underbrush thicker. Animals started to appear in the trees, and on the ground, and soon there was dry earth beneath their feet.

Night fell and darkness pressed in on them and the rain stopped. They made camp under a tree bow, but had no fire as there was no dry wood to be found. They ate jerky, drank some water, and passed out.

Hawk had the first watch, and he climbed into the bows of a tree to get a better vantage point. Clouds fleeted by overhead as the weather cleared, and stars blinked through the gaps. Everything was damp and smelled of rot and rotten eggs. Eggs. Hawk sure could go for an omelet. Perhaps in the morning he'd go on an egg hunt, though climbing trees to find nests was arduous work.

He rested the remaining Ash 12 within a crook in the tree trunk. The weapon was loaded with the last eleven bullets, and it had been agreed that here on out only single shots would be taken and all efforts would be made to conserve ammunition, though Hawk had no illusions. Soon the guns would be useless and that would be the beginning of the end.

His eyelids were heavy, and as comfort spread over him he fell asleep.

He woke to screaming.

Svet and Max lay on the ground at the base of the tree Hawk sat in, and a foot of water covered the ground. The bags of supplies floated in every direction, and Hawk's mates were just getting to their feet and rubbing sleep from their eyes. As daybreak came on, the inland sea had risen and pushed further into the jungle.

"Max, grab those bags," Hawk said.

The scientist looked up, his face distraught. "Wha—"

He didn't finish because two raptor-like dinosaurs poked their heads through the foliage twenty feet from where Svet and Max stood. Hawk brought up the Ash 12 and sighted the weapon on the nearest beast, but before he could pull the trigger Max turned tail and ran into the jungle.

Svet, standing alone before the beasts, backed away, never taking her eyes off the green and red dinosaurs that hadn't moved since they'd seen the travelers. Their heads nodded side-to-side, cold blue eyes blinking with curiosity.

Svet fired one shot from the Viking into the air and ran after Max, disappearing into the jungle and leaving Hawk alone. Seeing their prey run energized the raptors, and they half hopped, half ran as they gave chase, squawking and growling as they went.

"Shit." Hawk scrambled out of the tree. Yelling could be heard ahead, and leaves and branches lashed him as he darted through the jungle, the water splashing and sending waves across the forest.

Hawk had a terrible thought, and he looked over his shoulder, trying to take a mental picture so he'd be able to find his way back to camp, and their supplies, but the trees mocked him. They all looked the same, and he had no idea which direction he'd run in.

"Hawk. Help." It was Max. Hawk adjusted his course and headed for his mate, losing all sense of his position in the jungle. He slowed, listening hard as the water sloshed around him. He worked through the trees, tripping over submerged underbrush and roots, until he reached a clearing where he found Max and Svet back to back, the two raptor-like dinosaurs watching them from ten feet away.

Svet held the Viking before her, her arm rock steady. She had five bullets left. The creatures' heads bobbed and weaved, and unless she made perfect headshots, it wouldn't be enough to take down the animals. Putting two bullets in each would most likely just piss them off and make them attack, so she held her fire.

Max held Hawk's spear, but it looked like a toothpick compared to the muscular, thick-skinned raptors. The beasts were ten feet tall, with large powerful legs and short arms below an elongated head. The things looked like mini T-Rex's. They clicked and slurred, as if communicating, and when the noises stopped, the beasts advanced, spreading out and encircling the travelers.

Hawk fired the Ash 12, its report sending birds spraying from a nearby tree where they'd been hiding from the foul weather. Both dinosaur heads snapped in Hawk's direction, their dark eyes narrowing. More clicking as the creatures looked at each other, and one advanced on Svet and Max, and the other turned its attention to Hawk.

He backed away, and hid behind a tree, training the Ash 12 on the animal's head, right between the eyes. The dinosaur came forward like a chicken, slow awkward steps through the flood water, head bobbing up and down, side to side. As it advanced, the beast chortled and it sounded like a big cat purring.

The dinosaur was ten feet away when it screamed. Its mouth sprang open and purple-blue bile streaked from its mouth. Hawk ducked behind the tree, and a mass of phlegm and mucus slapped against the tree trunk like a wet towel, spattering Hawk's arm.

It was believed by scientists that certain dinosaurs had a defense mechanism built into their saliva that incapacitated their prey. Hawk had no doubt that was what the stuff was and he was careful not to touch the discharge.

Hawk couldn't see the dinosaur from his hiding place behind the tree trunk, but the animal moaned again and more phlegm smacked against the tree. Hawk stepped out, sighted the Ash 12, and fired one shot at extreme close range. The bullet struck the dinosaur in the forehead, and it stood suspended in time, its large wet eyes rolling back in its head.

The beast staggered back and fell into the water with a splash. Hawk came forward, using the fallen beast as a shield as he sighted the other dinosaur, which stood still before his companions.

The creature's attention was on Hawk, and Svet saw the opportunity and seized it. She stepped forward and aimed the Viking at the animal's head and squeezed off two shots. The dinosaur's head exploded in a hail of blood, bone, and skin. The beast dropped to the ground, all life gone.

"Are you guys all right?" Hawk asked.

"We're fine," Svet said. "Now."

The sea water at Hawk's feet turned red with the animal's blood, and in that moment an immense sorrow crept over him. These animals had done nothing to deserve this. The universe had thrown them together with man for the first time, and they were doing their best to survive. None of this was fair, but what was fair anymore? By all accounts Hawk and his friends should be dead.

The gray haze of dawn crept over the jungle as day broke. The fight over, the constant sound of insects, the bleating of lizards, the cries of *pterosaurs*, and the tittering of birds again filled the forest.

"We need to find camp. See if we can salvage our supplies," Hawk said. The faces that stared back at him had no hope. They'd been beaten, and it was disconcerting. Through all their tribulations his friends had remained confident. If their supplies had floated away they were screwed and there was no sugarcoating it.

"Let's try and follow the path that brought us here. Find our way back to camp that way," Max said.

"I hope you guys paid attention to trees as you were running for your life, because I didn't," Hawk said.

"No footprints in water," Svet said.

The rising sun cut through the tree canopy, shinning spotlights on the flooded jungle floor. A creature yelled in the distance, and that faint cry was a reminder the party would soon have to deal with the masters of this world. A spray of insects dive bombed

Hawk as the cloud zipped past. Hawk almost hit himself in the face swatting at them and Svet laughed.

The bite on Hawk's arm hurt, but it wasn't bad. The seawater-soaked bandage had dried and it chafed and needed to be changed, but he pressed on. Conifers mixed with palm trees filled the jungle, and giant ferns and bushes with broad yellow leaves covered the ground like snow. They began marking trees, spreading out and calling to each other to cover more ground.

"Climb tree?" Svet said.

Hawk surveyed the height of the nearby trees. He couldn't get high enough to see anything. "Not here," he said. "But keep looking. Thicker and taller."

"Da."

Hawk couldn't shake the feeling he was getting further from his goal. How far had he run while chasing his friends? At least a mile, and he changed direction twice. When Max found their first marked tree they changed direction. The trees were further apart and Hawk remembered the area. The forest was afire with light, clouds of gnats and flies filling the air.

"I recognize that tree," Max said. "The odd T where those branches come together. I remember thinking how strange it was when we passed it."

"So we've gone in circle?" Svet asked.

"Ja."

Svet said, "At least we know where to go now."

"Let's hope all our stuff hasn't floated away," Hawk said.

The water had receded as the tide went out, but there were patches of deep mud, and other impediments that couldn't be seen, so Hawk went slow, more feeling his way than using his eyes. The sky had cleared, and sunlight blazed down upon the land, but under the tree canopy it was cool and dim.

"Here," Hawk said. He squeezed through a stand of trees that was tightly packed and emerged into the clearing where they'd slept.

"What?" Max said.

All their supply bags were stacked haphazardly atop a pile of stones above the waterline. Hawk and his friends stood in silence, trying to come up with a scenario that explained what they saw. As usual, his companions were ahead of him.

"If the wind blew a certain way they could have been blown into the crux of the rock pile, and when the water receded they would have been left high and dry."

"Luck? Da?" Svet said. "About time."

She stepped forward and grabbed her bag off the pile and pulled out some jerky.

"Most likely the water's currents are to blame," Hawk said.

# 23

The castaways collected their stuff and pushed inland. Svet's mini-guitar was lost in the flotsam, and their food was gone. Animals had pillaged their supply while they were running, but thankfully the creatures hadn't taken their water bottles. The four stainless steel containers had been key to their survival, and without them, carrying any significant amount of water would be difficult.

"Oh, well," said Max.

"What?" Hawk asked.

Max looked at Svet and frowned. "Our bag with the… it's gone."

Svet said, "Our pills?"

"Ja."

Now Hawk knew what they were talking about. "Your say goodnight pills are gone?"

"You know of this?" Svet said.

Hawk reached into this pocket and drew out his plastic vile and held it up. "Thought about taking this thing so many times…" He looked at his companions. "You guys are what stopped me. Our friendship."

Svet and Max said nothing.

Hawk now felt guilty that he had this easy way out, and his friends didn't. Plus, who was he kidding? He didn't have the guts to kill himself, and maybe that was good. He tossed the plastic vile containing his pill into the jungle, and smiled.

"Whatcha do that for?" Max said.

"We're in this together now, for better or worse," Hawk said. He felt better immediately, like he'd dropped the ring of power in Mount Doom. The pill no longer could taunt him, entice him to pass into the peaceful black beyond.

There were signs everywhere that the inland sea penetrated further than they'd believed. Hawk noticed several piles of nuts against a stone, the ebb and flow of the sea collecting them there.

There were piles of debris and leaves, and Hawk felt more at ease about their supply bags being gathered by the sea.

Max looked exhausted. He'd been incapacitated for so long he was out of shape. Hawk's arm throbbed with pain, and it was getting puffy and red. Svet said she thought the best thing to do was cut the wound open, clean it well, and cover it with her homemade salve, but that idea made him nervous. He'd been wounded many times over the years, and there was one consistent piece of medical advice he'd received: if you don't need to open a wound and expose it to infection, don't. He feared infection had already set in and he didn't know what else to do.

When Max tripped over a root and fell, Hawk knew they needed a break.

"Svet, you see any footprints or signs of big guys?" Hawk said.

"Nyet. Water scare them off maybe. No scat. No scratches on trees. Nothing."

"Ja," Max said. "The animals instinctually would stay away from the tidal areas, though it looks as though the sea hasn't come this far inland in some time."

"Good place to lay up for a bit, then? Restock, rest up and get healthy?"

Max's face tightened with pain. "As much as I don't want to stop, I think that might be best in the long run."

Hawk nodded. The forest was packed with trees even Max was having trouble identifying. Mixed in with the conifers, giant ferns and palms were thick trees with gray bark and purple leaves with thin green veins. A clear sap leaked from these tree trunks like syrup. The bows of these trees were wide and thick, with tightly spaced branches. When they came across a stream that flowed toward the inland sea, Hawk called a halt.

Hawk chose one of the trees with the gray bark that had a broken lower branch. The limb was still attached to the trunk via bark, and with a little effort the party covered the fallen branch with palm fronds creating a small shelter. Svet cut sticks, sharpened them, and drove them into the ground around their hovel, while Max gathered nuts and fruit.

They'd lost their bows, all their arrows, the spears, and all that remained was Hawk's bolas, which was saved because it had been dangling from Hawk's waist during the disaster of the prior day. Hawk crouched within the underbrush, waiting for unsuspecting vermin, or a small dinosaur or lizard to venture by. He sat concealed until the sun passed noon, when he gave it up. He'd seen nothing except a few birds, and some very small lizards that fought a battle with the ants on the tree he hid beside. He should have cut some meat off the two dinosaurs they'd killed the prior day, but he'd been frazzled from the fight and hadn't thought to.

When Hawk got back to camp, Svet cleaned his wound and replaced his dressing. He'd decided to push off the decision about opening the cut for another day. Svet had gotten adept at handling cuts and gashes, and she was the group's defacto doctor, though Max knew more about anatomy. Svet had the touch, which Hawk constantly ribbed her about. Russians weren't known for their sensitivity. Especially women who'd been forced to fight through the glass ceiling in Russia's military, which was one of the worst in the world when it came to sexism.

They ate fruit and nuts, drank some of their freshly boiled water, and lounged in the shelter. Outside, the chorus of insects buzzed, but they heard no *pterosaur* cries, or growling dinosaurs.

Ten days passed without incident, but on the eleventh day the party woke in the deep of night to a flooded ground. They quickly packed, and exited into the pitch black. Stars blinked against the darkness, but the moon was nowhere to be seen. They stopped and Hawk lit a fire, and the companions of the International Space Station huddled from the night chill, the ground around them becoming damp as the sea crept silently across the land.

When a puddle of standing water formed beside them, Hawk said, "Time to go. Sun will be up soon."

"Ja." Max got up with an effort, and Hawk wondered if perhaps they should move to a dry spot and continue their convalescence. There was no great rush, or was there? What were the odds the extinction event was in the near future? Most likely, it was hundreds, maybe thousands of years in the future, and whether it took six months or six years to get to the beacon it didn't really matter.

But it did matter. Increasingly, Hawk believed the quest was the only thing holding their tiny band together. Had it not been for the beacon, Hawk was certain Max would have given up already, and though Svet still put up a good front, the lines on her face, the dark rings around her eyes, and her sunburned complexion said something else. He had to keep them moving forward. That was all Hawk knew how to do.

The ground rose as they struggled through the forest. The underbrush grew thicker, and their progress slowed to a crawl. The water didn't reach this far inland, and the sounds of animals increased as they fought their way through ferns, weeds, and flowers of every color. The air smelt like perfume, and Hawk sneezed. His arm felt better, but his legs ached and his stomach grumbled.

They broke free of the jungle and hit a pond—a giant puddle really—with brackish brown water. Hoof prints, claw marks, and the wavy lines of alligator-like tracks led to the watering hole, and the party moved away from the puddle as fast as they could, but didn't go far.

"Why don't you guys rest under the thick fern there?" Hawk said. "I'll go hide in a tree by that waterhole and get us some meat for dinner." They needed it desperately. They'd exerted a lot of energy, and fruit and nuts didn't replenish the body like meat.

"Should be easy to find dry wood," Max said.

"Da. I get fire going," Svet said.

"Cool. Keep an eye out for wood to remake our weapons," Hawk said.

"Ja, will do," Max said.

Assignments given, Hawk sharpened a stick into a spear and disappeared into the jungle.

The waterhole was still deserted when he arrived, so Hawk hoisted himself into a nearby tree and waited. He had the Viking with him, but it was tucked away and he didn't plan to use it unless he had no other option. His bolas hung over a branch at the ready, and he rested the spear on his shoulder, prepared to fire should dinner come to get a drink. But nothing came, the hours stretched on, and the heat and humidity soaked him through.

Hawk's mind wandered, and he tried to calculate how long ago they'd crash landed. Knowing he might be off by a factor of five, Hawk estimated he and his partners had been traipsing around the Cretaceous for four months. It was hard to believe. They'd gone from one crisis to another, though their time spent on the shore of the inland sea wasn't too bad. If that's what he and his companions had in store for the rest of their lives, there were worse ways to live. If only his wife and kids were with him, he thought he might be at peace.

He was stirred from his thoughts by a flock of animals hooting and screeching as they approached the waterhole. Perhaps this was a way of telling any smaller creatures to clear out, but when he saw the beasts who'd come to drink he didn't think that was the case.

To Hawk's untrained paleontologist eye the animals looked like ostriches, but they were green and yellow, and their feathers were small and tight like hair. Their bony legs were nothing like their arms, which looked muscular, but short. Red eyes shifted and rolled as the creatures looked at nothing and everything at the same time.

The beasts moved forward in a wave, together in a way that reminded Hawk of a flock of birds. The creatures didn't notice him as they clustered around the puddle, lapping up the brown water as if they hadn't drunk in days.

The beast's midsections were plump, like a turkey's, and Hawk judged they might be good eating. He drew back his spear, and something over his shoulder squawked. A huge multi-color bird sat within the dense canopy of the tree, and it startled Hawk and he teetered, dropping the spear and gripping the branch he sat on to stop his fall.

He was unsuccessful. He pitched off the branch, hung there for a second by one hand, and fell to the ground with a crash. All eyes turned Hawk's way, and all drinking and jabbering ceased. There were twenty-two of them, and the Viking had four bullets in it. Despite this, Hawk slowly drew the weapon out. Taking out one or two might dissuade the rest.

The animals inched forward, led by the tallest of them, which was mostly green, and had jagged scars all over its body, presumably from past battles.

Hawk put his back to a tree as the flock advanced. He sighted the leader.

"Yoooooooo," came a call from the jungle.

The flock of beasts paused, all heads turning toward the sound. Hawk ran, weaving in and out of trees like a race car through traffic. A cramp tightened his leg, but he pushed on, the sounds of pursuit driving him forward. Not wanting to lead the animals back to camp, Hawk twisted, turned, and backtracked, and by the time he was too winded to continue, the creatures had given up the chase.

The day was getting on, and Hawk didn't want to go back to camp empty handed. Whoever had helped him out was nowhere to be seen. Svet or Max had probably headed back to camp rather than search for him in the woods and risk getting lost.

He stalked the underbrush and managed to snag a squirrel-thing with his bolas, but it was mostly skin and bones. Maybe Max or Svet could work their magic and make a soup or stew.

When Hawk arrived at camp Svet and Max sat by the fire, looking tired and disheveled. Why his friends found the need to hide their love making from him he didn't fully understand, but he knew there was a layer of guilt there, as well as a wish to not remind Hawk constantly about what he didn't have.

"Which one of you do I owe the thank you to?" Hawk said.

"For what?" Max said.

"The distraction you… or Svet, provided saved my ass."

Max and Svet looked at each other. "What are you talking about?" Svet said.

"Just a few minutes ago. In the forest. One of you yelled and got the beasts off my trail."

"I'm sure neither of us did. We were… preoccupied," Max said.

"The wind?" Svet asked.

"Don't think so," Hawk said. He looked back into the jungle the way he'd come. "Must have been the cry of an animal, but man it sounded like a person."

"I had a cat that sounded just like a baby when it cried," Max said.

"Indeed," Hawk said.

# 24

Hawk and his friends lived under the large fern for six days, and in that time Hawk's wound got much worse. The gash was swollen and red with white pus around its edges. The cut was infected, and it was spreading.

"What I wouldn't do for an antibiotic," Hawk said.

"Da," Svet said. "You ready to do this? Or you wait until it gets worse?"

Hawk had waited long enough, so he nodded his consent.

"Good. Max, boil water and gather large leaves and vines for bandage. I boil knife blade."

"Ja."

Hawk sat with his back to a large tree trunk, his arm throbbing in rhythm with his heart. "You sure you know what you're doing?"

"Da. Trust me. I sew many people back together."

Soon the water bubbled over the fire and Svet held her blade within, sterilizing it. She made some of her special cream with aloe, mud, and crushed leaves and flowers of *calendula*. The marigold-like plant had yellow flowers and deep green stems and leaves. Svet had found several herbs and medicinal plants since their arrival. She had a version of thyme, mint, and a sweet purple herb Max thought was a relative of saffron.

"This hurt, da?"

"Yup," Hawk said.

Svet took his arm and placed it on a log they used as a table. She said, "Max, hold down his hand." Svet put one hand on his elbow, and with her other pulled the knife blade free of the boiling water.

Steam filled the air, and the scent of earth and rot.

"Try not to move, da," Svet said.

Max gave Hawk a stick to bite down on.

She looked at Max with eyes that said, "Make sure you hold him down."

Svet went to work, flaying back Hawk's skin around the bite. Hawk bit the stick as pain surged through him and he fought the urge to jerk his arm free. Blood poured from the wound, and as Svet cut deeper white pus ran through the blood like vanilla syrup through strawberry ice-cream.

Hawk whimpered, but managed to stay conscious as pain rattled him. It seemed like hours had passed when Svet put down her knife and started cleaning the wound. That hurt just as bad as the cutting, but when she rubbed a generous supply of her salve on the cut, the pain lessened.

Svet wrapped leaves over the wound and tied them in place with vines. When she was done, she leaned back and sighed, sweat dripping down her face into her raccoon eyes. She looked haggard, her beauty hidden by months of dirt, stress, malnutrition, and lack of sleep.

"Thanks," Hawk said. He rotated his arm and stretched his shoulder.

"We keep close eye on, da?"

"Da," Hawk said. He felt stronger already.

Rested, fed, stocked with water, and as healthy as they were ever going to be, the party pressed on through the primordial jungle like three giant ants, heads down, a stark determination and stubbornness driving them forward.

After a couple of hours, they halted to rest and eat.

"How does your arm feel?" Max asked.

"Much better," Hawk said.

"What's that?" Svet asked. She pointed through the trees to the west, where the forest seemed to open up and sunlight filled the underbrush.

"Don't know," Hawk said. He grabbed the Ash 12 and got up, checking the weapon to ensure it was ready to fire. There were nine bullets left in the magazine.

The trees thinned out, the underbrush became less thick, and the ground turned the color of coal. A section of the forest was burnt-out. It was a wasteland of black tree trunks, charred groundcover, and scorched earth. The devastation stretched into the distance in all directions. Creepers encroached upon the black patch, but they hadn't made much progress which told Hawk the fire had been recent. The scent of smoke and ash pervaded the air, but nothing smoked and Hawk saw no cinders.

"Damn," Max said.

"What stopped it?" Svet asked.

"No idea. Maybe rain?" Max said. "What else could it be?"

"Sometimes the vegetation is so moist it doesn't burn," Hawk said.

"We cross? Go around?" Svet said.

Going around would take them way out of the way, but Hawk didn't like being exposed on the fire blasted plain. Like the inland sea, every creature for miles would see them pass. The charred land stretched as far as the eye could see to the north and south.

"I think we have to cross it," Hawk said. "Good news is we should be able to see the beacon light without the tree canopy hampering us."

"Maybe," Max said. "We're at or below sea level."

"Do you want to spend night in open?" Svet asked.

A good question. The sun was starting its descent to the horizon and in three hours, dusk would cover the land. "Good point. Let's head back into the woods and make camp for the night."

The next morning, they rose with the sun and headed out across the blackened earth. Small green saplings poked from the charred dirt, and within months the area would again be covered in green.

"Life finds a way," Max said.

"Burning can be good for the forest. It will grow back stronger and thicker than it was before," Hawk said.

"In your country they do on purpose, da?" Svet said.

"Yup. The forestry service often does controlled burns to replenish the forest, but it's a risky business. If winds kick up, or shift, control can easily be lost."

They hiked on, the sun baking them with no tree cover, nothing to absorb the heat. By midday Hawk was drenched and called a halt. The companions rested beside a burnt tree, its skeletal remains dark and forlorn. A thin line of jungle cut across the horizon to the west, but it looked a long way off.

“You think we make it by night?” Svet said.

Hawk didn’t know and said nothing. He was in a heat induced haze and thought he saw a flash of light from the jungle in the distance, but he said nothing to his friends because it didn’t reappear.

The jungle was closer than he’d figured, and it looked like they’d make it there just as the sun went down. What Hawk hadn’t planned for was the herd of *stegosaurus* that blocked their way. The mountainous beasts lounged just outside the tree break, enjoying the shade the trees provided as the sun sank, leaving an orange-black sky that looked like dirty sherbet. The huge hippo-ish beasts had long tails with triangle spikes along their backs and down the tail, which ended with a spike. They’d dealt with this type of monster before. Their hides were armored, the heads protected by bone shields and horns.

“What now?” Max asked.

“We sneak around them.” He didn’t like that plan, but he saw no other path.

With no cover to conceal them, Hawk led Svet and Max north, where they’d turn west again once they were passed the herd. If the beasts charged them they were done. With nowhere to hide, and no cover, they’d be run down, but the beasts didn’t seem to notice them. The day waned, the sky grew cloudy, and a light rain fell.

The weather was getting colder, but Hawk didn’t fear a harsh winter. The landmass they were on was on the equator, so he didn’t think snow would be in the forecast. Hawk’s head snapped up at a great braying and whinnying. The herd of *stegosaurus* was moving toward them.

“Run for the trees,” Hawk said. In the tight confines of the jungle, the large animals would be unable to maneuver.

Black soot kicked up as they ran, and Hawk choked on it, the ash filling his eyes and stinging his throat. The herd was nothing more than a black dust cloud as it got closer, and Hawk didn’t think they were going to reach the woods before they got run down. He looked back at his friends and Svet was running beside Max, who looked exhausted. Max threw himself forward in long looping strides, and every few seconds Svet would put a hand on him to steady her lover.

"Let's split up," Hawk said. "You guys head further north, and I'll continue toward the forest. Maybe they'll chase me and leave you guys alone because I'll be closest."

"Nyet."

"That's an order," Hawk said. The words sounded strange coming from his mouth. An order. What a joke.

Svet looked at him with betrayed eyes, but she obeyed. Grabbing Max's arm, she steered him northward, away from Hawk.

Alone, with only his breathing echoing in his ears, Hawk recounted his life as best he could. It had been a good life, if short, but all his regrets came rushing back like the tide. All the baseball games he'd missed. The dance recitals. The anniversaries. Had it been worth it? As he ran for his life from extinct creatures that were going to trample him down, he couldn't help but feel that he had wasted his life, and now it would end in this burnt-out land, where his bones would rest until they turned to dust.

A gunshot rang out, then another, and another. Hawk looked over his shoulder. One of the *stegosaurs* had gone down and the others had stopped, and they stood around their fallen mate. Hawk turned it on, pumping his arms and legs as fast as he could, head thrown back. Max and Svet had bought him some time, and it might be enough.

He entered the forest at a full run and jumped onto the nearest tree and climbed, pulling himself branch to branch with the practiced ease of a monkey. When he was up twenty feet he spared a glance for the blackened plain. The herd hadn't moved. They stood around the dead dinosaur, their somber cries chorus-like.

Svet and Max were nowhere to be seen, and Hawk judged they'd made it to the jungle and were working their way to him. They knew he was inside the tree break to the north of their position, so he'd wait for them to find him.

There was movement out of the black plain as the herd moved back toward the jungle at a leisurely pace. Behind them, the fallen *stegosaurus* looked like a boulder on a dark desert. Already a squadron of *pterosaurs* circled above the carcass, dive-bombing the dead animal and pulling flesh from its bones.

The light rain stopped, but the wind picked up. A thick mist hovered just above the forest floor, the humidity increasing. It felt good to Hawk, and his tightened muscles loosened. Dust settled over the forest, and the blackness of night came on. The desolate plain looked even more barren in the half-light. The scene reminded Hawk of an old black and white photo.

Svet and Max appeared in the forest below, and Hawk climbed down. The forest was an out-of-tune orchestra. The constant buzz of insects. Birds chirped and shrieked, lizards bleated, and the trees and underbrush brought confinement and security.

Hawk said, "Who do I have to thank for that awesome cover fire?" Three shots had been fired, and at least one of them had struck home, freezing the rest at a critical moment.

"That would be me," Max said.

"Only two shots left for the Viking, eh," Hawk said.

"Should be three." Max slipped the magazine from the gun and thumbed out the shells into his palm and held it out to Hawk.

Three bullets lay there, the brass shining in the sunlight.

# 25

They stopped for the night in a hollow filled with giant ferns and water reeds. The area was dry, but smooth sections of dried mud and piles of sticks and leaves showed the outline of a large puddle. They camped beneath a spreading dwarf palm, sheltered by the thick fronds that were so tightly packed it was hard to see the stars.

Svet lit a fire, and the time travelers sat around the roaring blaze. The shallow notch in the land hid them well, and for the first time since they'd left the treehouse at the edge of the inland sea, Hawk felt at ease, or as much at ease as he'd ever be. The evening symphony was going full tilt, and it was hard to talk over the nightly tremors of chaos.

"So, are we going talk about the missing bullet?" Max said.

"Not now," Hawk said. They'd finished eating and Hawk had one more thing to accomplish before they settled in for the night. "I'm hiking back out to the burnt plain and see if I can catch a glimpse of the beacon light."

"Da. I go with you," Svet said.

Max said nothing. Someone had to stay back at camp and watch their stuff and keep the fire going. They couldn't leave their essentials unguarded.

"Ok, let's go then. Sooner we leave, sooner we can get to sleep." Max and Svet exchanged glances, and Hawk said to himself, no worries, there'll be time for a bump, though he couldn't imagine where. Their teenage bullshit was getting on his nerves, like the two had never had sex before. Then Hawk remembered that in a way they probably hadn't. Both had been married for a long time, and he believed both had been faithful spouses, so for them this was like high school.

Torches in hand, Svet and Hawk threaded through the forest, backtracking the way they'd come. When they reached the burnt landscape, they snuffed out their torches. Nothing moved on the open plain. Starlight and moonlight lit their way, but shadows scampered in the jungle behind them.

They walked out onto the clearing three miles. In the west there was an intermittent glow of light, but it was hard to tell if it was the beacon or the glow of moonlight on the horizon. The pillar of light they'd seen from the mountain top wasn't visible.

"You think that is it?" Svet said.

"I think so. If you look in any other direction the light is much less intense. Plus the way it pulses. If it was natural light it wouldn't do that, I wouldn't think."

"But why we no see better?"

"We could be below sea level, plus the trees block our line of sight."

"Da." She didn't sound convinced.

Hawk said, "Also, it's a little cloudy over there, and we don't know the contours of the land. We could be standing in a depression."

No 'da' this time, just silence.

"Let's head back." As they walked, Hawk stared at the pulsating glow in the west, and with each step his resolve grew. The light was from the beacon. It had to be. Nowhere else could the pale white light be seen, like a star crashed to Earth and was hailing them in Morse code.

As if reading his mind, Svet said, "That must be it, nyet?"

"Da," Hawk said, and she smiled, her teeth flashing white in the blackness.

When they got back to camp they filled Max in, and Hawk announced he was going to take a walk, and his companions smiled like teenagers at his courtesy. Hawk wandered into the bush, the Ash 12 hanging on his shoulder, Svet's knife stuck in his belt.

He found a tree and sat with his back against it, his mind conjuring pictures of Svet and Max entwined, naked atop a pile of sticky green leaves next to the fire. The torch stuck in the ground beside him sputtered and went out, and he sat in the darkness, listening to the sounds of the jungle, trying to pick out the cries and bellows of the various creatures.

When he got back to camp, his friends were sitting before the fire. Max had his arm around Svet, and when Hawk approached, Max let his arm fall to his side.

"I told you guys I'm fine with you two. The fact that you're uncomfortable makes me uncomfortable."

Svet and Max said nothing.

When Hawk was seated by the fire, rubbing his hands together for warmth, Max said, "So, about that extra bullet."

Hawk hadn't given the events on the plain much thought. So they'd miscounted the bullets. Of all the things that had happened in the last few weeks, this didn't register. "What is there to talk about?"

"You no understand," Svet said. "Max did not shoot the beast."

Hawk laughed. "Really. Who the hell did? Guns won't be for sale in these parts for a hundred million years, and I'm not sure dinosaurs have the dexterity to fire a weapon."

"No make fun, he—"

"I only fired two shots," Max said.

"Max, I was in a battle once. Nasty firefight that lasted three days. A sniper held a tower, and the guy was a good shot. Picking off anyone he could get a bead on. You know how many bullets we fired in those forty-eight hours? Two thousand four hundred and twelve. You know what I thought we fired? A thousand or so."

"That's different, and you're missing the bigger point."

"Da."

"Which is?"

"I never aimed at the beast. I fired into the air."

Silence fell between them and the insects and lizards filled the gap in the conversation. Something big was moving through the forest to the south, and the sound of crunching leaves and breaking limbs echoed over the forest. The beast didn't sound close; insects trilled, and the ground didn't tremble.

Hawk said, "You must have aimed in your frenzy. Things happen in stressful situations that appear different when the adrenaline stops flowing. How many heated arguments have you had where you can't recount exactly what you said five minutes later? Because you'd been angry, or nervous, or scared?"

"I hear you, but—"

"But what? If you didn't shoot the beast, who did? I didn't fire at it."

Hawk knew his friend wasn't comfortable with his explanation, but he'd experienced this kind of thing before. The frenzy of battle clouded the mind.

"You're right," Max said. He sounded beaten and tired. "I thought I'd killed a man once, and it turned out I had nothing to do with it."

"Do tell," Hawk said.

"I was driving my Porsche—my wife hated the thing. Said I looked like an old shriveled ass driving it." At the mention of his wife, he looked sidelong at Svet, who stared into the fire. "It was dark. I'd had a little too much to drink, and I came around a curve and hit a man walking along the side of the road. At least that's what I believed. I panicked and took off. When I got home I checked the front of the car for the person's blood, or a dent, anything, but all looked good. I put the car in the garage and tried not to think about what had happened. In the morning the local news said a young man walking home from a party had been struck and killed along the road I'd driven the prior night."

"Dear god," Svet said. She'd pulled her attention from the fire and was staring at Max.

"I tortured myself for days, and it wasn't until a week later that I turned myself in to police to discover someone had already confessed to the incident, and the man's account had been confirmed via blood and hair on the driver's bumper. I went back to where I thought I'd hit the man, but there was nothing in the road on its shoulder that gave any indication as to what I'd hit. Nothing."

"Yeah, like that," Hawk said. "Humans do strange shit when under stress, and the mind works as if in a dream."

The fire crackled, and gray smoke ran to the heavens, sparks and ash floating within the gray cloud like stars.

"Let's knock off for the night. I want to make some time tomorrow. I'll take the first watch." He got up and went to the edge of the firelight and sat on a stone. Svet and Max huddled together by the fire, and both were snoring loudly within minutes.

Seeing Svet and Max sleeping together, embracing, made him think of home and everything he'd lost. All the things he'd never be able to do again. All the time he'd lost and that he'd never get back.

He looked up through a gap in the tree canopy, and stars wheeled, the lights of a million other worlds. Had the beings who put the beacon come from one of those stars? Were they still here? All signs pointed to them being long gone, but there was always hope.

Hawk rested the Ash 12 against the tree trunk and settled in, folding his arms across his chest. The hours ticked by, but he wasn't tired, so he didn't wake Max for his shift. He looked so peaceful, a thin smile cutting across his sunburned face. Svet talked in her sleep, and the words, while out of order and in Russian, sounded calm and loving. She was a having a good dream.

Dreams. That was another reason Hawk didn't like to sleep. His wife and kids were always there, saying how much they missed him and how they wished he could come home. But he would never be able to go home, not unless the last few months were nothing but a dream. Some nights Michel would come to visit, and in many ways seeing him was worse. He'd seen Michel's dead face. The cloud had killed at least one person, Michel Fulcello.

An hour before sunrise, several creatures crept to the camp's edge. They had white glowing eyes, and when Hawk threw a pebble in their direction the beasts didn't scatter and run. They watched him with unblinking eyes as one would observe an animal in a zoo. The creatures looked like birds, but they didn't have feathers. They reminded Hawk of the strange chicken-like thing they'd seen in the caves.

He threw a bigger rock and this time the creatures scattered with a series of squeals and squeaks. The commotion woke Svet, and she disentangled from Max and came to sit by Hawk.

"Why you no wake me? You tired?"

"Not really."

"How possible? You should be dead on feet."

Hawk loved her accent. Her hair was clean and brushed, and she looked amazing in the glow of the fire. “Just… my mind never stops anymore. I’m always running overtime. Worrying about tomorrow. The next day. Will we find any peace?”

Svet didn’t answer right away. She ran her fingers through her hair, looked up at the stars, then down at the fire. “My ma used to say peace is an illusion for the ignorant.”

Hawk laughed so hard he woke Max. “What are you two gabbing about?”

“Just discussing the purpose of our existence. You know, nothing important,” Hawk said.

Svet said, “You sleep well?”

“Ja. I’m going hunting with the spear. You want to come?”

“Da.” Svet got up, and the two lovers disappeared into the underbrush at the top of the gully.

Hawk was alone again with his thoughts, and his kids’ faces filled his mind. He went through his mental album of events and special moments that kept him sane. The Christmas Jonah got the game system he wanted and was so grateful he hugged his father like he’d never hugged him before. Hawk lived on that hug like food, recalling it daily, reliving the moment again and again.

The gray of dusk permeated the forest, and Hawk cooked some meat they’d gotten from a bird Svet had nailed with his bolas. She was getting adept at using the weapon—better than Hawk. He had to make her one as soon as the opportunity presented itself. He stretched, rolled his shoulders and cracked his knuckles.

# 26

Another day passed as the three time travelers fought their way through the twisted jungle, the green creepers, underbrush, and trees fighting for every inch of earth and every beam of sunlight. The party was forced off their path several times, twisting and turning through the forest as if they had no idea where they were going. Which they really didn't. They were heading west toward the sunset, and had no other markers during the daylight hours.

Hawk strapped the Viking to his leg. It had three bullets left, and he didn't know what he'd do with the gun when it ran out of shells. He was thinking of burying it and if it was ever found—which would be highly unlikely—it could be one of those great mysteries his kids would read about on the internet.

Sadness washed over Hawk at the thought of his kids and he looked over his shoulder at his friends. Svet had the Ash 12 slung across her back. It had nine bullets left. Max trudged behind her, looking exhausted. Hawk called a halt next to a huge fern with a porch-like area beneath a roof of tightly packed fan leaves.

The party dropped bags, stripped off spacesuit boots, and drank some water. Max shuffled off to go to the bathroom and Svet went to look for a stream or watering hole. Hawk sat and leaned back, hands behind his head. In moments he was asleep.

Hawk woke to screaming and vaulted to his feet. It sounded like Svet and he ran toward her voice.

"Screeeeeeeeeeee. Screeeee. Screeeeeeeeeeeeeeee."

The forest canopy obscured the sky, but the trees were thinning out as Hawk ran through the jungle, jumping over roots and ant hills. Birds tittered and chirped and the song of the jungle urged him on, its rhythmic buzz like electricity. Palm fronds and fern leaves lashed his face as he threw himself forward, heart in his throat, lungs stinging with pain. A gunshot rang out, and the jungle went quiet. Every insect and beast pausing in its conversation, startled by the noise.

Ahead, the trees gave way to a watering hole with a thin pebble beach that ran half way around its oblong shore. The other half of the shoreline was packed with vegetation, and as Hawk broke free of the jungle he saw Svet fleeing, a dark shadow descending on her. Smaug's massive wings snapped as they closed and the giant *pterosaur* dive-bombed the cosmonaut.

Hawk drew down and fired twice, both bullets landing in the back of Smaug's neck. The dragon screeched an earsplitting cry, and rolled as would a wounded bird, twisting in the air like a kite with a broken wing. The beast pulled itself from its tumble right before crashing into the ground, and the great flying reptile spread its wings and sailed over the pond, a picture of its terrible face reflected in the still water.

Smaug arced in a circle and headed back toward Svet.

Hawk holstered the Viking and burst out onto the shoreline, running toward the fray, twirling his bolas. He couldn't bring himself to fire the last bullet. It was a line within him that once crossed was un-revocable. That bullet was the only insurance he had with his pill gone. The only proof that if things became too much, or he was badly injured, or…

"Yo. Dipshit!" Hawk yelled. He ran along the rock beach, bolas hissing through the air.

The dragon banked toward Hawk and let loose with its loudest and longest scree. He'd pissed Smaug off, that was certain, and if the flying reptile was truly a dragon he'd be cinders.

But Smaug wasn't a real dragon and couldn't breathe fire.

Hawk dodged into the jungle, zigzagging through the trees, hiding behind the trunk of a thick conifer. Smaug wailed, and a dark shadow extinguished the light beams cutting through the tree canopy. The buzz of the insects rose in a crescendo, as if the scene was coming to its climax.

Hawk couldn't see what was happening, and ran back to the watering hole. Smaug circled overhead, and Svet was nowhere to be seen. Hawk figured she'd made it to the jungle.

"Screee. Screeeeeee." The *pterosaur's* wings snapped in the wind as it picked up speed, its razor teeth bright against its dark beak.

"Yo. Dipshit." Hawk fired his bolas, aiming at Smaug's eye as the dragon missiled at him.

The bolas made of vines and rocks flew, spinning so fast it was nothing more than a round blur. Like Aaron Rodgers firing a timing pass over the middle, the bolas caught the dragon in the side of the head. The beast jerked from the impact, flew off course, and almost crashed into the forest, only recovering at the last instant as it pulled up hard and banked over the jungle.

The dragon wailed as it flew in a tight arc, tucking its wings and turning its bleeding head toward Hawk. In his peripheral vision, Hawk saw Svet step from the jungle and take aim at the *pterosaur*'s face with the Ash 12. Smaug dove at Hawk with a single-minded hatred, and didn't appear to see Svet. Hawk held his ground, the creature's bulging eyes and sharp teeth a hundred yards away.

The cosmonaut waited to the last second, drawing the dragon in as far as possible. She opened up with the Ash 12, the chatter scattering every creature for fifty clicks. Svet's finger lingered on the trigger for an extra instant as she screamed with rage, and six shots peppered Smaug's chest.

The dragon kept coming, blue blood dripping like rain.

Hawk dove for cover but didn't make it. A shadow fell over him and he felt at peace. He'd see Andrea, and… but he wouldn't see Andrea. That was all bullshit. She was lost to him, and giving up wouldn't change that, no matter how much he might wish it did.

A spear hit Smaug in the eye and the beast screamed and rolled through the air like it had been hit with a shotgun blast. The flying reptile flipped and tumbled, crashing onto the rock beach and coming to a stop against trees and underbrush.

Max rushed to Hawk's side. "Hurry now." Max helped him up and the two astronauts headed for the cover of the trees where Svet hid.

"You OK?" Max said.

"Yeah. Nice throw, Tarzan."

Max smiled. Even he knew Tarzan.

The three companions hid behind a tree trunk and watched Smaug. The dragon trembled and shook, but didn't get up and fly away. The beast rested, crumpled and beaten, for several minutes, the sound of its deep breaths sharp and rhythmic.

"Let's go," Max said.

Hawk put out an arm. "Not yet." Hawk searched about for a stone and found a golf ball sized rock the color of slate. He waited a few more minutes, and when Smaug didn't make any moves he threw the rock into the jungle in front of the dragon. The stone crashed through the leaves and underbrush, making a racket as it went.

Smaug sprang toward the noise with the agility of a cat. Blue blood splattered the jungle, and the *pterosaur* crashed into the forest with a screech, beak snapping.

"Playing possum," Hawk said.

"Ja."

When the dragon didn't find its prey, it roared in anger and lifted into the air, pounding its wings and kicking up a gale. The great beast soared over the jungle and disappeared from view.

The party stayed hidden, afraid the beast might double back, but it didn't. The two astronauts and one cosmonaut stood in silence, the pounding of Smaug's wings fading. Hawk thought he heard a cry in the distance, a great exultation of joy. His eyes snapped to his companions for confirmation and received none. If there had been a cry, his mates hadn't heard it.

Finding camp wasn't easy, and Hawk worried the entire hike that their supplies would be pillaged. They went in circles for hours, the thick green fortress of jungle unvaried and dense. They found an animal's trail Svet remembered, and using it to backtrack, they found camp. The canvas bags appeared against the wall of green and everything was where they'd left it. Hawk stepped into camp and froze.

Svet's ukulele was propped against her supply bag.

"What is—" Max's mouth hung open, eyes locked on the instrument.

"Not possible," Svet said.

"And yet." Hawk drew the Viking. It had one shot left. He eased behind a tree, scanned the area, and slipped forward into camp. As he walked, he holstered the gun, and knelt next to the ukulele, but didn't touch it. There was nothing attached to it, and it didn't appear booby-trapped.

Hawk picked the instrument up and held it out to Svet. "It is yours?" He shook his head. "Not that it matters."

"Da." Svet took the ukulele from him and strummed its strings. A gentle twang of music floated on the air and Svet slammed her hand across the strings, silencing them. Her gaze shifted to the jungle.

"That's it then. Something or someone is tracking us," Max said.

"Something? Like a monkey?" Svet said.

"Monkeys are mammals and didn't appear until the Tertiary period, but it's possible something is missing in the fossil record. We are talking about a hundred million years," Max said.

"So this monkey has a gun and can fire it? Moves like smoke and leaves no trace of itself?" Hawk said.

"No trace that we've noticed? Have you been looking? I haven't," Max said. "There is another possibility. Scientists speculated that a dinosaur man may have evolved if the extinction event hadn't occurred."

"Dino-man?" Svet said.

"Indeed, very odd, but not that crazy. They argued there could have been dinosaurs that walked mostly erect. With larger brains and better cognitive abilities with keen eyes and agile limbs. There is no fossil record for any of this, however."

"Which isn't that odd, according to you," Hawk said.

"True. Such fossil evidence, especially if the species was new, could have been missed or lost due to the extinction event."

"What we cannot deny is whoever or whatever tracks us has tried to help us. Nyet?" Svet said.

"Like I said before. No monkey can fire a gun. Would have a gun," Hawk said.

"Are you saying there's another person like us here?" Max said.

"It's possible."

"How?" he pressed. "We were in space. Everything that was on Earth is gone."

"True, but we know nothing about how we got here. Maybe some burp in space-time threw back another unlucky bastard?"

Max said, "Then why not announce yourself? What's with the sneaking around? Living in the shadows?"

"Also true." Hawk had another idea, and it was crazier than his last. "It could be an alien from the beacon station. An outcast? The creature could be AWOL. Afraid of us, but watching, waiting for the right moment to show itself."

Max and Svet said nothing.

The breeze picked up and wind pushed through the fern leaves, the whistling of their sharp tips creating a sad melody that made Hawk think of a crackling fire.

Max coughed, and said, "Say the missing bullet and me not remembering aiming at the dinosaur was a coincidence and went down the way you said. So that one is on me. What of the other two?" Max said. "The yell in the woods and our supplies being saved? Those our dino-man could have done. Or some being hitherto fore unknown. A creature of intelligence missed by the fossil record. I must remind you again, we knew very little this far back. There was much evidence to support what science believed to be true, but they didn't know for sure. Colors of dinosaurs being the perfect example."

Hawk didn't know what to make of it, but Max's explanation made the most sense. He said, "Alright? What do you propose we do?"

"We set a trap," Max said.

# 27

Hawk searched the forest, his unease growing. How close was their stalker? Close enough to listen to their conversations? Hear them breathing at night as they slept? Had their prowler been in their shelter while they were sleeping? Stood over them while they dreamt? Hawk didn't think so. A lookout was posted every night, though he fell asleep on his shift most nights.

Svet and Max's eyes darted from each other to the dark forest, the endless trees, creepers, weeds and flowers somehow different than they'd been just moments before. Out there in the green void something watched them. Something that didn't want to hurt them, yet Hawk still felt stalked. Nobody likes being followed, their every move observed and dissected, but military veterans felt the presence of watchful eyes more keenly as their internal radar was more acute. Hawk didn't like that his radar hadn't picked up whatever this thing was.

Hawk whispered, "We have to assume from here on out that we're being watched."

"Why do you whisper?" Svet said. "You think our tracker is that close?" She looked at the jungle again, then back at Hawk. The tough-as-nails Russian looked rattled, and that more than anything else put the hair on the back of Hawk's neck on end.

"Ja." Max answered for Hawk. "The jungle hides much."

Hawk found his voice. "Maybe close, maybe not. We must assume we are being monitored at all times and possibly in danger, though I feel obligated to say that if whoever or whatever is tracking us wanted us hurt, or dead, that end could have easily been achieved a long time ago."

"Logical," Max said. He hadn't reverted to his Spock-self in sometime and Hawk thought the Vulcan had departed for good, yet here he was. "How else would…" Max stopped, a new thought making him frown. "How the hell could whatever's tracking us understand English?"

Hawk sucked in a breath. He hadn't thought of that. Dino-man, a monkey, or an unknown lifeform wouldn't know English.

"Who knows. If it's a being from another planet perhaps it has a way to understand us."

Svet laughed. "Like E.T.?"

"Not like E.T. at all," Hawk said, but he smiled.

"What kind of…" Max lowered his voice so only his companions could hear him. "What kind of trap should we make?"

Hawk motioned with his hand, and the three companions huddled together within a spreading fern. The buzz of the jungle, the push of the wind, and the constant chatter of birds, reptiles, and dinosaurs made it impossible for the party to be heard without a high gain microphone.

"The question isn't what will trap our friend, but what will draw it in," Hawk said.

"Da. Food not good," Svet said.

"No, and that's normally what we'd use, but I agree, food isn't an issue here," Hawk said.

"What about one of us as bait?" Max said.

"No understand?" Svet said.

Hawk said, "There have been numerous opportunities for our shadow to take one of us, and it hasn't."

"No, I mean do you think if one of us were alone, hurt and needed help, do you think our stalker would assist? Or leave the injured party be and stay hidden?" Max said.

Their shadow hadn't showed itself and there had been numerous opportunities. Hawk rolled his shoulders and cracked his neck. The stalker had helped them. Had intervened multiple times. On the burnt-out plain, in the flood, and when Hawk was under attack in the jungle. In all three of those instances their pursuer had helped. Hawk said, "I think it would help just like it has so far."

"How?" Svet said.

"Depends on the situation. I think our friend is crafty, and a traditional trap probably won't work."

"Unless we have good bait," Max said. "The fact that we've seen no signs of pursuit other than the ones we were intended to find tells me we're outmatched in this game."

"Maybe, but we must try," Hawk said.

"Why?" Svet asked.

To that there was no logical answer, so Hawk said nothing. What would meeting another person mean? Not much. Everything. What knowledge would said person possess? Any individual on their trail would be in the same predicament. Survival, and the fact that their pursuer had the time to follow them around, meant daily necessities had been handled and no longer served as a challenge.

In the end, Hawk and crew agreed it would be impossible to construct physical traps without first securing the area, so it was decided that Hawk and Svet would create a better perimeter around camp. A web so tight nothing bigger than a rodent could get through it undetected. Once they were sure nobody was watching, Max constructed four basic snares using sinew line and nearby trees.

Svet was the bait. It was believed she could achieve maximum sympathy via her acting. She'd played the Lady in Macbeth in secondary school and that gave her more experience than Hawk and Max. The sexist boys made like they were going hunting, loudly proclaiming that they'd be gone for hours.

Hawk and Max circled around and hid in the underbrush where they could see the entire camp. Svet pretended to get hurt, tripping over a rock and landed by the fire. It was a brilliant performance. She cried out in pain, called for help, and then pretended to pass out. While she lay still, Hawk and Max watched. They gave it a couple of hours, but when nothing happened they decided to try again the following day.

The sun lifted its purple head above the horizon. Hawk and Max made a show of leaving camp, telling Svet they were going hunting, but circling back and hiding in the boughs of a conifer tree with thick spreading branches. Unless their stalker had the nose of a bloodhound, they were well hidden. They'd changed their position from the prior day because Hawk wanted a better vantage point and the direction of the sparrow fart wind had shifted.

Max made a cooing sound, the signal to Svet that they were ready. She pretended to fall, this time less dramatically and violent than the prior day. She made up for her poor acting with a loud dramatic scream that would be heard for a mile. She whimpered loudly for half an hour, then fell still.

They waited. The sun crept past noon, thin beams of sunlight pierced the tree canopy like spotlights. Svet cried in pain until she was hoarse, and when the sun started its descent to the horizon they gave it up again.

At the end of a third day of failure, Hawk said, "Maybe our friend has moved along and awaits us on the road ahead."

"Ja. I think we should move. Try again in a new spot," Max said. "If it's been tracking us it knows what direction we're going in."

The party packed up, dismantled their snares, and plunged into the primordial jungle once more, this time shouldering an unease bolstered by the idea they were dealing with something much more adept at surviving in the jungle than they were.

They hiked for two days until they reached a large depression in the ground. "This spot looks good," Max said. "We can create a solid perimeter here."

"Will that scare our friend off?" Hawk said.

"Unknown, but I think we should try."

"Da."

They set up camp within the stump of a fallen tree similar to their first shelter. Svet made a large fire pit and the companions settled in, cooking some bird meat they'd caught on the trail and collecting green stuff, which they'd all become good at spotting.

Svet and Hawk searched the perimeter of the gully as Max set his snares. They'd try their play again the next morning when Hawk and Svet went hunting. This time Max would be the bait.

At sunrise, Svet and Hawk climbed the embankment out of the depression and split up, Hawk going south and Svet east. They met around the opposite side, and Svet and Hawk tucked themselves in the bows of a tree with large yellow fan leaves and a trunk with thick shedding bark like a palm.

Hawk nibbled on jerky, and drank some water. Below in the hollow Max put on his best show, falling with a shriek that sounded like he'd really been hurt. He lay prone on the ground, not moving. Then he rolled over and cried for help.

Hawk and Svet sat. And sat. And sat. Nothing happened. Even the critters seemed to realize something was afoot and stayed clear.

"I have to take a leak," Hawk said. He shuffled off into the underbrush, leaving Svet alone. Getting through the thick vegetation without making noise was a challenge, and it took Hawk fifteen minutes to go twenty feet. He slipped behind a scrub palmetto tree, unzipped his fly and urinated.

He was about halfway done, his puddle of urine running toward his feet, when he saw a figure creeping through the jungle toward camp. The dark shape was vaguely humanoid, and amidst the dense foliage Hawk couldn't tell whether the intruder was human or beast.

He covered up and dropped to the ground, disappearing beneath a spray of thick fern leaves and crawling through his urine. Hawk wished he could warn Svet, but there was nothing he could do. The stalker was close, and any sound he made would bring scrutiny to his position.

He waited, breathing in and out, calming himself as the newcomer vanished within the sea of green. Max cried for help, and Hawk circled around, staying out of sight behind tree trunks and within underbrush as he made his way back to Svet, who sat where he'd left her.

"You see our friend?"

"Nyet."

"I did. He—"

At the edge of the gully, directly across from where Hawk and Svet crouched, the outline of a dark figure hid behind a bush, watching Max as he rolled around on the ground. Max must have sensed something was up, because he threw them a fast hand signal and screamed louder, weeping and wailing for help.

The shadow inched forward, its features still hidden by the shaded jungle. The intruder went to the ground, and army crawled over the dirt and through the groundcover toward Max.

Svet said, "Should we stop him? Do something?"

"Not yet."

A dinosaur roared in the distance and the mystery man disappeared from view. Dark green leaves, palm fronds, and spreading fern branches swayed and bent as something unseen moved through them.

"We're losing it," Svet said.

"Wait," Hawk said.

The vegetation stopped rustling, and other than the constant sound of insects, the jungle went still.

Svet gasped.

A figure the size of an adult slipped from the forest, working its way toward the center of the gully where Max and his traps waited. The person appeared male, mostly bald, with the telltale facial features of a person from the Orient. His sunburned skin glistened with sweat. He wore a red t-shit that was brown with age and torn in many spots. He had no shoes, and his pants were so torn there was barely anything left to them.

The stranger was ten feet away from Max when he stepped in a snare, and it pulled tight as the man's foot was caught. The stranger went down, a thin tree snapped back, and the man was dragged across the ground. He yelled and wailed in what sounded like Chinese, and pulled at the snare as if it burned his skin. Hawk and Svet rose and showed themselves, and Max got up, brushing himself off.

For the first time since their arrival, the party would have a guest for dinner.

# 28

As Hawk approached, the man stopped struggling and looked up at his captor with contempt. His eyes flashed with anger, and Hawk said, “Easy. We don’t want to hurt you.”

The man ranted in a language Hawk didn’t understand.

Max, who spoke several languages, shrugged and said, “Some form of Chinese or Japanese. Unfortunately, I don’t speak either.”

“What’s your name?” Hawk asked.

The man shrank back, confusion cutting across his face. He stammered and stuttered like a child, as if he hadn’t spoken in a long time and had forgotten the right words.

“Name?” Svet said in a soothing voice.

Hawk looked at Max who lifted an eyebrow. They’d never heard that tone from her, but it worked. The man’s face softened and in a hoarse voice straining from lack of use he said, “Enyo.”

“Nice to meet you, Enyo. I’m Jonah Hawkins. My friends call me Hawk, and this is Svetlana Savitska. Svet for short, and over there is Dr. Maximillian Schleggal. He prefers Max.” When Enyo said nothing, Hawk added, “Are you hungry? Thirsty?”

Enyo nodded vigorously and Max gave him his water bottle. The man drank greedily, water spilling from his mouth and down his chest. Hawk cracked his neck, but said nothing. It pained him to see water being wasted when they had so little, but now wasn’t the time to disturb detente.

“Let me take this off you,” Hawk said. He stepped forward with the intention of taking the snare off Enyo’s leg and the man sprang back, throwing up his hands to ward off a blow. “It’s OK. I just want to take this off. OK?” Enyo looked wary, but acquiesced. Hawk knelt and carefully removed the sinew twin knotted on the man’s leg.

When Hawk was done, Max said, “Come sit by the fire.”

Hawk led the way and sat on a log they used as a bench, staring into the fire and trying not to look at Enyo. Svet and Max followed, but Enyo sat watching them, his gaze shifting from them to the forest.

"No need to run. You can come and go as you please," Hawk said.

"Go?" Enyo said.

"If you wish," Hawk said.

Enyo rose and looked around as though he was seeing his surroundings for the first time. His eyes lingered on the three snares that still lay strewn about. He sat where he was, not running, but not joining them by the fire either.

"Stay there, that's fine," Max said.

Hawk had so many questions he didn't know where to begin, so he waited. How long had it been since Enyo had shared the company of another human? When was the last time he'd had a conversation? Was he alone? The man looked like he'd been to hell and back, but then Hawk remembered what he and his friends must look like.

Enyo had cuts and bruises all over his exposed skin. His clothes were rags, his thin beard a matted mess of dried food and dirt. His eyes gleamed like cinders, and he smelled rank. He watched Hawk and his friends, his eyes falling on the leftover fruit from breakfast that rested on a flat stone they used as a cutting surface.

"You want?" asked Svet, noticing the same thing Hawk had.

Enyo nodded. Svet rose, lifted the stone, and placed the food a few feet away from Enyo. He cringed whenever anyone got close, and it was clear he'd suffered a trauma, though it might be no more than isolation. Being alone for long periods of time has adverse effects on a human's mental state. Extreme isolation was known to cause a variety of mental and physical issues.

They all sat like that a long time. Enyo watching them, them staring at him. Birds chirped, insects buzzed, and the world didn't seem to notice or care that they'd added a member to their party. Or had they? Hawk still had the feeling Enyo might bolt at the first sign of danger, and Hawk didn't know how to put the man at ease.

Hawk decided to start simple. "Do you speak English?"

To Hawk's surprise, Enyo answered. "Yes. I studied at Oxford for a year." The man's voice cracked, but was steadier than before.

"Oxford?" Max said. "Are you alone?"

Enyo stared off into space. "Yes."

"How did you come to be here?" Hawk said. That was the million-dollar question.

Enyo surprised Hawk by laughing. Not a chuckle, or casual amusement. He laughed like a madman, no control, over responding as would a child. Hawk and his mates were silent. It looked like this man had been alone a long time, and it would take time for him to rejoin humanity, if he ever fully did.

"How did you all come to be here?" Enyo asked.

Hawk saw this as progress so he told the man their entire story from first to last. The physical pain caused by the cloud, the throwback and their fall to Earth in the Soyuz capsule, and the subsequent struggles. The markers they'd found in the jungle. Enyo listened without interrupting, his face softening, muscles relaxing, as the realization struck him that Hawk and his friends were in the same predicament he was.

"You're from the ship in the sky? I've been looking for it every night, but it's not always visible," Enyo said.

"You can see the space station from the ground?" Hawk asked. "I didn't even think to look."

Enyo chuckled, his face twisting into a grin for the first time. "You can see it if you know where to look. And have lots of time."

"How did you get here?" Svet asked.

Enyo looked hesitant, as if he still didn't trust his captors. He said nothing, but his hands no longer shook and his face had shed its mask of defiance.

"How did you find us?" Hawk asked. He'd learned that sometimes a question was too big and breaking it down into smaller pieces helped.

At this question Enyo brightened. "I saw…" he stammered, his voice cracking. "I saw your fires across the sea. Thought I was going crazy." His eyes strayed to the ground. "Crazier."

"You not crazy," Svet said.

Enyo smiled again, but said nothing.

"She's right," Max said. "We've all been through an unparalleled hardship."

"I would go to the edge of the sea each night, expecting to not see the bright flames, but night after night they blazed, and with them brought hope that I wasn't alone." Enyo took a deep breath, like that many words strung together came with great effort. "I thought they were natural, at first, then…" His voice got steadier, his eyes less glassy. He was already on his way back to mankind.

"Yes, we stayed at the edge of the inland sea for many nights. I was injured," Max said.

Pain cut across Enyo's face. "Hurt?"

"It's OK. I'm fine now."

Enyo stared up at the tree canopy and rubbed his ankle where the snare had grabbed him. The excitement over, the jungle had returned to its state of constant chaos. An army of ants marched past, insects hummed, and the thunderous roar of a great fight not far off made the ground tremble.

"So, it was you who shot the dinosaur on the plain and saved me? You who gathered our supplies in the flood by the sea? And you who provided the distraction when I was being attacked?" Hawk said.

Enyo nodded.

"Why you not show yourself?" Svet said.

"Afraid," he said. "I'd been alone for so long. And you… Hawk, are American."

The talk of shooting the dinosaur made Hawk think gun, and he visually searched Enyo for the weapon, but saw nothing.

"Afraid of us? Why?" Svet said.

Enyo shrugged.

Hawk said, "Where is your gun?"

"Camp."

"You don't carry it with you?"

"No. It is out of bullets. Used last one to help you."

"Thank you for that."

"My pleasure." The man's English was getting better.

"And how did you come to be here?" Svet asked again.

"I don't know," Enyo said.

"You must know something," Max said. "What were you doing when you arrived here? How did you arrive here?"

"I came to Earth in my capsule. From orbit. Just like you."

"From orbit? When?"

Enyo looked embarrassed, sighed and said, "What I tell you now is highly classified, though I can't see how that matters any longer."

Hawk, Svet, and Max waited patiently, saying nothing.

"My name is Enyo Liwei, and I am… I was, an astronaut on a mission for the China National Space Administration, who were partnering with the military."

"But how can that be?" Hawk said. "You were in orbit around Earth when the cloud passed?"

"I was."

"And what happened?"

"After the cloud passed everything on Earth was gone, and I lost all communications. I only had food for a few days, so I put the capsule in a decaying orbit and crash landed about fifty miles from here."

"Not possible," Max said. "NASA and Roscosmos would have known about your mission."

"My capsule was equipped with a new stealth technology my country was testing. That was the main purpose of my mission. And to monitor the cloud like yourselves. Most of the higher ups in government didn't even know I blasted off. I left from a secret location."

"I guess it worked," Svet said.

"Guess so," Enyo said.

The group sat in silence, the sounds of the jungle rising in a tumult. A fly landed on Hawk's arm and he slapped it away, and Enyo jumped. A swarm of gnats blew through camp like a rain cloud, its dark outline shifting and expanding as the bugs changed direction.

"You were in space at the same time as us, and got thrown back in time like us?" Svet didn't appear to believe the man, despite his story making sense.

"Indeed."

"What have you been doing down here all this time?" Hawk asked.

"Living at the temple. Hunting. Looking for water. Same things as you I'd imagine," Enyo said. "It was very hard at first, but one learns to live without certain… luxuries. If I hadn't found the temple I don't know what I would have done. I had my capsule, but it drew so much attention I covered it in palm fronds, but when I found the temple it made too much sense not to live there."

"The temple?" Max said.

"I was wandering the jungle, staying clear of this time period's larger inhabitants, when I came across a temple-like building covered in creepers, but built on a sturdy foundation. It was barely visible in the dense forest, but what I found therein is the true mystery."

Hawk and his friends waited patiently for him to continue, and when he didn't Svet said, "Mystery?"

"There are hieroglyphs all over the place, but I can't figure out what they mean," Enyo said.

"Any signs of other people? Or, anything unlike people?" Max said.

"I'm not sure, but many of the pictures show figures with seven fingers and tails."

"Have you found any markers in the jungle?" Hawk asked.

"No."

"The markers are why we came this way. All the way from over the mountains in the east." Enyo looked confused. It struck Hawk at that moment that perhaps the markers pointed at the temple, not the beacon. "You've never been across the inland sea?"

"No. Why would I? I was fishing there when I saw your fires." He paused, and his head tilted. "Where are you all going?"

"To the beacon light," Hawk said.

Enyo looked perplexed. "The pictures in the temple…"

"What? What do the hieroglyphs in the temple show?"

"Something about a light, but it makes no sense."

"The beacon light! We saw the light from space and are trying to find it. Have you seen it? Do you have any idea what it is?" Max said.

Enyo's eyes glazed over and he looked like he had when they'd first caught him; a confused and scared child. "Beacon light? What beacon light?" he said.

# 29

"You didn't see the bright light? From space?" Max said.

Enyo rubbed his chin, and looked toward the jungle. His eyebrows knitted and he frowned, but he said nothing.

"You didn't see it?" Hawk said.

Enyo ran his fingers through his hair and said, "No. There is a moonglow in the west on clear nights, but I never thought more of it than that. Now some of the hieroglyphs make more sense, though."

Hawk said, "When we were in orbit we saw a bright multi-colored pulsating light shining at the center of this continent. It didn't appear natural."

"And from the mountains we saw a pillar of light, like a spotlight shooting into space, that appeared to blink in an odd rhythm," Max said.

Enyo looked more confused than ever. "What do you think it is?"

"We believe it's a beacon," Hawk said.

"Or a monitoring and recording device," Max said.

"What would it be recording?" Enyo asked.

Hawk, Svet and Max exchanged glances.

"Do you know what time we're in?" Max said.

Enyo chuckled. "Long, long time in the past judging by the inhabitants."

"We estimate the throwback sent us seventy-five million years into the past, give or take twenty million years," Max said.

Enyo shrugged, still not understanding.

"The dinosaurs all died off around this time," Hawk said.

Enyo's eyes widened as he recalled his high school science. "The extinction event?"

"Exactly. We believe the beacon is in place to record the extinction event, and send the data off world," Max said.

"Off world?"

"Da," Svet said.

"To who? Who placed the beacon?"

Hawk and friends said nothing.

The group sat in silence for a long time, the jungle erupting around them as though they weren't there. Hawk got up, threw more wood on the fire, and gave Enyo more water.

After a time, Enyo said, "What's next? Where do we go from here?"

Hawk sighed. "As we've told you, we're on our way to the beacon, but now I think a detour to your temple is in order."

"Affirmative," Max said in his Spock voice. "Those hieroglyphs might tell us something about the beacon."

"Da," Svet said.

"If there is any connection at all," Enyo said.

"What do you mean?" Svet said.

"There must be a connection, no?" Max said.

"Not necessarily," Enyo said. He clasped his hands and placed them on his knee. He was growing more comfortable by the minute. His voice was recovering, and only cutting out every fifth word. "Perhaps the beacon was placed by one race, but discovered by another?"

"Like us finding the pyramids centuries after they'd been constructed?" Max said.

"Exactly. Some of the cave pictures appear to show a worship-like relationship with the light," Enyo said.

"Like praying to it?" Svet said.

"He does call the place a temple," Hawk said.

The buzz of the jungle filled the silence, and in the distance the scree of a *pterosaur* made Hawk think of Smaug. Were they free of the beast for good?

"Should we leave or camp here tonight?" Max asked.

Hawk said, "Enyo, how far is the temple from here?"

"Twenty miles. Maximum."

"How do you feel?"

"Physically, fine, but…"

Hawk understood. They were like a group of strangers riding the subway, all separate individuals, riding to work or school in the light, but not paying any attention to each other. Then the train loses power and the lights go out and suddenly all those people are together, until the lights come back on. “Must have been hard living alone for all that time.”

Enyo nodded. “I’m used to being alone in space, but that’s different. I talk to ground control, get messages from my family, even though I know most of what I read is fake, it was still comforting.”

“Fake?” Svet said.

“My government is a bit… paranoid,” Enyo said.

Hawk chuckled. “I don’t think you need to worry about that anymore.”

“Ja,” Max said. “We’re here for you.”

“Thank you,” Enyo said.

None of them said what Hawk was thinking: and we’re stuck here together for the rest of our lives so we have to get along, no matter how we may feel.

Max put his arm around Svet, and smiled at Enyo. He smiled back, message received.

They busied themselves around camp, and decided to spend the night and strike out fresh in the morning. They ate, talked, and one by one drifted into sleep. Hawk stayed on watch the entire night. Enyo slept soundly and made no attempt to leave, or otherwise search the camp or their belongings. He’d been watching them for weeks, and probably knew what everyone carried better than Hawk.

He felt at ease with the mystery solved. Of all the explanations they’d talked about, the Chinese having a stealth spacecraft wasn’t one of them. With that type of technology, China could control the world. Hawk chuckled to himself. No worries for him, it wasn’t his world anymore. His stomach tightened. But it was his world because that’s where everyone he loved lived. Maybe.

Other than what might have happened to their families, Hawk and his friends hadn’t discussed future Earth much. What had the cloud done to those on the surface of Earth? Were they thrown back in time? Where? Had his family ended up in Ancient Rome? Or in the future? If so, he hoped they found a life wherever they were.

What he hadn’t considered was the cloud causing destruction. That he couldn’t think about. Wouldn’t think about. He would never know, so worrying about it made no sense. He replayed his mental photo album, closed his eyes, and waited for morning.

An hour past sunrise the party followed Enyo through the thick greenery. He appeared to know exactly where he was going, and trudged forward with a single-minded purpose. He asked for no water, and no food, and said they'd soon hit an animal path that would let them travel much faster.

Hawk was strapped with the Viking and its single shot, and Svet held the Ash 12, which only had three bullets remaining. It was hot, and perspiration dripped down Hawk's back and over his face into his eyes. The tree canopy provided shade, but the humidity was stifling. Hawk wiped his face with a rag, and took a pull of water.

"Where you from?" Svet asked Enyo.

"Originally from Henan Province, but I've spent most of my life in the military, so I was transferred around a lot. The last few years I lived in Beijing."

"I've been there. A beautiful city. So much history," Max said.

"Yes, not all of it good."

"What country is all good?" Hawk said.

Enyo nodded acquiescence.

"How did you end up in the space program?" Max said.

"I volunteered and was chosen from a cohort of my colleagues."

"Did you choose to join the military?" Hawk said. He understood China was still a communist country, and choice had a different meaning there.

"Yes and no. My aptitude evaluation said I was suited for science, and in China the best way to do science is through the military. They get all the money for the truly cutting-edge projects, but I got tired of working on weapon and spy tech research, and when the slot came available for the space agency I leapt at it."

"Current predicament aside, how'd that work out for you?" Hawk said.

Enyo shrugged. "Same as military, but more fulfilling and exciting. At least I got to be an astronaut."

"At least," Hawk said. "What of your family?"

Enyo looked at the ground. "No wife or kids. I never had time, and felt it would be unfair to a woman to marry her and then abandon her."

It was Hawk's turn to look at the ground.

"Both my parents died young, and my work has been my life. Until now," Enyo said.

To that, nobody had anything to say, and they threaded quietly behind Enyo as he led them through the thick jungle. Everything was damp, and dew dripped from leaves, the scent of earth and decaying vegetation filling the forest. Hawk smelled smoke, but the sky was clear and there was no other sign of fire.

The party walked most of the day before they reached the path Enyo told them about. Footprints of every size and shape decorated the dried mud, and Hawk said, "You run into traffic on this highway?"

Enyo laughed. He'd relaxed during their trek, and as he got to know his new partners he smiled more, and appeared to have partially recovered from his isolation. "Most of the time, no. We'll hear big guys coming, and the smaller beasts tend to shy away."

The weather turned sour on the second day, and the party holed up beneath a dense fern and waited for the deluge to end. The patter of the raindrops on leaves was maddening.

"Would you like to see my capsule?" Enyo asked.

"Is it far out of the way?" Hawk said.

"No," Enyo said.

"Sure," Hawk said.

They turned off the main thoroughfare, fighting their way through the thick jungle that seemed to go on forever. In Hawk's time the rainforests were dying, and the great jungles suffered as well. In his day there was no spot left on the planet that humans hadn't occupied, even the poles. In this past, animals ruled the world, and from what Hawk had seen so far they were much better stewards.

The party broke free of the dense forest onto a trail lined with broken trees and squashed underbrush. It looked similar to the trail of destruction the Soyuz capsule had left when they'd crash landed. They hadn't gone far up the blazed trail when they came upon Enyo's space capsule.

Unlike the Soyuz, it was intact and mostly undamaged. Stars on a red background adorned the front of the craft, and the hatch stood open. The vehicle was much smaller than the Soyuz, and could only accommodate one person.

Hawk eased in slowly, wary of creatures that may have taken up residence in the capsule, but there was nothing. Hawk dropped into the capsule, and marveled at how old the equipment was.

Max stuck his head through the hatch. "For a high-tech machine, it doesn't look like it's very current," he said.

Enyo's head appeared over Max's shoulder. "It is one of our older models. It was deemed expendable."

Hawk almost asked, are you expendable? But didn't.

They drank water and moved on. Enyo had already transported everything of use to the temple, so the capsule was useless to them. The day wore on, the sun started to go down, and the gray of dusk filled the land as they crested a hill overlooking a shallow valley.

"We're here," Enyo said.

"Where?" Svet said.

Enyo pointed to the center of the depression.

"I don't see… Wait, that mound of green?" Hawk said.

"Yes." Enyo didn't wait for any more questions. He started down the incline into the shallow bowl, not looking back. Hawk was on his turf, and Enyo knew it.

"Can we make it before dark?" Max asked.

"No." Enyo stopped walking.

"Da." Svet dropped her bag of supplies and sat down next to it.

"I guess here is as a good spot as any," Hawk said. "Is there fresh water nearby?"

"Yes. I'll show you," Enyo said.

"Max, can you go with him? Fill the bottles?"

"I'm shot, boss."

Hawk said, "Good enough. I'll go, but while I'm gone get a fire going and make camp."

"Yes sir, captain my captain," Max said.

Svet laughed.

"Commander, and don't forget it," Hawk said.

He followed Enyo into the forest, torch held before him, the dusk of the prehistoric jungle engulfing them.

# 30

When Hawk and Enyo got back with the water they joined their companions around the blazing campfire. Darkness closed in around them, nothing but blackness beyond the firelight. The night symphony roared, buzzed and chirped. It had become the melody of their lives. The elevator music that kept them on the edge between sane and insane.

Hawk wanted a martini so bad he could taste it in his mouth, which gave him an idea. “Hey, how about I mix us some drinks? Liven up this party.”

“What kind?” Max said. “We’ve only got water.”

“I can mix you up anything you want.”

“You can’t make—”

“I can. Trust me.”

“OK, I’ll play.”

“Me too,” Svet said.

Enyo said nothing. He shook his head and squinted.

Hawk stood before his fellow time travelers and pretended to pull a towel off his shoulder and wipe an imaginary bar in front of him. “OK? Svet, what can I get you?”

“You go choknutiy?” Svet said. “How you do this?”

“If you do what I tell you, you’ll see.”

“Da,” she said, and threw up her hands. “I want a martini, dry, straight up with olives on bamboo skewer.”

“Coming right up.” Hawk took down an invisible glass and rubbed it with his imaginary towel. He set the glass on the invisible bar and started making a fantasy martini. Between making ice rattling sounds, Hawk said, “I want you to close your eyes and think of the last martini you had. Get it in your mind. Think about how it tasted. Bite the olive.”

“Da.”

“Your drink is done. Take a sip,” Hawk said.

Svet opened her eyes, took the faux martini off the bar and brought it to her lips. She took a long sip, closing her eyes. "Thank you, Hawk. Thank you very much."

"I'll have a scotch on the rocks," Max said.

"Saki hot," Enyo said.

They all sat at the make-believe bar, in the middle of the jungle like crazy people, sipping drinks in their minds. Hawk took a pull of his own martini, and felt the burn of the alcohol in his throat.

After two rounds Hawk said, "Let's turn in. Long day tomorrow."

"Can you make any drink?" Svet asked.

"Most," Hawk said.

"You working tomorrow night?" Max said.

"Sure."

They set out the next morning refreshed, but with no hangovers. Hawk felt like he'd had a night out, some time away from the constant grind of survival and the never-ending quest for the beacon. Enyo's trails were well worn, and they made good time through the jungle. The Chinese astronaut narrated as they walked, pointing out certain flowers and food sources. The tree canopy was full, but patches of sky were visible, and the jungle baked in tunnels of light. The party stopped in one of these areas to soak in the rays.

"Science has proven that humans need sunlight. Without it the odds of depression go up in orders of magnitude, and lack of sunlight can inhibit the body's ability to process resources," Max said.

"Sun with cold beer better," Svet said.

"You had to go say that?" Hawk said.

"Sorry."

The ancient temple didn't look ancient at all. Hawk had formed a mental picture of crumbling stone and root-cracked slabs of rock, but that's not what he saw.

Creepers covered everything, and flowers and small ferns protruded from every gap and ledge. Large open windows looked out like dark eyes, and great trees with wide trunks surrounded the temple. They were in ordered rows, as if planted as a barricade. The building sat on a foundation that looked pristine. It was white and smooth beneath the creepers, and was clearly made of a different material than the structure.

The place had an air of age, but if the creepers were stripped away Hawk thought the building would look in excellent shape. Nowhere did he see polyhedron shapes, like those of markers.

Hawk understood why Enyo thought the place looked like a temple. It had an oriental temple feel to it, as it tapered from a square foundation to a pointed peak in stepped levels. Not like a pyramid, but more of a layered wedding cake. Each section looked to be made of a different color stone, and the rock had a smooth sheen like that of polished granite despite the vines and their little claws.

"Whoever built this place meant it to last," Hawk said.

"Ja."

"Hold up here," Enyo said.

They approached the building across an open area between the protective cover of the trees and the temple. Ferns and scrub palmetto covered the ground, and small dinosaurs skittered away on their hind legs, running through the foliage with heads bobbing.

"Hold up," Svet said. "Why—"

Four mini-tyrannosaurs rexs stepped from behind a large fern, blocking their way.

"Meet Xio, Grog, Mixie, and Clint. Stay gemen. Sit. Sit," Enyo yelled.

One of the dinosaurs came forward, one stayed where it was, and two sat.

"Clint and Mixie always listen. Grog does when he's scared, but Xio is a bitch," Enyo said.

"What the fuck are you talking about, Enyo? You know these monsters?" Max said.

"They're not monsters. I think they're a type of carnosaur. I'm not sure—" Xio chomped at air and took another step forward. "Hey, Xio, I said sit. I mean it now. Sit." Xio roared, but didn't advance. "They are my watch dogs. I killed their mother and when I found the eggs I just..."

"Whatever. Just send them back to their doghouse," Hawk said.

"So, one minor thing, no matter at all really," Enyo said.

"What?" Hawk said.

"A slight flaw in my training. They were trained like military guard dogs, but they're not as smart."

"And?"

"Xio will attack anything other than me, and Grog will follow her. Eventually the other two will join in and I won't be able to stop them," Enyo said.

"What are you saying?" Svet said.

"I'm saying I'll hold them off, you run," Enyo said.

Xio took another step forward and threw her yellow head back in frustration. Her baseball sized eyes burned, and saliva dripped between sharp teeth. She snapped at the air again and came forward.

"Halt," Enyo yelled. The beast stopped.

Hawk dove behind a tree and Svet dropped and rolled. Max didn't move, like a spider that freezes when the lights come on in hopes that nobody will notice it. After a moment Max's muscles unlocked and he raised his spear.

Grog had fallen in behind his sister, and the two dinosaurs inched forward toward Enyo, who stood palms outward, trying to hold the beasts back. Clint and Mixie also inched forward, but they appeared less hostile. Their mouths were closed and their eyes blinked innocently.

Hawk moved away, using trees as cover, limiting his movement and going as slow as his frayed nerves would allow. Svet propped herself up on her elbows and worked her way backward in a reverse army crawl. Max took another approach. He stabbed forward with his spear, attempting to intimidate Xio, but the eight-foot dinosaur had different ideas.

A yellow-black streak moved toward Max, flying past Enyo as the astronaut yelled for the beast to stop. The dinosaur leapt at Max, who blocked the blow with the point of his spear as he fell to the ground. Xio wailed, the spear tip catching the beast with a glancing blow on its chest. Blood trickled from the gash, but the beast came on, straddling Max between its legs and biting at him.

Enyo still stood before the other dinosaurs, but Grog was screeching and yelling, throwing his head back like a panicking horse trying to break from its bridle.

"Shit," Hawk said. He drew the Viking, and worked his way back toward the fray. He hid behind a thick conifer and yelled as loud as he could, every strange sound he could come up with. Beeping horns. Dogs barking. Explosions. Laughter. The sound of a crashing plane. Like a clown at the circus Hawk made as much of a commotion as he could.

All the dinosaur heads jerked in Hawk's direction as if controlled by one mind, and that mind was hearing things it had never heard before.

Max inched backward, and vaulted to his feet. Xio noticed the movement and swung her yellow snout back his way, jaws opening to take a bite.

Max parried two of the beast's bites with his spear, but a third strike snapped the spear and the beast's teeth sank into Max's shoulder. The physicist screamed as he hit the ground, and crabbed back, trying to get away from the beast's chomping jaws.

Svet threw a rock and it hit Xio in the head and the creature wailed, throwing her head up, eyes rolling back. Max got to his feet and staggered behind a tree.

The scene froze. Animals and people alike stood their ground, eyes darting around, waiting for something to happen.

"Max, are you alright?" Hawk yelled.

"Yeah. I'm bleeding bad."

Hawk said, "Enyo, what should we do?"

The Chinese astronaut still held back Grog, Clint and Mixie, but all three beasts were abreast of him and would spring past him as soon as someone hit play and then everything jerked back into motion.

Xio's head flicked between where Max hid behind his thin tree, and Hawk, the beast not sure who to pursue. Svet appeared next to Max and she gave him her spear. As she retreated behind a tree of her own she trained the Ash 12 on Xio, prepared to fire into the beast's face should she come on.

Grog sprang past Enyo in a blur, followed by Clint and Mixie.

Max threw his spear at the charging Grog, and he caught the animal in its open mouth, and the spear's point protruded out the back of the beast's head like a unicorn horn. The dino fell to its knees and toppled over on its side with a crash and puff of dust.

Clint and Mixie had enough, and they ran squealing into the jungle like pigs. Xio wouldn't be scared off so easy. The dinosaur came forward, sniffing the tree Svet hid behind.

Max stepped out from his cover and threw a stone at the beast's head, and it hit home, catching the creature in a bulbous eye. It screeched and snapped, lunging toward him.

Hawk eased forward, trying to get a bead on the dinosaur through the trees. He got a few feet and stopped short. Clint and Mixie's heads poked through the foliage, watching him with confused eyes.

Max grunted as he hid behind a tree that didn't provide enough cover, so he backed away slow, Xio coming at him, head dodging right and left like a boxer looking for a spot to strike.

Hawk smiled at Clint and Mixie and pushed through the foliage, gun held out before him. Clint and Mixie darted past Hawk and fell in behind their sister. Then seeing Svet, moved toward her, cutting Max off from help.

The jungle fell silent. The ground shook. The commotion had caught the attention of something bigger.

The dinosaurs paused, and Svet ran, cutting through the forest like a blur.

Max tried the same thing, but tripped on a tree root and went sprawling to the ground, blood spurting from the wound on his shoulder. Xio screeched and came forward, her siblings behind her.

Hawk brought up the Viking, and sighted it on the lead dinosaur. A headshot should take the beast down, but what difference would it make? He only had one bullet, and there were three beasts. When Grog went down it had enraged the animals, so maybe a warning shot into the air? Freeze them one more time to give Max a chance to get up and run? Hawk took too long to decide.

Enyo blocked Hawk's view. He was a flash of white as he jumped between Max and the raging dinosaurs he'd raised.

# 31

Enyo put his palms out, bowed his head, and said, "Stay, Xio. Stay." The dinosaur sprang forward and clamped her jaws on Enyo's leg, shaking him and tearing skin and muscle. Enyo yelled, and Xio tossed him to the ground like garbage, then dove in for another bite.

Hawk tried to get a clear shot with the Viking, but branches, leaves and palm fronds blocked his view. There was a flash of yellow in the foliage ahead, but Hawk hesitated and didn't fire.

Clint and Mixie scattered, and Svet disappeared into the forest. Xio bit and tore at Enyo as Max backed away, scrambling to put space between himself and the fray. Enyo's screams of pain filled Hawk's mind, his heart pounding in his head.

Svet appeared from behind a tree and drove her spear through Xio's bulbous left eye and it came out on the opposite side of the beast's head. Svet jerked the spear free and stabbed at the beast again, and again, until the dinosaur went down, blood and brains oozing from holes in her chest and skull. Clint and Mixie were still nowhere to be seen, but their clicking and moaning could be heard just inside the tree break.

Enyo was unconscious when Hawk reached him. He was covered in blood, his torso ripped open, a bad bite mark on his leg, and he was missing two fingers on his left hand. The dinosaur's razor-sharp teeth had cut through his muscle and sinew, the white of his bones visible in the gashes.

Svet went to Max, who said, "I'm fine. Help Hawk." He was pale and held his shoulder, but his eyes were bright.

She peeled off and came to Enyo's side. "Get leaves. Water." Svet wiped away the blood and pulled off the torn shirt. She pressed her hands on the wounds, trying to stop the bleeding, but blood pulsed through her fingers. Hawk returned with wide green leaves and Svet used them as bandages, wrapping them around the wounds, tying them in place with palm fronds. "We need to move him. Clean wounds good."

"Ja," Max said. "Hawk, let's make a stretcher."

"You up for it?" Hawk said.

"I'm fine." Max winced. His shoulder was red with blood, but he was on his feet and moving.

"Still two out there," Svet said.

Enyo was on the edge of consciousness, but he forced out, "Clint and Mixie will leave you be." Enyo moaned and grimaced with pain. "I'm going to be unconscious soon, so listen. When you get through the main entrance make a left, go to the end, then make two rights. Got that?"

"A left, to the end, and two rights. Got it," Svet said.

Hawk went into the forest and hunted for two straight branches while Svet pulled down creepers, and ten minutes later Enyo was on a makeshift stretcher. Hawk hid their gear and helped Svet carry Enyo, and Max stumbled before them, clutching his shoulder. Hawk would come back for their gear.

The party crossed dark hardpan in front of the temple, the entire area surrounded by a thick stand of soldier trees. The temple was covered in creepers, and patches of white stone stood out against the uniform pale green. Vines trailed through open windows, but there appeared to be only one entry.

The party gathered beneath a large overhang of stone that covered the entrance. Several torches sat propped against the wall, their black tips staining the fine stone. Hawk and Svet put Enyo down and Hawk tried to light one of the torches with the spark stones. He'd only been tapping a minute when Enyo came awake with laughter, blood bubbles and saliva dripping from his mouth.

"Be here all night," Enyo said. He pointed to a ledge above the entryway. "Up there." He shook his finger, pointing.

Hawk felt along the sill and came down with a disposable lighter.

"Holly Hanna," Hawk said. He held the yellow lighter up to the sun and saw that the fluid was almost gone.

"Bring it," Enyo said.

With three flicks of his thumb, Hawk got the torches going and the party prepared to enter through smooth stone doors that were mounted on pin counterweight hinges. Enyo motioned at a metal latch with a lift handle held fast with a pin. Hawk removed the pin, lifted the latch, and the heavy stone doors arced open with a gentle push and a puff of dry air.

Once again Hawk's mental image didn't match reality. Inside no creepers clung to the smooth stone walls, and the floor was free of dirt. The foyer was adorned with a huge mosaic etched into the smooth stone wall that showed the progressions of the moon. It was detailed, and showed other star systems than Earth's.

Passages trailed to the right and left, dark tubes that led into the structure. There were no statues. No benches or seating, it was plain and unadorned. Hawk went left, his heart racing. He felt like Indiana Jones, except a plane didn't wait to whisk him away home. The passageway reminded Hawk of the subterranean levels beneath the buildings at NASA headquarters; sterile, dark, and cold. Hawk searched for light fixtures on the ceiling, but there were none. He knew that was a crazy thought, but there was nothing old about the interior of the structure.

The companions shuffled on through the darkness, diving deeper into the building. They'd seen no doorways, few windows, and the walls, ceiling, and floor were smooth and free of blemishes. To Hawk, the stuff looked like poured concrete, but of a very high grade. There were no cracks, no pock marks, no lines from the forms that would have been needed to shape it.

When the party reached the t-intersection, they turned right as instructed. Hawk and Svet carried Enyo, while Max went on point, leading through the darkness, the Ash 12 under his arm and a torch held high.

They made another right and ended in a vast chamber that reminded Hawk of a dining hall. Long tables with thin stone tops filled the outside of the room, but at one corner the tables had been rearranged on their sides to make a privacy barrier.

Firelight danced on the walls and the ceiling above disappeared into blackness. The torchlight revealed walls covered with pictures. The term hieroglyphs didn't do them justice. They were stone etchings with detail so fine it looked like the work had been done with a laser cutter.

In the far corner, behind walls of stacked tables, was Enyo's living quarters. Hawk and Svet placed the Chinese astronaut on his bed of bamboo and dried grass and covered him with his dirty and torn spacesuit. There was a jungle kitchen with an assortment of nutshell bowls and bamboo containers, a metal pot and a skillet made of steel from Enyo's ship. Hawk was surprised to see the pot. Apparently, the Chinese had been more practical with their worst-case-scenario planning.

Along the wall there was a stone water basin and at the far end a fire pit had been constructed and blackened wood rested therein. Hawk held the torch above his head, trying to get a sense of the ceiling height, but it wasn't bright enough. There was a raised dais in the center of the space, and torches were mounted in sconces on the walls. Hawk walked around the chamber and lit torches one by one with flicks of his thumb.

The lighter brought him back. The feel of the plastic in his hand, the blue-orange flame floating above the stainless steel. Such a simple thing. Something he'd taken for granted his entire life. All the time he'd spent the last few months smacking rocks together to get a spark, all the energy exerted and wasted.

The glow of torchlight lit the chamber, revealing its vastness. The ceiling stepped inward as it went up, and open corridors ran along the walls as the ceiling tapered away into darkness a hundred feet up. Great balconies stood out at each step, as the structure narrowed to a point. Hawk thought it was a gathering hall, and the center dais was the stage.

Hawk got water boiling and Svet cauterized Enyo's wounds and used sinew thread and a curved fish bone to stitch him up. Then she used leaves and palm fronds to bandage the wound. The Russian cursed frequently as she worked, and thankfully for Enyo he'd passed out. When she was done she moved on to Max and said, "It would help to have that vodka now." They had salt to make saltwater, and Svet's healing cream, but that was it.

"You will be fine," Svet said. She kissed Max's forehead and cleaned the bite on his shoulder.

"And Enyo?" Hawk said. He knew the answer, but he hoped he was wrong.

"No good. He lost lot of blood, and I can't stop infection," Svet said.

Exploration of the temple would be put off until necessities were taken care of. Svet devoted all her time to Enyo, while Max and Hawk hunted, prepared food, searched for herbs, and helped Svet. They also guarded at the main entrance at night, which left little time for anything other than survival.

A week passed in this way, the routine consuming them, weariness turning the time travelers into zombie machines. Enyo was doing much better. His fever had broken, and his cuts were healing. Max's wound festered, and he developed a low-grade fever, and was tired and hungry all the time. He'd taken to laying before the fire most of the day, only getting up to go to the bathroom, eat, and drink.

Svet played her ukulele on the eighth night, and Max and Enyo fell asleep, snoring and wheezing like little kids. Svet plucked at the strings, playing in rhythm with the night symphony that buzzed like electric inside the temple. The open windows let the sound in, and the conical interior enhanced it like a speaker.

She stopped playing, laid the instrument aside, and sighed.

Hawk said, "Where are we Svet?"

Svet sighed again, and ran fingers through her hair. A tear slipped down her face, and she wiped it away in anger and her face tightened. "I think Max caught some parasite or pathogen in his open wound when the thing bit him. He is getting worse and there is nothing I can do for him." She sniffed and wiped her face again. "Enyo. I don't know how he's not dying from the same thing, but he's not. He's healing and might live."

"Will he ever be able to travel?"

She looked away and said nothing.

Luck is a funny thing. As soon as you get some you start worrying about when it will run out, like luck was blood and without it death would soon come. In this case Hawk knew that to be a literal truth. He and his friends had been very lucky thus far. While they'd watched what animals ate before they tried it themselves, the party had been extremely fortunate to have avoided getting sick from some toxin or poison unknown to their immune systems.

Hawk had no doubts that with the proper equipment Max could find hundreds of unknown pathogens in the jungle just waiting to try out the human body as a host. They were fresh meat.

Meat that had been cut, scraped, stabbed and beaten, but somehow none of these viruses had taken hold.

Until now.

Losing Max was unthinkable, but their immune systems were on twentieth century time, and Hawk had feared from the outset this greatest of threats, and was why his first reaction had been for them to wear their spacesuits when they came down.

"There really is nothing you can do for Max?"

She looked at him, her icy blue eyes searching his, then her gaze dropped to the Viking.

Hawk said, "After everything we've been through. All the monsters we've fought off. It might be the smallest of them all that gets us in the end."

# 32

A week later Enyo was much better and Max had gotten worse. Svet tended to her lover constantly, but there was only so many times she could dampen the cloth on his forehead. He was burning up, and his shoulder wound was red and puffy with pus at its center. Hawk and Svet hadn't spoken about it, but Hawk could see the Russian was slowly losing it, her love for Max and the fear of his loss tearing her apart.

If Max had no luck, Enyo had all of it. His wounds had closed, and though he would be forever without his fingers, he'd already learned to work chopsticks with the three-fingered hand, and was up and about, even helping around camp.

Max moaned and cried most of the time, and Hawk took to taking long walks to get away from the misery. He felt for his friend, but at the same time there was no happy ending to this story and the physicist was grating his nerves.

Hawk's initial evaluation of the temple had turned out to be accurate. All the hallways led to a viewing platform or an open hallway that looked out on the vast cavern with the dais at its center. Who had gathered here and why? Where had they all gone?

As to where the people came from, there was an etching in the main hall that showed a massive door with starburst decorations around its edge. In the picture the door stood open, and odd seven fingered beings with tails were depicted coming through the door. In the open door a great staircase descended into the earth, implying that the people who gathered in the temple had come from underground.

Hawk's mouth almost hit the ground when he'd discovered the door existed in a subbasement below the dais. It reminded Hawk of the secret hatches used by magicians to perform their escape tricks. It was set in a stone wall, and had no handle, no lock, and no hinges were visible. Hawk tried to pry it open, but made no progress. Whatever was hidden below the temple would stay a secret. Was there a connection to the light beacon? Hawk wandered the dark halls of the temple, reviewing the etchings, many of which made no sense and showed scenes of upheaval and destruction.

The sound of Max screaming echoed through the stone corridors, and Hawk worked his way back to the main hall. Max tossed and turned as Svet tried to hold him down. "He got very agitated suddenly," she said.

"Dreaming probably," Enyo said. He'd appeared from behind the wall of tables that made up their living space.

Max was yelling at someone named Michele. Hawk didn't know who that was, but Max sounded angry and betrayed.

"Why?" Max sputtered. "What did I do? I did not kill him. I did not!" Max yelled, and then let loose with a string of German curses.

"What are we doing here?" Enyo said. "He is in pain."

Svet's eyes strayed to the Viking strapped to Hawk's waist.

"Is there no hope at all?" Hawk said.

"If you believe in God now be the time to ask for favor," Svet said.

Hawk fingered the Viking. He knew what needed to be done, he just couldn't bring himself to do it. "Enyo, how do you feel? Can you travel?"

Enyo looked at Max, frowning, thinking exactly what Hawk was: does it matter? Enyo shook his head, and said, "I can. My leg still aches when I walk for a long time, but if we take breaks I think I'll be alright."

"Not yet," Svet said. She wiped Max's brow with a wet cloth and kissed his forehead.

Another week passed in this manner as Max slipped closer to death, and Enyo built up his strength. They restocked their supply of dino-jerky, made new bows and arrows, a supply of spears, and searched the area around the temple, but found nothing unusual. If the people who'd lived below the earth were still here, there were no signs of them.

Hawk and Svet wandered the temple, discussing the etchings, trying to make sense of the one that they both felt provided them their biggest clue.

It was a picture of a wooded scene, with lines depicting light rays shining through the trees. In the distance, a column rose into the sky, a block of dots and dashes that looked like fire or light. Crowds of beings walked through the trees, toward the light. It was the only etching that provided a clear message. All the others showed scenes from the jungle, the odd figures performing menial tasks, as if the etchings had been provided to teach those who viewed them how to do basic things like light a fire, cook food, and defend oneself by making weapons.

Svet said, "It's almost like these were created to teach their young."

This made sense, but why wouldn't the elders teach the younglings themselves? The bigger question for Hawk was where had they all gone?

He recalled the pueblo dwellings at Mesa Verde National park in Arizona. The Anasazi had lived in elaborate cliff side dwellings high above the valley floor. Hawk remembered wondering what had scared the Indians so thoroughly that they'd gone to such lengths to protect themselves.

Then they all just left. Pots still hanging over fire pits. Utensils resting on work surfaces. By all accounts the Indians ran, leaving most of their belongings behind. Is that what happened to the ancient people that had once lived in, or under, the temple?

What they hadn't found was any etching, symbol, anything in the shape of a polyhedron, like the markers in the jungle. If there was a connection between the two, Hawk expected to find something in the etchings, a clue that tied the shape to the temple, but he found nothing. None of the etchings showed a polyhedron, or any clues as to the markers.

"Svet, we need to move on," Hawk said. They were falling into a rhythm that would lead to dotage. Hawk understood that to be his fate, but not before reaching the beacon.

The Russian sighed as Hawk watched her emotions play across her face; anger, frustration, and then fear. Fear of losing another person she loved. "What are you to suggest?" Her eyes fell on the Viking.

"How soon can we be on our way?"

"What about Max? I can't leave him."

"Can you bring him awake?"

"Da."

"Will he understand what I tell him? Answer questions?"

"Maybe. I see where you going and I don't like it."

"I don't like it either," Hawk said.

Three days later Svet brought Max awake with the pretense of feeding him. She spooned soup into his mouth and wiped his chin after each spoonful. Hawk sat beside Max's bamboo rack, and placed the Viking on the bed next to the German. Max eyed the weapon and gurgled.

"Max, can you hear me?" Hawk said.

Max nodded. He was pale, sweaty and dark rings circled his eyes, which were red cinders shrunken into his head.

"We need to move on, Max. What can we do for you?"

Hawk and Svet had discussed how to broach the situation with the scientist. Asking someone if they'd like to be murdered was a touchy conversation. Both Svet and Hawk said there was no way they could ever put their friend out of his misery, so they'd agreed to let him do it himself if that was what he wanted and they believed he was of clear enough mind to make the call.

"There… noth you can do for me," Max said. "I'm on fire inside." Tears leaked from his eyes.

Svet wept, wiping Max's forehead with a damp cloth. "No, my love, there isn't."

Max picked up the Viking. "Wish we ha… get rid of pills," he said. His bony fingers gripped the gun and he brought it to his chest and held it tight against his breast. "Go. Thank you. Both of you."

Max was no longer recognizable as the man Hawk had known and respected. His ankles and wrists were swollen, and he was as white as powder. He shivered and shook, even as sweat rolled off him and his shirt darkened. He'd lost so much weight there was literally nothing left but skin and bones, and Hawk didn't understand how his friend could still be alive.

Hawk put his hand on Svet's shoulder and squeezed it. She wanted to stay, tend to Max until there was nothing left but dust, but Max had made it clear he didn't want that. He wanted to be remembered for the man he was, not the skeleton he'd become, and he didn't want to hold them back.

They left Max with the Viking, strapped on their supply bags, and exited the temple for the last time. It was possible they'd be back, but Hawk wasn't ready to think about that. They made their way through the dark hallways in silence, the pictures of a forgotten race from a long-lost Earth reminding Hawk he knew nothing. Enyo trailed after, coughing every few seconds, but having no trouble keeping up. Hawk had his arm around Svet, and the Russian cried until there were no tears left.

When they got to the entrance the party paused under the stone overhang. Sunlight drenched the jungle, and Clint and Mixie were nowhere to be seen. The dinosaurs had kept their distance since their siblings had been killed, but Hawk saw them at night patrolling around the temple, and when Hawk had revealed himself, the beasts paused in confusion, not knowing if he was friend or foe.

Hawk had decided to sneak past the animals, and as they came around the side of the temple to head west they found the carcass of a mid-sized dinosaur that had been killed, but not eaten.

"That's for me," Enyo said.

"What is?" Hawk said.

"My watchdogs bring me offering," Enyo said. Then seeing the confusion on Hawk's face, he said, "Like bird dog. They think they're bringing me food."

The animal carcass was several days old and badly decayed. The eyes had caved in, and rib bones were visible under the corpse's leathery skin. The smell was horrid—that well known scent of something that's been dead too long and gone unburied.

With a look back, Hawk took a mental picture of the vine-covered temple. The wedding cake of green creepers sat on its strong foundation, and Hawk had the strange feeling he'd seen the building somewhere before. How hadn't he noticed it before? Where had he seen it?

Svet sniffled. Hawk still struggled with leaving Max behind. He'd been drilled his entire life to never do that. Never leave a mate behind, no matter what. And what had they left Max for? Nothing. A light in the sky that would most likely turn out to be nothing at all. An illusion. A freak of nature that wouldn't help them one bit.

But he didn't know that. Hawk ran fingers through his hair and cracked his neck. The quest for the beacon was their life. Getting there was all that mattered, even if it meant shedding those they loved. It had been Svet who pointed out there was really no decision to make. Stay and wait for Max to die a painful death, or let him go out on his own terms.

The path thinned out, and large green leaves reached out to grab them as they passed. They hadn't gone far when the faint sound of a gunshot froze them in place, and Svet wept anew.

# 33

Hawk lost track of how long he trudged through the jungle. The forest was a uniform green, thick patches of ferns and conifers packed so tight the party was forced to squeeze through thick stands that left them scratched and bloody. Svet didn't talk much, and Enyo talked too much. The Chinese astronaut never shut up, and after Hawk snapped at him he became shy and reserved, as if Hawk had disrespected him. Hawk apologized, but the damage was done.

The three time travelers walked on in a daze, sleeping, foraging, walking, repeat. The jungle density kept most of the big predators away, and they'd been left undisturbed for the most part. Smaller critters stole food and things from camp, but Hawk felt comfortable in the forest. He'd become part of the never-ending jungle.

Hawk climbed a tree one night to confirm they were still on course, and the beacon light was closer, though still some ways off. Hawk's feet were blistered, bug bites covered his face and arms, and he'd caught a nasty stomach virus that made him puke every eight hours. He didn't have a fever, yet he still worried that some prehistoric pathogen worked its way through him looking for a place to set up camp, the memory of Max's simple bite never forgotten.

"How long have we been walking?" Svet asked one morning as they traversed a stream that cascaded down a series of rock steps where the land had never settled after an upheaval.

"A couple of weeks," Hawk said.

"Twenty days," Enyo said. "Give or take a day or two."

"Any idea how far we've come? How far to go?" Svet asked.

Hawk ran his fingers through his hair and stared back down the trail they'd just cut through the dense jungle using stone hatchets. "I don't know. When I checked three days ago I'd say we'd gone maybe half the distance?"

Svet let out a long-exasperated sigh. "Twenty more days?"

"If we're lucky and don't run into trouble," Hawk said. "And what are the odds of that?"

Svet and Enyo said nothing. The odds sucked, and Hawk knew it.

As Hawk's partners pushed through the forest they looked beaten. Svet's head was always down. She had two dead lovers to think about now. Two losses to torment her. Enyo hardly spoke since his confrontation with Hawk, and he felt horrible about it and tried to patch things up more than once, but it was clear Enyo's feelings had been hurt and he had no interest in making amends, at least not yet. Unlike in their former lives, Enyo would have to get over it. Hawk was a third of the population.

On what the party believed to be the twenty-eighth day since leaving the temple, the jungle opened up and the trees became more spaced out. Sunlight streamed into the forest as the canopy thinned, and by lunch the party was at the edge of a large clearing.

Bones of all shapes and sizes littered the plain, which stretched out in all directions and was several miles wide. Giant ribcages, skulls, and piles of bleached white bones of all shapes and sizes marked the area as a graveyard, a place where prehistoric beasts came to die.

"Boneyard," Svet said.

"Yes," Enyo said. "I've seen other places like this, but not as big."

The vastness of the graveyard was an awesome sight. Hawk estimated that the skeletons of thousands of dinosaurs covered the clearing. It was a paleontologist's dream, a viewfinder into the past that could occupy teams of scientists for their entire careers.

Hawk called a halt and they made camp within the tree break. Svet got a fire going and Hawk and Enyo foraged. There wasn't much green stuff, but there was plenty of jerky and water, so the travelers ate their fill and decided to rest the remainder of the day and continue on the next morning. Hawk hoped to cross the boneyard in full daylight, and hide within the carcasses of the dead inhabitants of this gone world.

"What you make of this?" Svet asked.

"There have been many species that went to a specific place to die," Hawk said. "I think that's what this is."

A flock of *pterosaurs* circled in the distance, most likely waiting to descend on a dying beast. The insects were thick, but no big dinosaurs appeared. On some level the graveyard might be safe because the animals respected the location in some primitive way.

Night came on and the light beacon was clear to see as it cut a path to the stars, a pulsing column of light piercing the darkness and sending out a deep glow that pervaded the land like fog. The ringing chorus of the night symphony was so loud it was hard to talk around the camp fire so they didn't try. Enyo went to bed and Svet sat staring back the way they'd come, her mind still with Max at the temple.

Hawk wandered into the field of bones, marveling at the size of some of the ribcages that were forty feet high, the thin rib bones arced together into a curved backbone made of vertebrae five feet across.

He had no torch. The boneyard was illuminated by a quarter moon and starlight, and long shadows stretched across the primordial landscape. Hawk imagined the beasts that came to the plain to die, the lives they'd led and how in the end they'd somehow known, by some instinct or internal clock, that they had to come to this place. The resting place of their mothers and fathers, so they too could rest. There was something romantic about the idea, and Hawk realized it wasn't all that different from how humans did things. What was a graveyard of tombstones if not a gathering place for the dead?

The next morning, they broke camp at first light and headed out across the bone-filled plain. It was hot and humid, and the savannah baked. Here and there flesh still clung to bones, and the smell of rot and decay made Hawk gag.

The boneyard was a museum of sorts. They saw *stegosaurus*, *tyrannosaurus*, the large skull of a *triceratops*, its largest head spike six feet long. The feeling of death and despair hung over the entire area like a shroud.

Svet appeared more dejected than ever. She didn't speak, and walked with her head down, staring at the ground. She tripped every few seconds and Hawk was afraid she was going to fall. She looked like she might cry at any moment, a sea of emotions simmering just below a boil. That broke Hawk's heart. Svet had been one of the strongest people he knew, and now she'd become broken and lost, her spirit gone with those she loved.

This was to be expected, Hawk knew, but it was disheartening. He'd tried hard to keep the party's spirits up. Keep them focused on the path ahead, not the path behind, but as the days wore on and hope fled, and their former lives receded further into the distance, the idea of having no reason to continue slowly took hold and all the old arguments were raised anew.

"Screeeeeeeeeeeeeeeeeeeeeeeeeeeee."

A shadow fell over the party and Hawk looked up to see Smaug descending toward them, giant wings open, mouth of razer teeth gleaming in the sunlight.

"Govnó," Svet said.

"This thing just won't give up," Hawk said. "It's like it knew we'd come here."

"Don't be ridiculous," Enyo said. "How could that be?"

"The thing has been on our ass since the mountains. There are *pterosaur* skeletons here, so..." Hawk said.

"It watches for us. Waiting til we come into the open," Svet said. She pulled the Ash 12 from her shoulder. It had two bullets left.

"Take cover there," Hawk said. He pointed toward a medium sized ribcage that wasn't missing any bones. It was the only cover Hawk could find. Most of the skeletons were broken apart, and provided little protection.

Svet went down as she ran, and Enyo helped her up. The party ran hard, the shadow overhead growing.

"Screeeeee. Screeeeeeeeeeeeee."

Hawk looked back to see that Svet had stopped running. She stood her ground as the *pterosaur* advanced, raising the Ash 12 and sighting the weapon on the beast as it came right at her.

"Noooooooo," Hawk yelled. He ran toward Svet, his flight forgotten.

The Russian was as still as stone, the Ash 12 trained on the dragon's head. The beast was three hundred yards out and Svet still hadn't blinked.

"Screeeeeeeeeeeeee. Scree—"

The Ash 12 erupted, two fast shots. Svet dropped the empty gun and sprinted full tilt at Hawk.

Smaug crashed into a large *tyrannosaur* skeleton, and the sound of cracking bones filled the plain. The dragon didn't move and laid still where it landed.

The Earth shuddered, and the vibration continued as if a stampede rumbled through the jungle.

Hawk stopped running and so did Svet, but Enyo didn't even slow up. The astronaut and cosmonaut stood in stunned silence for a few seconds, then Hawk said, "How the hell did you do that?"

Closer inspection of Smaug's corpse revealed that Svet placed bullets in each of Smaug's eyes, blowing out the back of the *pterosaur*'s skull. Hawk felt sorry for the beast. They had invaded his home, and the great flying reptile was only doing what millions of years of evolution had trained him to do; protect his kids. What scared Hawk was the realization that he wasn't very different from the beast.

A block of ice shifted in Hawk's stomach. Killing Smaug had been necessary, so why did he feel like he'd betrayed a worthy adversary with unfair play? He had. Guns had no place in this time, with these creatures, but without this advantage Hawk didn't know how things would have gone.

They left the *pterosaur* where it lay, blood leaking from its massive head. The irony wasn't lost on Hawk that Smaug had ended up in the boneyard, even if that hadn't been his intention.

The sun burned, the day dragged on, and the time travelers left the boneyard behind. They didn't say any words, or prayers, but Hawk made the sign of the cross and mumbled some bullshit about peace.

Now they had no guns, and Hawk knew that would mean their death. Maybe not today, or tomorrow, but soon. They'd been lucky, but the luck had been Vladimir shipping guns to the International Space Station, something that under normal circumstances would be deemed a major breach of international relations. In this case, it had bought them life. How long that life would be remained to be seen.

# 34

The ground vibrated and the jungle vegetation at the clearing's edge swayed and shook. Two *stegosaurs* ran onto the boneyard, a massive *tyrannosaurs rex* on their tails. The thirty-foot T-Rex lunged forward on its powerful hind legs, its large dark eyes blazing, mouth snapping at the *stegosaurs* as they trundled through ribcages and past piles of broken bones.

Hawk dropped to the ground and rolled under a large breast bone that lay askew atop a massive femur that had once belonged to a beast so large Hawk couldn't picture it in his mind. He lay with his nose in the dirt, the ground trembling beneath him, dust obscuring his view. His heart pounded, every cut and scrape he had stung and throbbed, and he was cold, despite sweat dripping down his face into his eyes.

The battle with Smaug had brought out the big boys and another *tyrannosaur* broke free of the forest, trees cracking, its loud roar bringing the first T-Rex to a halt. The two beasts eyed each other. The newcomer, whose skin was oddly black as if the beast had been burned, screamed with a fury that froze the other dinosaurs, but not for long.

No longer interested in the *stegosaurs*, the T-Rex's squared off, circling each other, looking for weakness and coiling to strike.

"Good time to go, nyet?" Svet said. She'd appeared next to him under the white slab of bone.

"I suppose it is," Hawk said. "Where is…"

Enyo crawled through the bones fifteen feet from them, but the Chinese astronaut didn't see them.

"Enyo," Hawk said, but Enyo didn't hear him. He kept crawling away from the battle that was seconds from getting underway.

The black T-Rex had enough of the dance. It opened its mouth and wailed again, its teeth the size of swords, its massive jaws big enough to crush a car. The animals lunged at each other as if their fight had been choreographed. The clash sent both fighters to the ground, and the massive beasts rolled and clawed at one another, jaws snapping.

Hawk and Svet crawled after Enyo, and when they saw him get up and run, they did the same. Behind them the sounds of the T-Rex battle filled the world. The ground shook under the weight of the giant beasts, and to the south the *stegosaurs* disappeared into the jungle.

When the companions reached the forest on the opposite side of the boneyard the party collapsed with exhaustion. In their haste to get out of the open and off the plain they'd run the entire way, giving it all they had. Hawk was shaken and weak, weeks of malnutrition and lack of sleep taking its toll on his forty-plus-year-old body.

They watched the battle unfold on the boneyard, but it didn't last long. The black T-Rex tired out its smaller opponent, and the yellow-striped beast fled before it was killed. The dust settled on the plain, the buzz of insects returned, and Hawk let out an exasperated sigh of relief.

The party spent the night at the edge of the boneyard and pressed on the next morning. The forest wasn't as thick as the prior section of jungle, and the scent of sulfur pervaded the air. They'd left the volcano behind, but as Pangaea continued to break apart there would be all types of unpredictable seismic activity as the continents continued to form. Hawk hoped the ground didn't literally disappear beneath his feet.

Ten more days they walked. Wake, eat, drink, walk, drink, eat, sleep, repeat. The party no longer spoke. What was there left to say? Soon they'd arrive at the beacon and their quest would be over. What then? Hawk trembled at the thought. They'd gotten through the last several months because they had a goal, something to get them off the rack each day.

Svet was a shell of her former self, and Enyo had turned inward. Hawk wished the man would talk like he used to. The constant struggle to survive, to find meaning in everyday menial tasks, was difficult, and Hawk didn't think he could keep up appearances much longer. When he gave up, would they?

Night fell and a deep glow filled the edges of the forest, creating a pale dusk that wasn't quite light, but not darkness either.

On the horizon the glow filled the world and the pulsating pillar of light shot into the deep black sky.

They were close. It was a matter of days now, maybe hours.

Hawk lay on his bed of leaves and stared up into the illuminated night sky. Fear filled him. Fear of the unknown. Fear that the beacon wasn't a beacon at all. That is was nothing. A trick of the eye or an odd feature of the landscape. What did it matter anyway? Even if the light was a beacon, what did that really mean for them? Most likely nothing.

After dinner the next day Hawk said, "We have plenty of light. You want to continue on for a bit?"

As if the Gods had heard the question, they answered with a resounding no. The sky opened up, and rain fell in a torrent. Hawk and friends huddled beneath a conifer tree protected by its thick branches and dense leaves. Thunder cracked, and the pounding rain leaked across the dry ground at their feet.

When the rain ended it was well after midnight and the party needed some rest, so they spent a damp night trying to sleep on wet leaves. The rain had brought out every bug and critter, and they slithered and crawled around and over the travelers as they tried to sleep. After an hour, Hawk gave up and took a walk.

The glow in the west had grown. They were no more than twenty miles from the light, and it dominated the land. Like an elevator to Heaven, the strobing white light pierced the night like a sword, fraying and fading as it rose.

Mist hung over the forest as the damp vegetation warmed. The fog was thick as smoke, and it snaked through the trees, around the fern leaves, and into every gap and crevasse. Hawk lit a torch with the lighter, but it didn't help much. Everything beyond ten feet was obscured in a damp white haze.

"Hey."

Hawk jumped.

"Sorry," Svet said. "Couldn't sleep."

"Me either."

She handed him a bamboo cup filled with clear water.

"Thanks." Hawk sat on a fallen tree and sipped his water.

"Why you no bartend anymore?" Svet said. "I miss my martini."

Hawk chuckled. "I don't know. Just didn't seem right to have fun and make-believe when..."

"When we're going to die?" she said.

Hawk said nothing. Svet nailed it on the head. What did they have to live for? Each other? That had gotten thin as paper.

"Maybe we won't," she said. "We not know what lies ahead. No idea, so why you take the worst road? The road that leads to misery and death. Why not take a better road?"

"Because I can't find the entrance ramp, and the road doesn't lead home."

"Build new road," Svet said.

Hawk harrumphed.

Back at camp, Enyo let loose with a loud snore, then he fell silent. The night dragged on, and the astronaut and cosmonaut stared into the light, and waited for the oncoming day.

The following night the beacon was so bright it lit the surrounding area like a klieg light. Every crack was illuminated with a pale white light that had no warmth, and brought no peace. The light strobed in a random pattern that made the party's movements look erratic and slow.

The forest thinned, and the tower of light stood at the center of a clearing. The ground was hardpan, and not a single creeper or weed marred its surface. It reminded Hawk of the area around the markers.

The light source was a round polyhedron shaped crystal structure the size of a small house. Light streamed from each flat surface, the crystal painting the area in a throbbing rainbow of colors. The crew approached with caution. Hawk's heart pounded in his chest and he was short of breath. There was nothing natural about the polyhedron crystal. It had been placed here.

The beacon sat on a platform of reflective metal that went into the ground like a foundation. When they got close, Hawk had to shield his eyes because the light was too bright. A foot-wide trench circled the foundation, and Enyo sighed as he examined it.

"What is it?" Hawk said.

"Looks like an isolation platform. They're used for scientific equipment and designed to remain stable and separate from surrounding vibrations," Enyo said.

"Whoever put this here knew there might be upheavals in the land and went to extreme length to keep the structure stable?" Hawk said.

"It would appear so," Enyo said.

Closer inspection of the giant crystal revealed a small opal colored stone at its center. The stone shined brightly, and the crystal structure around it refracted and magnified the light.

"Looks like the petroglyph monument you found," Svet said. The Russian stared at the crystal with awe, eyes the size of quarters.

*Beep. Beep.*

"What's that?" Hawk asked.

*Beep. Beep. Beep.* The faint beeping sound persisted, and Hawk and his companions split up and headed around the beacon in search of the noise.

A keypad with strange symbols on the buttons was set in a stainless-steel frame and mounted on the far side of the crystal. There was a small monitoring screen filled with odd symbols, and a red light that blinked in rhythm with the light.

"What the shit do you make of this?" Hawk said. The light beacon towered over them, bathing the group in colored light. A low hum came from the crystal, as if some machinery quietly toiled within. The pillar of light rose into the sky and disappeared into darkness. A long black pole, like a lightning rod, protruded from the top of the crystal. To Hawk it looked like an antenna.

Svet sighed but didn't answer.

Enyo said, "Sure seems like some kind of transmitting device. The antenna on top tells us that. The keypad is more of a mystery. I wish I knew what the symbols meant."

"I no recognize any of them from the temple," Svet said.

"No. I don't think they're connected, not directly anyway," Hawk said.

"You base this on?" Enyo said.

"I base it on I didn't see a single polyhedron in the temple. Not one, so unless whoever placed the beacon meant to confuse any who found their work, I can't see how the same race built both things."

Hawk turned away from the beacon. His eyes couldn't take the light any longer. The opal stone inside the crystal pulsed and changed color, and strengthened, then dimmed, as if a power drain was restored.

"We made it," Svet said.

"Now what?" Enyo said.

"Now we try and sleep and take a better look at this thing in the morning. We may have missed important details," Hawk said. The strong light created deep shadows, and Hawk's night vision was shot from the bright light.

With great reluctance the companions backed away from the light beacon, transfixed by the rainbow of color that pulsed and invaded the sky. Hawk needed to think and process everything he'd seen. It was clear another race had visited and possibly lived on Earth millions of years in the past and might return. What that meant for him and his friends, he didn't know, but tomorrow was another day, and in that, at least, he had faith.

# 35

The next day dawned sunny and clear and the glare of the beacon blended into the brightness of the day. Hawk and his friends searched the entire area, but found nothing new. The red light on the control panel beeped, its display screen showing gibberish, and the opal within the giant crystal glowed. They'd made camp at the edge of the clearing under a large tree with wide spreading branches and green leaves with yellow tips. They ate some fresh roasted meat Svet had killed the day before with her bolas.

What should they do now? This was the question that dominated Hawk's thoughts. He drank the last of his water and tossed his bamboo cup onto the pile of bowls that needed to be cleaned. "What do you guys think? What's our move here?"

Svet sighed and rolled her shoulders and cracked her neck, but said nothing.

Enyo said, "Well, I guess it depends on what we think this thing is. Are we in agreement it's a monitoring device?"

"Maybe, but what is it monitoring? The extinction event?" Hawk said.

"Who knows. That makes the most sense, but is that relevant?"

"I'd think so," Hawk said. "The event could be tomorrow or a million years from now."

"True," Enyo said. "But what could we do about it?"

To that, Hawk had no response. He said, "What if we disable the beacon so that whoever placed it here sends a repair team to investigate why it isn't transmitting?"

Svet perked up. Hawk had voiced this idea before, but sitting a hundred yards from the massive beacon the statement had taken on a new meaning. Svet said, "Unless whoever placed beacon lives close, it could take years for them to travel to Earth and investigate."

"Yes, and they might not even bother," Enyo said.

"Why wouldn't they?" Hawk asked.

Enyo said, "It's that time thing again. If they placed the monitoring device to record the event, that implies they had some knowledge of when that event would occur. If they can't make it here in time, why bother?"

"True," Hawk said.

"Or, if the event is still years off the investigation of the outage might not be the highest priority. They might not come to repair the beacon for a long time."

"All true," Hawk said. "I guess my question is what do we have to lose? Also, we have no clue what this mystery race that placed the device and monuments are capable of. For all we know they can travel faster than light and might zip here in five minutes."

"Maybe they have transporter like Star Trek?" Svet said.

Enyo sighed. "You guys are reaching for shit."

Hawk and Svet said nothing.

The debate over for the moment, Hawk got up and stretched his back. A dinosaur roared in the distance, but Hawk barely noticed. It was like having an annoying dog next-door that never stopped barking. You eventually tuned it out and didn't hear it anymore.

Hawk walked to the beacon and slid his hand over the smooth crystal surface. It was somewhat warm to the touch, and vibrated slightly. Was this his decision to make? He eyed the control panel, the red flashing light, the rhythmic thrum of the beacon's energy pulsing through the crystal. Was he still Commander? He didn't feel like it. So much had happened he thought the old hierarchy was a distant memory, and now they were equals in all ways.

The day wore on as Hawk's thoughts tormented him, poking and prodding for action. Prior planning helps support strong performance. That was the military motto he'd lived most of his life by, but what planning could be done? This was the end of the road, one way or another, and if tampering with the beacon caused some type of catastrophe, then so be it. What did they have to lose? That was really the question.

The companions spent most of the day on their own. Svet wandered off, but Enyo sat in camp, his head in his hands. When dinner rolled around Hawk thought they'd had enough time. He said, "Do we vote?"

"What are choices?" Svet said.

"Unless I missed something, it's a thumbs up or down on disabling the beacon," Hawk said.

"How would you do this?" Svet asked.

Hawk chuckled. "With a rock."

"You think that will work?" Enyo said.

"Only one way to find out, but yeah, I think it will work."

"I think destroying anything at this point is premature," Enyo said.

"So that's one thumbs down," Hawk said.

"What's the rush? Other than an event that may or may not be coming in our lifetime? Why not study the thing a little? See if we can make sense of the symbols. Maybe go back to the temple and see if we missed—"

"I'm not going back there," Svet said.

"I'm sorry, I didn't—"

"I know," Svet said.

"Svet, where do you stand?" Enyo said.

"I not sure," Svet said. She stalked around camp, running her fingers through her greasy blonde hair. Her face was smeared with dirt, her eyes hollow, her once muscular arms skin and bones.

"You have to vote," Hawk said.

"You decide," Svet said.

"No. We must decide this together. That's the only way I'll be comfortable with our decision."

Svet stopped pacing, raised her head, and a smile spread across her emaciated face. "I vote to disable," she said.

Hawk laughed. "Well played. Well played."

They had a tie. He was the deciding vote and the decision ended up being his after all. He thought he knew what needed to be done, but he wasn't a hundred percent sure and he didn't like the feeling. Usually his decisions were clear in his mind before they needed to be made, but this, perhaps the most important decision of his life, floated in his mind like a noxious cloud of confused ideas and thoughts that wouldn't stop twisting his judgment.

Night came on and the light from the giant crystal polyhedron filled the clearing and forest like a giant strobe light. The party ate under its glare in silence. Enyo and Svet hadn't asked what Hawk planned to do, which Hawk was thankful for. He knew what to do, he just needed to bring himself to the final decision.

After they'd eaten, Hawk said, "It's time." He walked around camp, looking for a rock, and when he didn't find one he strayed into the forest. White light cast long intermittent shadows, and the night symphony seemed strangely out of tune. He found a black rock the size of a football and he picked it up, turning it over in his hands. Having determined the rock should be sufficient, he headed for the crystal. Enyo and Svet fell in behind him.

Hawk stood before the panel for a long time, staring at the blinking red light, listening to the beeping sound and the hum of the power within. Enyo and Svet said nothing, but simply waited for Hawk to do what he had come to do.

Hawk slammed the rock into the panel, throwing it as hard as he could. The rock bounced off the steel and fell to the ground. The light was still red, the beeping sound continued, and the energy hum remained. He picked up the rock and pounded the panel, over and over, letting out all his frustration and hatred that had built up over the past nine months. He heaved the rock with such fury and abandon, Svet and Enyo took a step back.

After what seemed like an hour, but was only a few minutes, the control panel sparked. Hawk dropped the stone and stepped back.

The red light went solid, then went out and the beeping sound shifted to a steady, unbroken beep that went up in volume before sputtering out with a burst of static. The opal stone at the center of the beacon dulled, the pulsing stopped, and it winked out. The great crystal blinked, sizzled, and went out. The area fell into a deep darkness.

What he'd done might make things worse, but Hawk didn't care. He felt as though a great burden had been lifted from him. Perhaps what he was feeling was false hope, but it was hope.

The party decided not to live at the edge of the beacon clearing because there were no good trees to build the treehouse

Hawk dreamed of. They picked a large conifer about half a mile from the beacon. If any green men came calling they were close enough, and it might not be a bad idea to be hidden when they arrived.

Construction on the treehouse was underway. It would have three bedrooms, a common kitchen area, and a recreational space that would eventually have bamboo chairs and tables. The rec room didn't have walls, and had a three-hundred-and-sixty-degree view of the jungle. At its center Hawk and Enyo had constructed a bar from dried wood and bamboo, along with five stools, the fourth and fifth being symbolic empty seats for Max and Michel.

Centered on the bar was the empty vodka bottle, which Svet had turned into a flower vase. The bottle was scratched and worn from its travels, but it brought back memories of home, for better or worse. Several chess pieces were also lined up on the bar. They'd lost the board, but a new one would be made and soon they'd be able to pass the time playing chess.

Another reason they'd moved away from the beacon was the cessation of the light had brought inquisitive animals to investigate, and the dinosaur traffic around the polyhedron crystal had grown ten-fold.

As with any life, whether it be in the past or the future, it simply rolled on. Time didn't care about your losses, your struggles. She was a fickle bitch that Hawk had come to respect. He would never forget his wife and kids, but he had come to terms with the idea of never seeing them again. They were in his mind, pictures of the past indelibly etched into his brain, and part of his mental picture album, and he would refer to them as needed, hoping his family had found peace, no matter what fate had tossed their way.

Nightly drinks at Hawk's bar had quickly become a ritual. Svet took a walk alone each night, as did Hawk, but they always found their way back home in time for a cocktail. They talked of old times, the memories of their former lives that had become their current lives. They'd stare up at the stars and try to find the International Space Station gliding around Earth, waiting for a time when people would again call it home.

The sun fell below the horizon and darkness settled over the land. A blackness so thick Hawk barely saw his hand in front of his face. On this night the two astronauts and one cosmonaut sidled up to the bar and took their seats. A gentle breeze stole across the jungle, bringing the scent of flowers and earth. Hawk sighed. His new world wasn't that bad once you got to know her, as long as you respected her children.

"We're going to have to figure out how to make some real alcohol," Hawk said.

"Da," Svet said. "You think we can?"

"I do."

Svet smiled, picked up her ukulele and strummed a mournful tune.

Hawk mixed them some imaginary drinks, and settled in to wait.

## THE END

facebook.com/severedpress
twitter.com/severedpress

# CHECK OUT OTHER GREAT DINOSAUR BOOKS

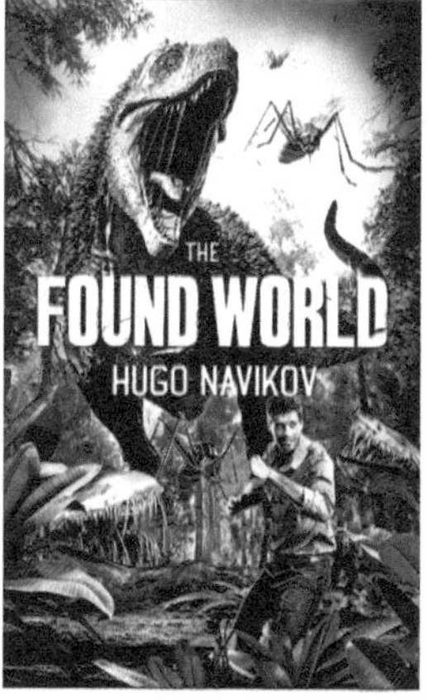


## THE FOUND WORLD
by Hugo Navikov

A powerful global cabal wants adventurer Brett Russell to retrieve a superweapon stolen by the scientist who built it. To entice him to travel underneath one of the most dangerous volcanoes on Earth to find the scientist, this shadowy organization will pay him the only thing he cares about: information that will allow him to avenge his family's murder.

But before he can get paid, he and his team must enter an underground hellscape of killer plants, giant insects, terrifying dinosaurs, and an army of other predators never previously seen by man.

At the end of this journey awaits a revelation that could alter the fate of mankind ... if they can make it back from this horrifying found world.

## HOUSE OF THE GODS
by Davide Mana

High above the steamy jungle of the Amazon basin, rise the flat plateaus known as the Tepui, the House of the Gods. Lost worlds of unknown beauty, a naturalistic wonder, each an ecology onto itself, shunned by the local tribes for centuries. The House of the Gods was not made for men.

But now, the crew and passengers of a small charter plane are about to find what was hidden for sixty million years.

Lost on an island in the clouds 10.000 feet above the jungle, surrounded by dinosaurs, hunted by mysterious mercenaries, the survivors of Sligo Air flight 001 will quickly learn the only rule of life on Earth: Extinction.

facebook.com/severedpress
twitter.com/severedpress

# CHECK OUT OTHER GREAT DINOSAUR BOOKS

## FLIPSIDE
## by JAKE BIBLE

The year is 2046 and dinosaurs are real.

Time bubbles across the world, many as large as one hundred square miles, turn like clockwork, revealing prehistoric landscapes from the Cretaceous Period.

They reveal the Flipside.

Now, thirty years after the first Turn, the clockwork is breaking down as one of the world's powers has decided to exploit the phenomenon for their own gain, possibly destroying everything then and now in the process.

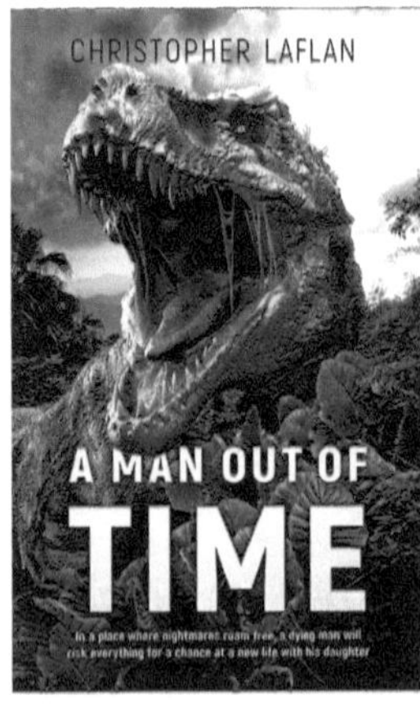


## A MAN OUT OF TIME
## by Christopher Laflan

Five years after the Chinese Axis detonated an unknown weapon of mass destruction off the southern coast of the United States, Special Ops Sergeant John Crider and the members of Shadow Company have finally captured what they all hope will lead to the end of the war. Unfortunately, the population within the United States is no longer sustainable. In an effort to stabilize the economy, the government enacts the Cryonics Act. One hundred years in suspended animation, all debt forgiven, and a chance at a less crowded future are too good to pass up for John and his young daughter.

Except not everything always goes as planned as Sergeant John Crider finds himself pitted against a land of prehistoric monsters genetically resurrected from the fossil record, murderous inhabitants, and a future he never wanted.

# CHECK OUT OTHER GREAT DINOSAUR BOOKS

## PRIMORDIA
## by Greig Beck

Ben Cartwright, former soldier, home to mourn the loss of his father stumbles upon cryptic letters from the past between the author, Arthur Conan Doyle and his great, great grandfather who vanished while exploring the Amazon jungle in 1908.

Amazingly, these letters lead Ben to believe that his ancestor's expedition was the basis for Doyle's fantastical tale of a lost world inhabited by long extinct creatures. As Ben digs some more he finds clues to the whereabouts of a lost notebook that might contain a map to a place that is home to creatures that would rewrite everything known about history, biology and evolution.

But other parties now know about the notebook, and will do anything to obtain it. For Ben and his friends, it becomes a race against time and against ruthless rivals.

In the remotest corners of Venezuela, along winding river trails known only to lost tribes, and through near impenetrable jungle, Ben and his novice team find a forbidden place more terrifying and dangerous than anything they could ever have imagined.

## PANGAEA EXILES
## by Jeff Brackett

Tried and convicted for his crimes, Sean Barrow is sent into temporal exile—banished to a time so far before recorded history that there is no chance that he, or any other criminal sent back, has any chance of altering history.

Now Sean must find a way to survive more than 200 million years in the past, in a world populated by monstrous creatures that would rend him limb from limb if they got the chance. And that's just his fellow prisoners.

The dinosaurs are almost as bad.

www.ingramcontent.com/pod-product-compliance
Lightning Source LLC
LaVergne TN
LVHW091140080826
845145LV00008B/2209

* 9 7 8 1 9 2 5 8 4 0 3 5 3 *